A CATERED
BAKE-OFF

Books by Isis Crawford

A CATERED MURDER
A CATERED WEDDING
A CATERED CHRISTMAS
A CATERED VALENTINE'S DAY
A CATERED HALLOWEEN
A CATERED BIRTHDAY PARTY
A CATERED THANKSGIVING
A CATERED ST. PATRICK'S DAY
A CATERED CHRISTMAS COOKIE EXCHANGE
A CATERED FOURTH OF JULY
A CATERED MOTHER'S DAY
A CATERED TEA PARTY
A CATERED COSTUME PARTY
A CATERED CAT WEDDING
A CATERED NEW YEAR'S EVE
A CATERED BOOK CLUB MURDER
A CATERED DOGGIE WEDDING
A CATERED QUILTING BEE
A CATERED BAKE-OFF

Published by Kensington Publishing Corp.

A CATERED BAKE-OFF

ISIS CRAWFORD

KENSINGTON PUBLISHING CORP.
kensingtonbooks.com

This book is a work of fiction. Names, characters, businesses, organizations, places, events, and incidents either are the product of the author's imagination or are used fictitiously. Any resemblance to actual persons, living or dead, events, or locales is entirely coincidental.

To the extent that the image or images on the cover of this book depict a person or persons, such person or persons are merely models, and are not intended to portray any character or characters featured in the book.

KENSINGTON BOOKS are published by

Kensington Publishing Corp.
900 Third Avenue
New York, NY 10022

Copyright © 2025 by Isis Crawford

All rights reserved. No part of this book may be reproduced in any form or by any means without the prior written consent of the Publisher, excepting brief quotes used in reviews.

All Kensington titles, imprints and distributed lines are available at special quantity discounts for bulk purchases for sales promotion, premiums, fund-raising, educational or institutional use.

Special book excerpts or customized printings can also be created to fit specific needs. For details, write or phone the office of the Kensington Special Sales Manager: Kensington Publishing Corp., 900 Third Ave., New York, NY, 10022. Attn. Special Sales Department. Phone: 1-800-221-2647.

KENSINGTON and the KENSINGTON COZIES teapot logo Reg. U.S. Pat. & TM Off.

Library of Congress Control Number: 2025933138

ISBN-13: 978-1-4967-3498-3

First Kensington Hardcover Edition: July 2025

ISBN-13: 978-1-4967-3501-0

10 9 8 7 6 5 4 3 2 1

Printed in the United States of America

The authorized representative in the EU for product safety and compliance
is eucomply OU, Parnu mnt 139b-14, Apt 123
Tallinn, Berlin 11317, hello@eucompliancepartner.com

*To my grandkids, Anna, George, Mila, Cora, Anya,
and Aiden.
May you live long and prosper.*

Prologue

I read somewhere that revenge is a dish best served cold. I think Shakespeare wrote that. I could look it up on Google if I wanted to, but I won't, because it really doesn't matter who wrote it. What matters is that I'm going to find out whether it's true or not. I think it is.

My father has been waiting for this moment for a long time. Decades. At least two of them. Okay. Eighteen years if we're being accurate. I made him a promise and now, finally, I'm going to carry it out. Yes, I am. I'm going to enjoy watching everyone squirm, and that's the truth. They're going to get what's coming to them. Especially after what a couple of them did.

Of course, they don't have to participate in the contest. No one is forcing them. They have a choice. They could have said no when the invitation arrived, but they didn't. They entered the contest, just like I knew they would. All so sure of themselves. Certain that they'd win. But I was counting on that as well. They always thought they were the best. In everything. Totally unchecked egos. Evidently, nothing has changed.

To be honest, I would have been very disappointed if

they hadn't accepted the invitation—not that I wouldn't have found another way to do what I need to do. They did, though, and I'm really looking forward to what's about to occur. In fact, I'm counting down the days waiting for the contest to begin. It's what I'm living for. In the last year, I've discovered that I have a talent I didn't know I possessed. A talent for making people afraid. Did you know that fear and hate have smells? Smells that are better than perfume. I didn't. I could bathe in them. The scents. I have bathed in them. The only thing better than that is the taste of blood. And I'm not talking imaginary. Just a drop or two on my tongue is enough. I know that seems weird, but everyone has their own idiosyncrasies. And no, I'm not a vampire. I'm real. Okay. I lied. I don't really do that. But it sounds really bad, doesn't it? The question is, what to do? Start small and ramp things up, or start with a bang—metaphorically speaking. Have some help? Do it all myself? That's TBD.

As someone famous once said, "Let the fun begin." Or was it the games? I can't remember. But it doesn't really matter, does it? The result will be the same.

To clarify: I'm talking about my fun, not theirs. The thing about cooking when you think about it is that it's a dangerous activity. There are sharp knives, food that can kill you, and fire. In short, there are plenty of opportunities for accidents to happen and, believe me, they will.

Chapter 1

"Can you imagine living here when Michael Billings was still alive?" Libby asked Bernie as they passed through the gate of the old Kenmore Estate. A onetime notorious bootlegger, Billings was renowned for his lavish lifestyle, but time had taken its toll and had reduced the estate to a shadow of its former self.

Bernie laughed. "Only if I had staff," she said as she drove down the winding paths that led to the tent, which, she decided, looked like a giant billowing marshmallow from the distance. "You'd definitely need them for a place like this."

"How big do you think the estate is?" Libby asked.

"Maybe an acre, two at the most," Bernie guessed as she parked the van, and then she and her sister hurried toward the tent. Everyone stopped chatting when they ducked inside. They were the last ones to arrive.

"I'm nervous," Libby whispered to her sister as she stopped at the entrance and surveyed the group.

"It's just a run-through," Bernie reassured her while she blinked sweat out of her eyes. Even though it was seventy-five degrees, the humidity made it feel as if it was in the nineties.

"I know what it is. I just wish you hadn't said yes," Libby continued.

"You agreed," Bernie reminded her.

"What if we lose?" Libby asked.

"We won't," Bernie replied with more confidence than she felt as she studied the people gathered together. All of them were around the same age as the Simmons sisters, all of them had the same skill sets as they did. There were nine in the group if she counted herself and her sister. There were six contestants, two judges, and one producer of *The Longely Bake-Off*. It was an interesting mix, not to mention a colorful one. Literally speaking.

There was Nell Pinto, wearing her signature polka-dotted leggings and blue hair. She owned a catering operation called The Best, along with Lori Peterson, who had recently dyed her hair neon green and complemented it with bright red lipstick and blue eye shadow. Then there was Mike Goodman, in his Hawaiian shirt and red hair. He ran a shop called The Cookie Corner, which specialized in late-night deliveries of warm chocolate chip cookies. Adam Borat was there, too—a short, round guy with a mustache, a pronounced limp from a motorcycle accident, and a penchant for plaid pants. He'd worked in several restaurants and was now the owner of The Sheffield, a wannabe English pub.

Bernie knew she and Libby had as good a chance as anybody here, if not better, to win the contest, but she'd never competed in anything like this before, let alone been on television as a contestant. She took a deep breath and let it out, trying to quell the butterflies in her stomach. Hopefully, the judges would be nice.

There were two of them: Ellen Green, who hosted a

cooking show on local TV, and Doug LaForte, who had owned a restaurant called The Potted Pig in Seattle and was now making a living teaching cooking courses at the local community college and judging culinary contests. Bernie was thinking about everyone's strengths and weaknesses, when the producer of the show clapped his hands, signaling for silence. Everyone stopped talking and focused on him.

"Thank you all for coming," Sam Levine told them, clearing his throat. He looked around, ran his hand over his chrome dome, and began to speak. "This run-through should take two hours, as will the next one—"

"I don't see why we need two run-throughs," Adam muttered, interrupting him.

"Because," Sam patiently explained for the second time, "I want you to be familiar with your environment." He pointed to the wires and cables snaking across the floor. "For instance, I don't want anyone tripping on those."

Nell rolled her eyes.

"People have, you know," Mike said. He'd been watching cooking shows ever since he'd been invited to participate in *The Longely Bake-Off*.

Hosted by a flour mill called Red Fern, the bake-off was supposed to take place over the course of three weekends. It was loosely based on a show called *The Great British Bake Off*, and each weekend's filming consisted of three baking assignments: the signature, the technical challenge, and the showstopper. However, there were differences between the two shows. For one thing, *The Great British Bake Off* had individual contestants pitted against one another, while *The Longely Bake-Off* had teamed people up with each other for the three episodes. Also, there were fewer people competing. Bernie was wondering why that was the case, when the producer started talking again.

6 *Isis Crawford*

"And," he said, continuing with his explanation, "I want to make sure everyone knows how to operate the equipment and where your supplies are. Don't forget you're going to be timed and there are going to be cameras circling you and bright lights to deal with."

Ellen jumped in. "And us coming around and talking to you," she said. She adjusted her rhinestone cat-eared headband. "Don't forget that. We know it can be distracting, but it's part of the show."

"I suppose it can be," Libby allowed as she studied her surroundings. Cooking here was going to be different from at their shop, A Little Taste of Heaven. There were three separate prep stations set up in the middle of the tent, while the pantry, the ovens, and the refrigerator were arrayed along the sides. She watched Sam point to the pantry and the refrigerator.

"Hopefully, this rehearsal will allow you to familiarize yourself with the equipment. Each team has been assigned a specific work area." He indicated who was going where, before he went on speaking. "We have done your shopping for you. Your ingredients are in the pantry and the refrigerator, along with everything else you might need to construct your dish, but"—here he paused for a moment to emphasize his point—"be advised that there are limited quantities of many items."

"Meaning?" Bernie asked.

"Meaning," Sam replied, "that if there's no more butter in the fridge, that's it. You can't get more."

"But what if we need more?" Lori inquired as she wound a lock of her hair around one of her fingers. "What if someone takes our portion?"

"Too bad for you," Adam told her.

Lori turned to Sam. "That doesn't seem fair."

Sam grinned. "Think of it as a test of your improvisational abilities."

Mike pointed to himself. "Improv. My favorite thing to do," he announced.

Nell snorted.

Mike turned to Nell. "What's that supposed to mean?" he demanded.

"I'm just remembering the Franklin wedding when the icing melted because it was so hot and you used Betty Crocker," Nell told him.

"No one could tell the difference," Mike protested.

"They most certainly could," Nell told him. "Lulu told me all about it. I heard they didn't want to pay you."

Mike rolled his eyes. He was about to reply, but before he could, Sam clapped his hands together again.

"Children," he said, "settle down." When everyone had, he continued with his advice. "As I was saying, make sure you take what you need on your first pass, because it might not be there when you come back."

"Good to know," Bernie said, making a mental note to take a few extra eggs—just in case. She and Libby were making a cheese soufflé, topped with a mushroom-and-sherry sauce.

"And don't forget to take the humidity and heat into account," Sam went on. "They can affect the way ingredients react. Flour absorbs moisture."

"What about the technical challenge?" Libby inquired.

Sam cleared his throat before replying. "I'm glad you asked. We're doing that tomorrow. We will be giving you the ingredients for a surprise dish that you will be expected to re-create."

Nell groaned. "And the recipe for it?"

"You'll be given a general outline," Sam told her. "The rest is up to you." He rubbed his hands together, then moved the ring on his forefinger up and down. "Today, because this is the first time you're doing this, we're holding off on the camera crew, but they will be in full attendance tomorrow."

"And remember, people," Ellen chimed in, "time is not your friend. Factor it into your calculations." She smiled, exposing the small gap in her front teeth. "I know you can do this."

"Appearance is also important," Doug added. He resettled the baseball cap he was wearing. "We expect your creations to be as wonderful to look at as they are delicious to eat."

Sam looked around. "Any questions?"

No one said anything.

"None?" he asked again.

"Not from me," Adam said.

Sam nodded. "Oh. One last thing. In case my two judges can't agree, I will render the final opinion."

Ellen stepped forward. "Are we all ready?" Everyone nodded. "Fine. Then let's do this." And she lifted the whistle that was hanging on a lanyard around her neck and brought it up to her lips. The contestants assumed a running position. Then she said, "Bakers, on your mark, get set, go," and blew the whistle.

The contestants took off.

"You get the eggs and the butter and cheese, and I'll get the wild mushrooms, chives, onion, and sherry," Libby told Bernie while they ran for the pantry and the refrigerator.

"Will do," Bernie said as she made for the pale blue vintage-style fridge. *I love this thing,* she thought as she grabbed a carton with a dozen eggs. She was just reaching for a wedge of Swiss cheese, when Nell slammed into her.

"Watch where you're going," Nell snapped.

A CATERED BAKE-OFF 9

"Watch where I'm going? How about you watch where *you're* going," Bernie squawked. "You ran into me."

"Did I?" Nell said as she grabbed the wedge of cheese Bernie had been reaching for. "Sorry about that."

"Hey, I was going to take that," Bernie protested. There was no more Swiss left.

Nell shrugged. "Sorry. I can't help it if you're slow," she told her. "I guess you'll just have to make do with the Romano. Maybe you'd be faster if you weren't wearing those heels of yours."

"What's wrong with them?" Bernie asked, looking down at her four-inch stilettos. Nell didn't answer; Mike did, instead.

"I like your shoes," he observed as Bernie took the wedge of Romano and stuffed it into her apron pocket, before grabbing a pound of salted butter sitting on the second shelf.

Bernie thanked him and closed the refrigerator door. Then she scurried off to her and Libby's workstation.

"Where's the Swiss?" Libby asked Bernie as she put the butter, eggs, and cheese down on the table.

"Nell took it," Bernie told her. "We get the Romano." She rubbed her side where Nell had bumped into her. Somehow she'd never thought of cooking as a contact sport. Then she went over to the nearest oven, set the temperature to four hundred degrees, and turned the oven on. Afterward, she went back to her workstation and began looking for a quart soufflé dish, a whisk, and a copper bowl in the cabinet next to the prep table.

Hopefully, they would have those—they should. They were pretty basic, but one never knew. If they didn't, she'd have to change her battle plan. Of course, she could use the electric mixer on the table, but using a copper bowl and a balloon whisk ensured a fluffier, lighter soufflé, es-

10   *Isis Crawford*

pecially since the eggs weren't room temperature. Plus, if she didn't use a copper bowl, she would need to use cream of tartar to stabilize the egg whites, and she hadn't seen any in the pantry.

"*Yes,*" she crowed a moment later when she found a soufflé dish, a copper bowl, a whisk, and a grater, then laid them on the table.

"So, I take it, you're doing the soufflé and I'm doing the sauce?" Libby asked her sister as she started cleaning mushrooms and separating the stems and the caps.

"If that's okay with you," Bernie said, reaching for the butter. She cut off a tablespoon's worth from the pound she'd gotten from the fridge and began smearing it all over the bottom and sides of the dish. Then she took a half cup of the unflavored breadcrumbs she'd found in the pantry and sprinkled them over the butter, after which she turned the dish upside down and tapped the bottom. Then she turned the dish right side up and inspected the inside. The inside surface was now evenly coated. That would ensure the soufflé would come out easily, as well as give it a little extra flavor and texture.

"I haven't had one of these in a while," Bernie noted as she put the prepared dish off to the side.

"Not since Dad's birthday," Libby said.

"And that was chocolate," Bernie said.

"God, was that good," Libby reminisced. She could still taste it. Sweet, with a tiny bite from the pinch of red pepper.

"Indeed, it was," Bernie agreed as she reached over, took a stick of butter, put it in a small saucepan, and turned the stovetop burner on to low. It wouldn't do to have the butter burn, she thought. Then she'd have to start all over and there wasn't time for that. Here every minute counted. She was about to begin measuring out the flour for the béchamel sauce when she noticed that Libby had stopped chopping mushrooms and was staring at one. She had a this-isn't-good expression on her face.

"What's going on?" Bernie asked her sister.

Libby pointed. "This mushroom."

"What about it?" Bernie asked, puzzled. "It looks perfectly fine to me."

"I think it may be a destroying angel," Libby told her.

Chapter 2

Bernie laughed. "Funny thing, it doesn't look like a destroying angel to me. Where's her flaming sword?"

"I'm talking about the mushroom, Bernie," Libby said.

"Oh." Bernie raised her eyebrows. "I thought you were telling me the zombie apocalypse had arrived."

"Ha. Ha. This is serious," Libby told her, holding up the mushroom.

"The mushroom's name is *serious*?" Bernie asked. "Is *serious* a new species?"

Libby ignored her and continued with what she'd been saying. "Or it could be a death cap. They're in the same family."

"What family?"

"The killing-people family."

"I knew you shouldn't watch those foraging videos on TikTok," Bernie told her sister as she walked over to where Libby was standing and took a better look at the mushroom in question. "Are you sure?" she asked her sister. The thing Libby was pointing to looked like a regular mushroom to her. "It looks okay to me."

"Of course, I'm not sure," Libby snapped. "If I were, we wouldn't be having this conversation."

A CATERED BAKE-OFF   13

Bernie sighed. "Where did you get it from, Libby?"

"Obviously, the paper bag marked mushrooms, Bernie." Libby grimaced. "Its stem is too long."

Bernie managed not to roll her eyes. "The stems on the mushrooms look the same to me. You know, we don't have time for this."

"For checking? Would you rather be dead?" Libby asked her.

This time, Bernie did roll her eyes. "Seriously?"

"Yes. Seriously." Libby held up the stem of the alleged destroying angel and the stems of two other mushrooms, then laid them side by side. "See the difference?"

"No, not really, Libby," Bernie answered.

"There's a quarter of an inch difference, Bernie. I measured them."

"Even if what you're saying about the height difference is true . . ." Bernie began.

"It is," Libby told her.

Bernie tucked a wisp of her hair behind her ear. "What you're saying seems unlikely."

"It's not that unlikely," Libby replied. "People make mistakes identifying mushrooms when they're foraging all the time. I looked it up on Google," Libby said, and she waved her phone in front of her sister's face. "See, the pictures look the same." She pointed to the mushroom on the table.

"Well, if Google says it, then it must be true," Bernie remarked.

"Take a look," Libby demanded.

Bernie sighed, took Libby's phone, and studied the picture on the screen. "You're right," she said after a moment. "These two do look similar," she conceded. Then she pointed to three other mushroom pictures. "But so do these." And she handed Libby's phone back to her.

14　*Isis Crawford*

"Okay. I could be wrong," Libby allowed, "but if I'm right and we poison the judges . . ."

". . . that would be bad," Bernie said, finishing her sister's sentence for her.

"What are you planning to poison them with?" Adam asked. "Cyanide? Atropine?"

Bernie and Libby jumped. Neither one had heard him coming up behind them.

"That," Libby said, pointing to the offending item.

"A mushroom?" Adam asked.

Libby nodded.

"What's wrong with it?" he asked. "It looks okay to me."

"That's what I said, too," Bernie told him.

"Hence, the problem," Libby said as she took out her phone again and showed him the pictures she'd found on Google. Then she said, "I'm calling Sam."

"You should ask Lori before you do," Adam suggested. "She's the one that picked them. She used to teach a course over at Monroe Community College on foraging, with an emphasis on fungi," he added. "Check with her."

"Check with me about what?" Lori called over from her workstation, having heard her name from across the room.

Libby held up the mushroom. "About this."

Lori put down the bowl with the eggs she'd been whipping, wiped her hands on the tea towel slung over her shoulder, and walked over. "Why?" she asked. "Is there a problem?"

"I think this might be a destroying angel," Libby replied.

Lori laughed. "The thing you have in your hand is just a look-alike."

"Are you sure?" Libby demanded.

"Of course, I'm sure," Lori told her, two spots of color

appearing on her cheeks. "Do you think I'd make a mistake like that?"

Libby opened her mouth to answer, but Sam walked into the tent before she could.

"What's going on?" he asked, looking around. "Why aren't you guys cooking?"

Lori pointed at Libby. "She thinks I'm trying to kill her." Then she explained why.

"I didn't say that," Libby protested.

"You implied it," Lori countered.

"I most certainly did not!" Libby cried. She pointed to the mushroom in question. "I just wanted to make sure this was safe to eat. I didn't realize you were so sensitive."

Lori put her hands on her hips. "I'm not."

"You're acting like you are," Bernie pointed out.

Lori turned and faced her. "Listen, I've been doing this forever and I haven't made a mistake yet. Did you know that specific mushrooms grow around specific trees?"

"Like truffles and oak trees," Bernie said.

Lori nodded her head in agreement. "Exactly. Although it isn't only oak trees, it's oak tree roots, too."

"What's the difference?" Adam asked.

"None really." And Lori explained. "After a tree dies, the tree's roots remain in the ground for a long time." Lori flicked a piece of pasta off her shirt. "So even if you don't see the tree, the roots might still be there, hence truffles. Which is why people use dogs and pigs to hunt them. They're not always visible. Sometimes, lots of times, you have to dig them out."

"What does that have to do with what they were talking about?" Mike asked.

Lori put her hands on her hips and leaned toward Mike. "If you had paid attention, you would realize that I was merely trying to point out that you can identify mush-

16   *Isis Crawford*

rooms by where and how they grow. A destroying angel is usually taller than most of the other mushrooms growing around here—"

Libby interrupted. "That's what I just said."

Lori turned toward her. "True, but you have to factor in the location as well, something you didn't say."

Libby opened her mouth to speak, but before she could reply, Nell did.

"So, partner of mine, is this or isn't this the angel of vengeance?" Nell asked Lori.

Lori corrected her. "Destroying angel."

Nell waved her hand impatiently. "Whatever."

"Of course, it isn't," Lori said. Then she went over to Libby and Bernie's workstation, gathered up the mushrooms, and threw them in the garbage. "There," she said, "now you don't have to worry."

"You didn't have to do that," Libby told her, thinking about how the sherry sauce was going to taste without the mushrooms.

"Yes, I did," Lori said. "I always tell my class, 'When in doubt, throw it out.'"

"If I didn't know better, Lori, I'd think you wanted to sabotage our dish," Bernie said, crossing her arms over her chest.

"How can you say that?" Lori said. "I'm just trying to make sure everyone is okay. Your sister wasn't comfortable and now she is." She shook her head. "It's amazing how such a little thing can cause so much damage to a living organism. There's no known antidote for eating one of those mushrooms, you know. Your organs start shutting down, one by one, and then you're done."

"I know," Libby said.

Sam looked from Libby to Lori and back again. "So, are we all right here?" he asked.

A CATERED BAKE-OFF   17

"I guess," Libby muttered as Doug appeared. The judge was holding a cup of coffee. "Sorry, I missed all the commotion. What's going on?"

Sam explained.

"Well, it would have made great publicity," Doug said. "I can see the headlines now: *Destroying Angel Strikes Again*. The tabloids would love it."

"That's a terrible thing to say," Mike countered.

Sam laughed. "But true."

Nell shook her head in disbelief. "You guys have sick minds."

Adam raised both hands in the air. "Hey, we're just saying it like it is. Death always brings the ratings up."

Lori grimaced. "And speaking of death, Mike, I suppose you're going to throw your mushrooms out, too."

Mike startled. "I wasn't going to. Should I?"

"So, you don't think I'm trying to kill you, too?" Lori asked him.

Mike smiled. "You would have done it a long time ago, if you'd wanted."

"Hey, I never said that," Libby protested again.

"You implied it," Lori said, repeating her last comment.

Libby took a deep breath and counted to ten before replying, "No I didn't."

"Then what would you call it?" Lori demanded.

Sam put his hand up before Libby could answer. "Let's stop bickering and get back to cooking," he said, looking from Libby to Lori and back again.

"Fine," Lori said. She was turning to go back to her station when there was a loud boom.

"What the hell was that?" Bernie cried out.

Libby pointed to the oven Mike and Adam had been using. The glass in the door had exploded. Everyone stared at it.

"Holy crap," Bernie said.

Mike swallowed. "You can say that again." He bit his lip. "All I can say is that it's lucky I wasn't standing there."

"Ditto," Adam added. "We could have gotten seriously hurt."

"Ya think?" Mike said, studying the pieces of glass spread out on the floor.

"At least it's safety glass," Bernie remarked.

"True," Mike agreed. He walked over and picked up one of the pieces from the floor, carefully weighing the little glass cube in the palm of his hand. "But one of these could still give you a nasty cut if it came flying at you. Not as bad as regular glass, but . . ."

". . . bad enough. Especially if it hit you in the eye," Bernie said, finishing the sentence for Mike.

"I gotta say, I hope the actual filming goes better than this," Sam said, staring at the chaotic scene in front of him.

Everyone looked at each other. Bernie was the first one to speak.

"I guess this is what the phrase *technical difficulties* means," she observed.

"No," Doug said, contradicting her. "This is what happens when you rent cheap equipment."

Everyone turned to Sam.

"I'm not dignifying that with a response," Sam told him before walking away.

Chapter 3

"Was the oven defective?" Brandon asked Bernie later that evening. It was ten o'clock, and since it was a weekday night, the only people left at the bar at this hour were a handful of hard drinkers, the Simmons sisters, and their boyfriends, Brandon and Marvin.

Bernie shrugged and took another sip of her scotch. She was on her second shot glass. It had been that kind of day. "Carl wasn't sure." Carl was the owner of Carl's Appliance Repair.

"How so?" Libby's boyfriend, Marvin, inquired as he ate a pretzel from the bowl in front of him.

This time, Libby answered. "He said that the explosion could have been caused by either faulty wiring or someone tampering with it. He wasn't sure, which was why Sam called the police."

"That seems a little overreactive," Marvin observed.

"That's what the cops said," Bernie told him.

"What did they tell him?" Brandon inquired.

"They said to call them if something else happened," Libby replied. "So now he has a call into Central Restaurant Supply about replacing the oven. That's where he got it from originally."

20   *Isis Crawford*

Marvin ate another pretzel. "It sounds like an exciting day," he noted.

"That's one way of putting it," Libby responded.

"On the positive side, you did get to see Kenmore," Marvin pointed out.

"True," Libby agreed.

"It's a pretty big piece of land for these parts," Bernie said. "I was surprised. It's in rough shape, though. The house could definitely use a couple of coats of paint and maybe a new roof."

Brandon stifled a yawn. He still had hours to go on his shift. "I heard at one time someone wanted to buy the property, tear down the house, and put condos up, but the zoning board nixed the deal. Now, though, I hear that might be in the works again." Then he changed topics. "So, what about those mushrooms you were talking about before?"

"No story. Libby made a mistake," Bernie replied. "That's what watching too many YouTube videos will do to you."

"So, the ones Lori picked weren't poisonous?" Brandon asked.

"Obviously," Bernie said.

"Maybe next time, you should specify cultivated mushrooms," Brandon commented. "It would save on the drama."

"It's just that wild mushrooms taste so much better," Libby told him. "I thought he was going to get them from Ralph. She sighed. "Now Sam says if we need more mushrooms, he's going to get them from John at Maybury Farm. They supply the grocery stores around here."

Brandon dried his hands on the dishtowel slung over his shoulder. "I can see that, given all the hullabaloo. How is Sam, by the way? He hasn't been in here for a while."

"Aside from having six-month-old twins and getting no sleep, he told me he's fine," Bernie told Brandon.

"Better him than me," Brandon observed as he reflexively wiped down the counter in front of Libby.

"You don't want kids?" Libby asked him.

"Not in duplicate," Brandon replied.

"I think it would be fun," Marvin countered before getting back to the matter at hand. "So, what do you think about what happened with the oven?" Marvin asked, turning to Libby. "Are we talking bad luck or something else?"

"Like what?" Bernie asked.

"The word *sabotage* comes to mind," Marvin replied. "Or am I being paranoid?"

"You're being paranoid," Brandon promptly replied.

"No wonder you and my sister are together," Bernie said to Marvin. "You have a lot in common."

"Ha. Ha. Ha. Very funny," Libby said. "But Marvin could be right."

"Meaning that Adam or Mike rigged their own oven?" Bernie posited.

"Maybe Nell or Lori did it," Libby said.

Bernie made a face. "Why would anyone want to sabotage a baking contest, for heaven's sake?" Bernie asked as Libby knocked back the rest of her wine and held out her glass for a refill.

"Who knows why anyone wants to do anything these days," Brandon said, taking the bottle of Pinot from the shelf behind him, refilling Libby's glass, and handing it back to her. Libby took a swallow and put the glass down. Then she ran her finger around its rim while she thought.

"How does an oven explode?" Libby mused. "In all my years of cooking, I've never heard of an oven exploding."

"That's not what Google says," Bernie pointed out.

22 Isis Crawford

"If Google says it, then it must be true," Libby observed, repeating Bernie's comment from earlier in the day.

"What does Google say?" Marvin asked out of curiosity.

Bernie picked up her phone from the counter, looked for the entry, and read it. "According to this, 'If during a pyrolytic cycle, the oven temperature increases too rapidly and the oven fails to switch into safety mode, it can result in a deformation of the glass and may cause an explosion.'"

"What the hell is a *pyrolytic cycle*?" Brandon asked.

"Glad you asked," Bernie said, reading a different entry out loud. "'Pyrolysis is the heating of organic material in the absence of oxygen.'"

"Well, that explains everything," Brandon said, wiping his hand on the towel slung over his shoulder.

"No need for sarcasm," Bernie told him.

"I wasn't being sarcastic, Bernie."

"You think you can explain it better, Brandon?" Bernie asked.

"As a matter of fact, I do," Brandon told her as he watched Bernie's sister take a gulp of the wine he'd just poured her. Usually, Libby was a one-glass-an-evening gal, but today's events must have really rattled her, he reflected.

Bernie extended her hand. "Be my guest."

"With pleasure," Brandon replied. "Something like that could be caused by faulty wiring or something could be wrong with the insulation—"

Bernie interrupted. "How could something be wrong with the insulation?"

"Well, for openers, mice could have eaten it," Brandon replied, remembering what had happened in his old apartment. "It's amazing the amount of damage they can do."

He nodded at a customer leaving and told them to have a good evening. "Also, the safety switch in the oven might not work."

Libby raised an eyebrow. "Ovens have safety switches?" she asked, taken aback. "Where? Ours sure doesn't, unless I'm missing something."

"They're built in," Brandon told her. "If the oven gets too hot, the switch is supposed to kick in and bring the temperature back down, but sometimes it doesn't. It's really rare, but it does happen." He took a sip of water. "One of my friends was roasting a chicken in the oven and the self-cleaning function came on and the oven door locked. She couldn't stop it."

"So, what happened?" Libby asked.

"She called the place where she'd bought it and the guy at the other end of the line told her to unplug it before it caught fire and/or exploded."

"For real?" Bernie asked.

"Yes, for real," Brandon said.

"Can you think of any other reason the glass in the oven might have exploded?" Libby asked.

Brandon considered the question for a minute. Then he said, "Well, someone could have put a different kind of light bulb in the oven."

"Like an LED?"

Brandon nodded. "Yes. Or maybe a small explosive device. Or—and here's another idea—the oven exploding could be a practical joke that got out of hand."

"Doubtful," Bernie said.

"It's possible," Brandon told her.

"I don't see how," Bernie replied.

"Let me tell you a story," Brandon said. "When I was in high school, we had to take home ec. One of my friends put a whole box of baking powder in the cake he and his partner were supposed to be baking."

"Why?" Bernie asked.

Brandon chuckled, remembering. "Because they wanted to see what would happen."

Marvin finished his beer and wiped his lips off with the back of his hand. "What did happen, Brandon?"

"What do you think happened, Marvin? The cake exploded."

"Did the oven glass shatter?" Bernie asked.

"No, it didn't shatter, but it did crack. And there was a fire." Brandon chuckled again. "I'll tell you one thing. It sure did scare the crap out of the class and Mrs. Connelly."

"What happened to your friend?" Marvin asked as he ate the last pretzel in the bowl.

"He was suspended from school for two weeks," Brandon said.

"Are you sure that person, wasn't you?" Bernie asked.

"How can you think such a thing," Brandon demanded, doing a reasonable approximation of indignation.

"Let's guess," Bernie said as Marvin moved his bar stool in a skoosh.

"How do you know about this oven stuff anyway?" Marvin asked Brandon.

"Oh, I had a part-time job in an appliance store for a couple of summers when I was in college," Brandon replied. "I learned more about ovens and washing machines than you would ever want to know."

"Great," Bernie said. Then she finished her scotch and Libby finished her wine. They both stood up.

"You guys leaving so soon?" Marvin asked.

Both women nodded.

"We're doing another run-through tomorrow, starting at eight in the morning," Libby explained.

"Hopefully, this one will go a little smoother," Brandon said.

"Well, it can't get any worse," Bernie observed. "After all, what else can go wrong?"

In retrospect, she realized this was not the thing to say. One should never provoke the kitchen gods. They had long memories.

Chapter 4

The weather was perfect the next day. It was sunny and sixty, going up to a high of eighty degrees, when Libby and Bernie left A Little Taste of Heaven at seven-thirty for the show's second trial run.

"Smells like summer," Libby said, sniffing the air as a couple of geese flew overhead, honking as they went. Somewhere nearby, someone was mowing their lawn. She took another deep breath, reveling in the odor of freshly mowed grass and the lingering aroma of honeysuckle.

"We couldn't ask for better than this," Bernie noted, echoing her sister's opinion as she drove up to the gate of the estate and showed her pass to the security guard Sam had hired the previous evening.

"You're right, we couldn't," Libby allowed. "Nervous?"

"About a repeat of yesterday?" Bernie asked as the guard checked her and Libby's names off his list and nodded them through.

"That and the technical challenge," Libby told her. "I hope the recipe they give us isn't too hard."

"That too," Bernie told her.

"I mean, things gotta go better than yesterday, right?" Libby replied.

"Fingers crossed, or as Grannie used to say, 'From your mouth to God's ear,'" Bernie replied as she studied the large white tent that had been set up last week for the bake-off. She reflected that Libby was right. Nestled among the estate's gently rolling hills, the tent really did look like a giant billowy marshmallow. When she and Libby walked inside, they could see that the damaged oven had been replaced by a purple one.

"That color is hideous," Bernie observed before she greeted the other contestants.

"But at least it's here," Libby replied. "It's probably the only one Central had in stock." Since the pandemic, things had been harder to come by.

"Or the cheapest," Bernie guessed.

A moment later, Sam and the two judges joined them. Sam cleared his throat, and everyone fell silent as he began to talk.

"After some discussion, the judges and I have decided to carry on with the second run-through as if yesterday's trial was completed successfully," he told the assembled group.

Nell frowned as she adjusted the waistband of her leggings. Today they were dark blue with large green polka dots.

"What about the ovens?" Adam asked. "Are they safe?"

"Excellent question," Sam responded. "First off, I want to apologize for yesterday's unfortunate occurrences. I understand how upsetting they must have been, and I want you all to know that we've taken steps to remedy the situation and I can promise you that nothing like that will happen again. I also want to assure you, we are doing everything possible to get to the bottom of the situation.

"As you can see," Sam continued before anyone could say anything else, "we've replaced the stove that was malfunctioning. In addition, we've also gone over all the other appliances to make sure they're in good working order,

28   *Isis Crawford*

and I am happy to report that they are. Hopefully, we will have no more equipment problems in the foreseeable future." He rubbed his hands together. "Remember, this is just a rehearsal, but that said, I want you to treat it as if it's the real thing." Then Sam nodded to the two judges. "Your turn," he told them, and he took a step back as Ellen took a step forward.

She smiled at the contestants. "To paraphrase: Your assignment, should you choose to accept it . . ."

". . . is to make a Battenberg cake," Doug told them as he took a step forward, too.

"For which, we will give you a bare-bones recipe," Ellen said, and she started handing out sheets of paper, with the recipe printed on it, to a member of each of the three teams.

"At least there are no mushrooms in this recipe," Mike quipped after reading it.

Doug ignored the comment and addressed himself to the matter at hand. "At first blush, the cake seems simple enough," the judge warned, "but bear in mind that it is a persnickety chore to put together."

"And that you only have an hour to come up with the final product," Ellen added.

"We want to see a clean, defined checkerboard," Doug told them. "Neatness counts—especially when it comes to something like this." And he began the countdown.

"Do you know the cake's history?" Bernie whispered to Libby as they hurried toward the pantry.

"As a matter of fact, I do . . . kinda," Libby told her. "I read it in an old cookbook that Mom had. It said it was invented to honor some royal's wedding."

Bernie nodded and studied the recipe Ellen had given out. Apparently, it consisted of two almond sponge layers. One was supposed to be colored yellow, while the other a pale pink. Once out of the oven, you cut the layers up to form a checkerboard pattern, glued them together with apricot jam, and iced the whole thing with marzipan frosting.

"It sounds simple enough to me," Bernie commented as she stopped reading and picked up her pace.

"I think there's a chocolate and vanilla version, too," Libby said as she and her sister got to the pantry just in time to see Nell grabbing the last two bottles of the almond extract, instead of taking just one.

"Excuse me," Libby said, pointing to the bottles Nell had in her basket, "but I think one of those belongs to us."

"Oh, sorry," Nell said, flashing a phony grin. "I guess I made a mistake."

"I guess you did," Bernie told her as she took the bottle of almond extract out of Nell's basket and put it in hers. "I wonder how that happened?"

"What is that supposed to mean?" Nell demanded.

"Exactly what I said," Bernie retorted.

Nell's eyes narrowed. "Are you saying I did it on purpose?" Her blue hair contrasted with her now-reddening face.

"If the shoe fits," Bernie told her. "You and your partner—"

"Are delightful," Libby said, elbowing her sister in the side.

Bernie opened her mouth to say something rude, but then she realized that now was not the time to get into an argument. After all, she and Libby only had an hour to get the cake done, and in the scheme of things, that really wasn't a lot of time, especially since the cake had to cool down before they could construct and ice it.

"You're right," she said, instead. At that point, she turned and helped Libby collect the rest of the ingredients

30   *Isis Crawford*

they needed from the pantry. Then they hurried back to their workstation. Hopefully, nothing else would go wrong.

A half hour later, something did.

"Goats," Bernie said later that evening when she was telling the story to her dad. "I would have expected a lot of things, but goats weren't one of them."

Chapter 5

In the beginning, things went well, she told her dad. Even though Sam had just assured everyone the ovens were safe, Bernie had still crossed her fingers when she'd set the oven temperature to 350 degrees and turned it on. When nothing bad happened, she'd let out a big sigh of relief and started greasing the cake tins and lining them with parchment paper, while Libby had ground the almonds and set them aside.

"You know, there's a special kind of pan for this kind of cake," Libby informed her sister as she started premeasuring the ingredients. "At least that's what the cookbook said."

Bernie raised an eyebrow. "Did you see one here, because I didn't."

"Neither did I," Libby said. She was attaching the paddle to the mixer arm so she could begin combining the butter and sugar, when she heard a bleat.

Libby frowned. "What was that sound?"

Lori looked up from measuring out the ground almonds. "Sounded like a goat to me."

"Me too," Michael said as he measured out the flour.

32 *Isis Crawford*

There was another bleat.

Bernie blew a wisp of hair out of her eyes. "Is that a goat?" she exclaimed.

"I hope we don't have to milk them and make cheese or something like that," Lori cracked. "I can see that happening now."

"Good idea," Adam remarked. "I'll have to suggest it to Sam. We can call it the milk-off."

Ellen laughed. She, Sam, and Doug were standing on the far side of the tent watching the contestants work. "Don't worry," she reassured Lori. "That's not going to happen. The estate manager uses the goats to keep the grass short. It's cheaper and doesn't pollute the way a lawn mower does."

"That's right," Doug added. "They're usually kept in the barn at the other end of the estate. Maybe a couple of them got out?"

Libby shuddered as she turned on the mixer. The paddle began to move. "I hope not," she said as she watched the paddle making patterns in the butter. This was another one of her favorite smells.

"You don't like goats?" Adam asked.

"No, I don't," Libby replied.

"How come?" Adam inquired. "What did they ever do to you?"

"Plenty," Libby said.

"Tell me," Adam responded.

"Why?" Libby asked.

Adam shrugged. "Just nosy, I guess."

"I'll tell you," Bernie volunteered when Libby didn't respond. "It's a pretty funny story."

"I don't think so," Libby said.

"I do," Bernie retorted, and she began. "When my sister

was six years old, we visited a petting zoo in Canada. Everything was going great until a group of goats mobbed her and began eating her shorts. Literally."

"Yeah," Libby continued, unable to resist taking up the tale. "My dad had to wade in and pull me out."

"It was quite the sight," Bernie said, starting to laugh. "He was lifting her up, but the goats weren't letting go."

"They actually pulled my shorts off me," Libby told Adam.

Bernie wiped tears of laughter from her cheeks with the back of her hand. "Which is why my sister hasn't liked goats ever since."

Libby glared at Bernie. "It wasn't that funny," she told her.

"Yeah, Libby. It was."

For a moment, everyone was quiet as they concentrated on what they were doing. Then Bernie saw shadows moving outside the tent. A moment later, she heard more bleats, followed by clomping. Next she spotted heads peeking in from underneath the tent. The sides of the tent began to shake as some of the goats grabbed the tent's guide ropes and began to pull on them, and the rest of the herd moved inside.

"What the hell," Libby cried as a goat ambled toward her, followed by another, and another, and another. Pretty soon, she and her sister were surrounded by twenty of the animals.

"I think they're Angoras," Bernie said as one reached up and tried to grab a stick of butter off the table, while another one started nibbling on the strings of Libby's apron.

"I don't care what they are," Libby told her sister as she began waving her arms around in the air. "Scat, get out of here!"

For a moment, the goat chewing on Libby's apron strings stopped. "Baa," the goat bleated.

"*Baa* to you, too," Libby said.

The goat gave her the side-eye, then went back to what she'd been doing; while another goat started licking Libby's apron; a third one began nibbling on Libby's polo shirt; the rest of the group just milled around.

"Help!" Libby cried while she tried to push them away.

"Ditto," Adam said as two goats started eating his socks.

Bernie studied the scene in front of her. She couldn't believe how many goats there were. At least fifty. Maybe more. The tent was flooded with them, all looking for something interesting to chomp on. Two of them were grabbing at Ellen's polo shirt, while Doug was trying to prevent a baby goat from nibbling on his sandals, and Sam was windmilling his arms around, attempting—and failing—to keep the horde at bay.

A moment later, a man came running into the tent. He was wearing a baseball hat, a T-shirt, cargo shorts, and a panicked expression on his face.

"I'm so sorry," he said. He rested his hand on his heart. "I don't know what happened. They were all in the pen and then they were out and down here."

"I don't care how this happened," Sam told him. "The question is, what are you going to do about it?" he asked as a goat grabbed a stick of butter off Adam and Mike's workstation and began to eat it.

"Hey, goat, give that back to me!" Adam shouted. "That's not good for you."

"Baa," the goat said, headbutting him.

Meanwhile, Libby continued trying to get the goats clustering around her to stop eating her apron. And failing.

A CATERED BAKE-OFF   35

"Just like old times," Bernie said to Libby as the man in the baseball hat began waving his hands in the air, trying to herd the goats out of the tent.

"Scat! Shoo!" he yelled.

The goats weren't impressed. Half of the herd continued clustering around the contestants, while the other half started gnawing on the bottom of the tent.

"Make them go away," Libby cried out as Bernie tried to get the Angoras off Libby's apron. It wasn't working. The moment she got one off, another latched on.

"I'm trying," the goatherd said as he attempted to lead three of the goats out of the tent.

"Well, try harder," Libby told him.

The man stopped and looked around. "This is impossible. I'm going to have to get the dogs," he told her.

"You should have done that in the first place," Sam snapped. Bernie noted that Sam's neck had turned scarlet.

"I thought they were here," the goatherd protested.

Sam gestured around the tent. "Obviously, they aren't."

"I don't understand how this happened," the goatherd said. "Someone must have left the paddock gate open." He scratched under his hat.

"Aren't your dogs supposed to control these creatures or something?" Sam demanded.

The goatherd nodded.

"Then, where the hell are they?" Sam asked.

"I wish I knew," the goatherd replied. "They should have been with the goats." He had been about to say something else, but the tent started to shake.

Bernie looked. Through the tent wall, she could see moving shadows outside. It looked as if some of the goats were still tugging on the tent's guide ropes. In the commotion, she'd forgotten about them.

36   *Isis Crawford*

She was just about to say, "We should do something about them," when it happened.

The tent collapsed.

Just like that.

One moment, it was standing; the next moment, it was flat as a pancake.

Pandemonium erupted.

Chapter 6

For a moment, everything went white. *Literally.*

"What the hell!" Libby exclaimed.

"I can't believe the tent fell down," Bernie said.

"I've heard of everything going black, but white?" Libby told her sister as she listened to the screaming and yelling and bleating around them. Evidently, the goats weren't too happy with the situation, either. "Is everyone okay?" she yelled out.

"Define *okay*," Lori yelled back.

"Uninjured," Libby replied.

"My shoulder hurts," Lori told her.

"I'm talking serious injury," Libby said as Doug screamed at a goat to stop headbutting him.

"This is your fault," he yelled at the goatherd. "You better round them up."

"I'm trying," the goatherd yelled back. "What do you want me to do? Wave a magic wand and make them disappear."

"Sounds like a good idea to me," Ellen said.

"How the hell do we get out of here?" Adam asked, changing the subject. "That's what I want to know."

38   *Isis Crawford*

"Try crawling out from the edge of the tent," Bernie suggested as she lifted the tent top over her head to give herself a little breathing room.

"*Crawl?* You want me to crawl in my white Capris?" Ellen squealed. "Are you kidding me! I don't think so."

"Well, aren't we Miss Fancy Pants," Lori told her.

"I've got a pocketknife on me," Doug said, speaking up before Ellen could reply. "I can cut our way out. It's got a six-inch blade."

"No, no, no," Sam cried. "Whatever you do, don't destroy the tent. That's three thousand dollars."

"Wow, they really overcharged you," Adam said.

"Thanks for the support," Sam told him.

The next ten minutes were complete chaos as everyone, human and caprine alike, fought their way out of the white nylon material shrouding them.

"I don't understand how the goats could have made the tent fall down," Sam bemoaned once everyone had gotten out and were recovering on the grass.

"You probably didn't put it up properly," Doug told him. "Did you put the pegs in deep enough?"

"Of course, I did," Sam replied. "Do you think I'm an idiot!" He sighed.

The tent now looked like a big sheet covering the lawn. A sheet that was moving as the last of the goats made their way out from underneath it.

"Can we settle this later and find those dogs so they can get the goats back where they belong?" Bernie asked.

"Good idea," Adam said, and everyone spread out and began searching. Ten minutes later, Bernie and Libby found the dogs.

"Over here," Bernie yelled as she followed the barks coming from the garden shed. Evidently, someone had closed the two Aussies in the building. She opened the door and the dogs came bounding out.

A CATERED BAKE-OFF 39

"Thank God," the goatherd said as they came running toward him. He bent down to let them lick his face.

"Do you think there's a chance, the dogs got in there by accident?" Sam asked Bernie as he watched the Aussies and the goatherd start rounding up the flock. Fifteen minutes later, the goats were all back where they should be, leaving nine bewildered human beings behind.

Bernie snorted. "And the goats just happened to get out at the same time as the dogs got shut in? Doubtful. I mean, what are the odds?"

"Minuscule," Adam answered.

"I'd say *nonexistent*," Libby replied.

"At least, very unlikely," Ellen chimed in.

"Why would someone do something like this?" Sam complained, gesturing toward the tent.

"Maybe they don't like reality TV," Bernie suggested.

"Or they don't like cooking shows," Libby said. "Or maybe they just don't want to see *this* particular show go on."

"At least this is better than what happened yesterday," Bernie pointed out.

"How do you figure that?" Mike asked. "One of us could have been hit on the head with a tent pole," he pointed out. "We could have gotten a concussion. It's amazing no one did."

"Well, at least no one is going to get cut with flying glass from an exploding oven door," Libby added.

Lori rubbed her shoulder. "One of the poles hit my shoulder," she said. "I wouldn't be surprised if I had a pretty bad bruise."

Adam rolled his eyes. "Always the princess."

"At least it's not broken," Bernie replied.

"You don't know that," Lori said.

"Believe me, you would know if it was," Bernie told Lori, remembering when that had happened to her.

40   *Isis Crawford*

"You should put some ice on it," Libby suggested.

"But why?" Sam wailed, taking control of the conversation again. "That's what I want to know."

"Why did the pole hit my shoulder?" Lori asked him.

"No," Sam cried. "Why is this happening?"

Lori snorted. "Poor planning?"

Sam put his hands on his hips. "Are you saying all of this is my fault, Lori?"

"You are the producer," Lori told him.

"Or maybe this is someone's idea of fun," Bernie hypothesized.

"Like whose?" Adam asked.

"Your guess is as good as mine," Bernie said as she bent down and rubbed her little toe. She'd stubbed it on something while getting out of the tent.

"Maybe we should smudge the place," Lori suggested.

"I don't believe in that stuff," Sam informed her.

"Do you have any enemies?" Bernie asked him when she straightened up. "Does anyone have a grudge against you?"

Sam shook his head. "Not that I know of."

Bernie turned to the other people gathered around. "How about you guys?"

Everyone shook their heads no.

Sam bit his lip as he studied the tent for a moment. He sighed. "I'm glad I took out extra insurance, I can tell you that." Then another thought occurred to him. "I wonder if this is what you call an act of God, because the policy I signed doesn't cover those." Sam turned and surveyed the damage again. He shook his head. "What a mess." He sighed. "It could be worse, though."

"It could always be worse," Doug observed. "That's not much comfort."

"You shouldn't say that, Sam," Bernie remonstrated.

"Getting superstitious in your old age, Bernie?" Libby

asked as she took her apron off and examined it. It looked like Swiss cheese.

"No more than you," Bernie pointed out as Sam sighed for a third time.

"I don't care who said it," he said as he started walking toward the tent. "I'd better take a look and see how badly damaged the tent is," he declared. "Hopefully, it's okay and putting it back up won't be a big deal." He frowned. "I don't think we have enough money left in the budget to rent another one."

"So, are we still doing this?" Bernie inquired, asking the question that had been on everyone's mind since the goat invasion. "Are we still going on with the show?"

"Definitely," Sam said. He looked around. "Unless anyone feels different. Of course," he continued, "I don't know if we'll have time for another practice run-through now. We'll probably have to go straight to air. That's if I can get the tent up in time."

There was a moment of silence as everyone looked at each other. Adam was the first to reply.

"I'm in, practice or no practice," he replied as he combed through his mustache with his fingers.

"Me too," Mike said.

"Make that three," Lori said.

"Four," Doug said.

"I guess I'm in as well," Ellen replied.

Bernie and Libby said the same.

"Then it's unanimous," Sam was saying, when Bernie realized something. Nell was missing from the group.

Chapter 7

Oh my God, Bernie thought. *Is Nell lying under the tent?* She hadn't stepped on her getting out, but then she probably wouldn't have.

Bernie squinched up her eyes and tried to remember when she'd last seen Nell. There'd been that confrontation over the almond extract, and she'd seen her turning on the oven, but now that Bernie thought about it, she didn't remember seeing Nell after that. She hadn't seen her when the tent had come down and she couldn't remember hearing her, either. In fact, she couldn't recall seeing Nell when the goats had stormed the tent. But then, everything was crazy, so maybe Nell had been there, after all, and she hadn't seen her because she'd been too busy fending off the Angoras.

"Hey, where's Nell?" Bernie asked everyone as she counted the people on the lawn, just to make sure she wasn't mistaken. Nope. No Nell.

Lori spoke up. "She's probably still in the bathroom," she informed Bernie. "Lucky thing she missed this. She's not a big animal person."

"Missed what?" Nell said, strolling into view. While everyone else bore marks of their recent encounter with the Angoras, Nell's clothes were intact. They didn't have any holes, rips, or tears in them.

"This." Sam pointed to the tent.

Nell put her hand to her mouth. "Oh my God. What happened?"

"Goats," Libby said.

"*Goats?*" Nell's eyes widened as she looked around. "What goats? I don't see any goats."

Libby answered her. "The goats that invaded the tent. They're gone now. The goatherd rounded them up."

Nell laughed. "I guess I lucked out."

"I guess you did," Doug said.

"So, where were you?" Bernie inquired.

"I was in the bathroom, like Lori told you," Nell replied.

Bernie raised an eyebrow. "For all this time?" she inquired. "You were gone for like what?" Bernie did a rapid calculation in her head. "A half hour?"

"Yes, for all this time." Nell looked around. "I have IBS, people, not that it's anybody's business," she added.

"Sorry," Bernie told her. "I was just worried about you."

Nell put her hands on her hips. "It didn't sound that way to me. It sounded as if you were suggesting something."

"Did you?" Bernie inquired.

"Like you think I had something to do with the goats getting loose," Nell replied.

"I didn't say that you did," Bernie pointed out.

"That's ridiculous," Nell countered. "Why would I do something like that? I don't like goats. They're dirty and smelly."

"I told them you didn't like animals," Lori said to Nell.

Libby jumped into the conversation. "Maybe this is your idea of a joke."

"Don't be an idiot," Nell replied.

44   *Isis Crawford*

"So, now I'm an idiot?" Libby snapped. "You realize someone could have gotten hurt."

Nell opened her mouth to reply, but before she could, Sam coughed. The four women turned toward him.

"Ladies," he said, "I realize everyone is upset. This has been an upsetting morning."

"Now, that's an understatement if I ever heard one," Ellen cracked.

Sam ignored her and continued with what he was saying. "I think we all need to go home, have a cup of tea, and think about the morning's events. Then I suggest we reconvene here tomorrow afternoon and discuss what we want to do. That will give me a chance to see about the tent and go over the equipment and make sure it's still in working order."

"So, no Battenberg cake?" Lori asked.

"Probably not. But that's TBD. If nothing is damaged and we can get the tent back up, we might have time for one more run-through. We'll have to check and see," Sam said.

Everyone nodded and began walking toward their vehicles.

"What do you think?" Bernie asked Libby when they reached Mathilda, their van.

"About what?" Libby replied.

"Nell."

"What about her, Bernie?"

"Do you think she let the goats out?" Bernie asked while she hopped in the van and started her up.

Libby turned the question over in her mind as she buckled her seat belt and turned on the air-conditioning. "Well," she said after a moment had passed, "she *was* gone for a while."

"Exactly," Bernie replied. "I don't remember seeing her

at her station after I was done buttering the layer pans. Do you?"

Libby thought for a moment. "Now that you mention it, I'm not sure. On the other hand, she was a little bit out of my line of sight. And anyway, to be honest, I really wasn't paying attention."

Bernie tapped the steering wheel with her fingernails as she considered the timeline. "She certainly had enough time to walk over to the paddock, shut the dogs in the shed, and let the goats out."

"If she walked fast," Libby said.

"It is a bit of a hike," Bernie allowed.

"But why would she do it?" Libby asked after another moment had gone by. "What's her motive?"

Bernie adjusted the strap on her sundress. "Well, this is the second rehearsal that has gone off the rails."

"And?" Libby questioned.

"And we haven't been able to rehearse."

"None of us have," Libby pointed out.

"True," Bernie answered, "but Nell was judging that children's baking show last year, so she's familiar with how cameras work."

Libby laughed. "So, you're saying all this stuff is happening because Nell wants an edge?"

"Okay. It is a stretch," Bernie allowed. She was silent for a minute. Then she remembered something else. "Didn't Adam and Nell have a thing?"

"You mean a *thing* thing?"

"Yes," Bernie replied.

"No. You're thinking of his cousin Greg," Libby informed her. "And even if they did, so what?"

"You're right. So much for that thought," Bernie remarked as she drove up the long, winding road that led to the estate's gate. On the way out, Bernie took a detour and

46 *Isis Crawford*

stopped at the paddock that housed the goats. She wanted to take a look at their setup for herself.

The Aussies ran up and started barking at them the moment Bernie and Libby got out of the van. Bernie was petting them and feeding them pieces of a leftover corn muffin from the breakfast that they'd eaten in the van that morning, on their way to rehearsal, when the goatherd walked out of the barn.

"You guys are going to be Starsky and Hutch's favorite people from now on," he told Bernie, indicating the dogs with a nod of his head.

"I hope this is okay," Bernie said.

The goatherd laughed. "Believe me, they've eaten a lot worse than corn muffins."

Without his hat on, the goatherd looked younger to Bernie. He reminded her of someone, but she couldn't figure out who that was. She hated when that happened. As she reflected on how unreliable memory can be, the goatherd apologized again for what had happened earlier in the day.

"I'm getting a padlock for the gate," he told them. "That way, this won't occur again."

"So, you think it was an accident?" Libby asked him.

The goatherd held out his hands in a your-guess-is-as-good-as-mine gesture. "You got me," he said. "Goats are smart. One of them could have figured out how to push the gate open and then they'd all come out. It's not impossible."

One of the Aussies barked, and the goatherd petted him. "I guess Starsky wants more corn muffin," he said.

Bernie laughed and fed the dog the last bit of the muffin. "He definitely is the food-driven one of the pair."

"How do you think the dogs ended up in the gardening shed?" Libby asked.

This time, the goatherd shrugged. "They could have chased something inside—there are rabbits and squirrels and chipmunks all over the place—and the door could have swung closed behind them. It tends to do that, and then they couldn't get out. The door's lock is funky, or . . ." Here he paused.

". . . someone could have lured the dogs into the shed, locked them in, and let the goats out," Bernie said, finishing the goatherd's sentence for him.

"That too. They certainly could have," he allowed. "But why would they? What's the point?"

"To disrupt things," Bernie suggested.

"Well, the goats certainly did that," the goatherd conceded, looking back at his charges while he rubbed the stubble on his chin with his fist.

"Anyone you know complain about them?" Libby asked. "Maybe this is their way of getting back."

"The next-door neighbor," the goatherd promptly responded. "In fact, this past spring, he went to the town board and complained after a couple of the goats wandered away and managed to get over to this guy's garden and eat his peonies."

"We should talk to him," Bernie said. "What's his name?"

"Howard Crohn."

"Haven't heard of him," Bernie said.

"He moved in last year," the goatherd told her. "But he's away for the summer. He has a beach house down in Hatteras. You can check if you want."

"We will."

Then Libby changed the subject. "I don't suppose you saw anyone around here before the goats escaped?"

"Now that you mention it, I think I might have heard someone coughing outside," the goatherd replied after a

48   *Isis Crawford*

moment's reflection. "But I'm not really sure, because I was in my cottage, getting something to eat. It's down there by the stream." He pointed toward the grove of birch trees. "Sorry I'm not much help," he said sheepishly. "I seem to be doing a lot of apologizing here," he added. Then he looked at his watch. "Hey, I've got to get going," he told them. "I've got the left half of the front lawn to graze today. Can't have my guys being late for work. They might get docked." And he laughed at his own joke.

Bernie and Libby thanked him and got back in Mathilda. On the way out, they waved to the security guard stationed at the entrance to the estate. He waved back. At the main road, they took a right and headed to the neighbor's house, where the goats had eaten the peonies. It was a short drive.

"Guess the goatherd was right," Libby said to Bernie after she'd knocked on Howard Crohn's door and no one had answered. She was turning to get back in the van, but she spotted a neighbor across the street weeding her flower bed. Libby decided to check in with her.

"He's away," the neighbor informed her after she'd straightened up and brushed the dirt from her hands. "Won't be back for another couple of weeks. You can leave a message for him with me if you want."

Libby thanked her, told her it wouldn't be necessary, and left. "Of course," she said to Bernie when she got back in the van, "there's nothing to prevent this guy from driving back, letting the goats out, and going back to Hatteras."

"Aside from the fact that it's a fifteen-hour drive and he has no motive," Bernie asked.

"Motive, schmotive. Who needs a motive?" Libby said as she rolled down the window. It was definitely getting hotter out.

"I hope this is the end of this—whatever this is," Bernie said as she took a right onto Avalon Avenue.

"I do, too," Libby agreed while Bernie stopped for a red light.

While she was waiting for the light to change, Bernie reached over and took a sip of the coffee she'd filled her thermos with this morning before she'd left for the estate. It had been a long day, and it was only two in the afternoon. She sighed. "I think I could do with something a bit stronger right now," she commented as the light turned green. "Like a really stiff drink."

"You and me both," Libby replied. "You and me both."

Chapter 8

The next day went by smoothly, or as Amber, their counter person, would have said, it was a no-drama kinda day. Except for the graduation parties and weddings, their day-to-day business was usually on the slow side this time of year, since this was when people went away on vacation or spent time at their summer camps. If that hadn't been the case, Libby and Bernie wouldn't have agreed to participate in *The Longely Bake-Off*.

This was the time of the year when they repaired the things that needed to be repaired in the shop, repainted the things that needed to be repainted, and tried out the new recipes they were going to sell in the shop in the coming year. This June, they'd ordered new chairs for the tables out front, painted the shop walls a soothing mint green, gotten new awnings for the front windows, filed their sales tax, paid their workmen's comp for A Little Taste of Heaven, and spent the rest of their free time practicing baking their signature dish.

"Maybe whoever did this has decided to turn his attentions to someplace else," Libby suggested to her dad later that afternoon.

Sean snorted. "I wouldn't count on that if I were you,"

their dad said as he ate a piece of the peach pie his daughters had brought upstairs from the shop. Of all the pies his daughters made, he had to say that this was one of his favorites, especially when the peaches were full of flavor, which these were. "By the way, this is excellent."

"You like the crust?" Bernie asked.

"I don't like the crust, I *love* the crust!" Sean exclaimed. "What's the difference?"

"Don't tell anyone, but I added a tablespoon of lard to the mixture," Libby informed him.

Sean grinned. "In this day and age, that seems like blackmail fodder to me."

Bernie laughed. "This is just for us. I can't imagine what our customers would say if they found out."

"They'd probably think it was worse than feeding them death caps," Sean said. "People are very strange these days. My mom used to make piecrusts with lard all the time and I'm still standing."

"Different time, different place, different beliefs," Bernie observed. She shook her head and changed the subject. "Tell me, do you think whoever is screwing around with us during our run-throughs for the show is going to stop?"

Sean shook his head. "That's hard to answer, considering we don't know what they're trying to accomplish."

"Stop the rehearsals?" Bernie responded.

"That's one possibility," Sean agreed as he savored his next-to-last bite of pie.

"Or they like playing practical jokes?" Bernie suggested.

"Then they have a strange sense of humor," Libby observed.

"A very strange sense of humor," Sean agreed. Just as he was about to eat the last piece of his pie, Sean heard the downstairs door open and someone coming up the stairs.

"Are you expecting anybody?" he asked his daughters.

52   *Isis Crawford*

They both shook their heads. A moment later, Lori opened the door and walked in. She'd dyed her bangs pink. Combined with neon green, the effect was jarring.

"Wow," Bernie said, unable to help herself.

"My hair, right?" Lori asked, looking abashed.

Bernie nodded.

"I know," Lori said. "It's what I do when I get nervous. Listen," she continued, "I want to apologize for the other day. I was . . . nervous."

"We all were," Bernie said.

Lori smiled. "Good. I probably should have called first, but I wanted to show you this." And she handed Libby a folded-up piece of paper.

Libby unfolded the paper, looked at it, and frowned. "So much for a quiet day," she said. Then she proceeded to read the note out loud. " 'Roses are red/Violets are blue/You stink as a cook/Your partner does, too.' "

"You didn't write this, did you?" Lori asked.

"You're kidding, right?" Libby said.

Lori giggled nervously. "I figured you didn't. It's just that after that last rehearsal, Nell said I should ask." Lori's voice dropped off as Libby handed the paper back to her.

"Where did you get that?" Bernie asked.

"It was slipped under my door. Mike got something, too," Lori informed her. "He told me his said, 'Roses are red/Violets are blue/Cookies are sweet/Unlike you two.' I already called Sam and told him about them," she said, anticipating Libby's next question.

"Was Mike's note slipped under his door as well?" Sean asked.

Lori shook her head. "No. It was left in his mailbox."

"I feel left out," Bernie commented.

"Don't worry," Lori told her. "I noticed an envelope on the windshield of your van."

"Guess I should go check it out," Bernie said as she lev-

A CATERED BAKE-OFF   53

ered herself off the sofa. "You want a piece of pie? Some iced coffee when I come back up?" she asked Lori.

"Pie?" Lori repeated, brightening.

"Peach and blueberry," Libby told her. They'd just finished off the last of the peach pie.

Lori grinned. Bernie grinned back. No matter what, it was impossible to be unhappy when eating pie. Pie just made everything better. It was just a fact of nature.

"I'll help bring everything up," Lori said.

"No," Libby said, "you sit. I'll get it."

"How come you want her to stay upstairs?" Bernie whispered to Libby when they stepped outside.

"I don't want to take the chance of her glancing in the prep room and seeing our"—she hesitated searching for the right word—"construction. I mean, it would suck to have to come up with something else at this stage of the game."

"It certainly would," Bernie said. "If there is a show. I tell you what, you get the envelope and I'll get the pie," she told Libby, who nodded her assent.

Five minutes later, the sisters were back upstairs.

"Boy, does that look good," Lori remarked as Bernie put half of a peach-and-blueberry pie on the coffee table.

"And it tastes even better," Sean said. "Not that I'm prejudiced or anything." He turned to Libby and nodded at the envelope she was holding. "Let me see," he said.

"Be my guest," Libby answered, handing the open envelope to him. He took out the sheet of paper, unfolded it, cleared his throat, and read aloud: " 'Roses are red/Violets are blue/Cooking is great/But not for you two.' "

"So, what do you think?" Bernie asked him.

"I think whoever wrote this needs to work on their poetry skills," Sean replied as Cindy, the cat, came out of his bedroom.

"Besides that, Dad," Bernie said as she watched their

cat jump on her dad's lap, turn around three times, and sit down.

"You need to report these to the police," Sean said.

"I already have," Lori told him. "They said to keep them informed and that there really isn't too much they can do for us right now."

"I don't see why not," Libby told him.

"Lack of resources," Sean replied promptly as he started rubbing the tips of Cindy's ears. Her purring filled the room.

"But this is harassment," Libby replied.

"They're not direct threats," Sean pointed out.

"But what about what's happened at the estate?" Bernie demanded.

"Well," Sean replied, "you could call those events practical jokes."

Libby snorted. "Be serious."

"I am. After all, no one was hurt," Sean pointed out.

"But property was damaged," Libby replied.

"True," Sean said. He paused for a minute, then said, "Lori, I seem to remember your partner, Nell, getting arrested for a series of practical jokes a couple of years ago."

"It was one joke," Lori protested.

Bernie turned to her father and asked what it was.

"She put a skunk in her ex's bedroom," Sean told her. "He couldn't go in there for a couple of weeks."

"He deserved it. He was a real stinker," Lori said, laughing. "Although," she added, "the person she got it from told her it was deskunked."

"And then there's Lucy," Sean continued. Lucy, aka Lucas Broadbent, was Longely's current chief of police.

"What about him?" Libby asked.

"He's probably unwilling to prosecute. He hates Sam

A CATERED BAKE-OFF 55

Levine's guts; so barring a major crime, he'll probably read the reports and let them sit on his desk."

"Why does he hate him?" Bernie wanted to know.

Sean smiled. "Something about his wife and your producer winning a dance competition," Sean replied. "At least that's what Clyde tells me."

"You're kidding," Bernie said. "Lucy is that petty and vindictive?"

"Yes, he is, along with some other words I can't say in polite company," Sean replied.

Bernie shook her head. "I don't get it," she observed as she began to slice the pie.

"What don't you get?" Sean asked.

"The goats, the oven, the notes," Bernie replied.

"The first two you could put down to accidents. It's a stretch, but you could. The notes, on the other hand, are childish, but you can't call them accidental." Sean scratched the tip of his nose. "You can't call them threatening, either."

"But you can call them old-fashioned," Lori observed.

Sean cocked his head. "What do you mean?"

"They're on paper. They haven't gone viral," Lori replied.

"So, you mean some old guy sent them?" Sean said.

"I didn't say that," Lori said.

"Well, not in so many words," Sean told her. He waved his free hand in the air. "Now let's get to the pie."

"You want another slice?" Bernie asked her dad after she had placed Lori's slice in front of her.

"Do I look like I'm at death's door?" Sean asked indignantly.

"I'll take that as a yes," Bernie said, cutting her dad a large piece and handing it to him.

56   *Isis Crawford*

"This is really good," Lori exclaimed after she'd swallowed. "Do I detect a pinch of ginger in there?"

"I'm impressed," Libby told her.

Lori nodded her head in thanks. "As well you should be." Then she said, "You're good, but not good enough. Too bad you're going to lose."

Bernie snorted. "Like they say, don't count your biscuits before they bake. How's Nell doing, by the way?" she asked, changing the subject.

Lori smiled. "Fine. Why are you asking?"

"Just making conversation," Libby said.

"How long have you had her for a partner?" Bernie asked, realizing at that moment that Lori looked uncomfortable.

"Awhile," Lori said as she glanced at the clock on the wall. "Oh, my heavens," she cried. "I didn't realize it was so late. I have to get a move on." She gathered up her belongings and left.

"I guess she didn't like the pie, after all," Libby observed.

"I don't think it was the pie. I think it was my mentioning Nell that freaked her out," Bernie replied. "I hear the two of them aren't getting along that well these days."

Libby blinked an eyelash out of her eye. "Do you think she came to hire us to find out who wrote the notes?" she mused as she listened to the downstairs door closing.

"Then why didn't she?" Sean challenged.

Libby shrugged. "Maybe she had a change of heart."

"Or maybe she came to see your reaction to the notes," Sean posited as he watched Lori get into her beat-up orange Kia and pull away from the curb.

"Why would she do that?" Libby asked.

"Because she wrote them," Bernie suggested. "What do you think, Dad?" she asked, turning to him.

"It's certainly a possibility," Sean responded. "But then, so could anyone else," he added as he tackled the pie. "You didn't use lard in this crust, did you?" he inquired, changing the subject after he'd taken a bite.

Libby shook her head.

"I can tell. I like the one with the lard better. It's flakier. Sometimes the old ways are the best," Sean pontificated.

Bernie was about to answer him, but her cell rang. It was Sam telling them that he'd gotten a note, as had Adam, and he was calling a meeting tonight at nine to discuss what they should do.

Bernie sighed. She'd planned on spending the evening with Brandon. Hopefully, the meeting would be short.

Chapter 9

Bernie and Libby pulled up in front of Sam's house a little before nine.

"It looks as if we're going to be the last ones to arrive again," Bernie said as she studied the cars parked side by side in the driveway.

"Nice to be consistent," Libby remarked while looking at the nondescript ranch in front of them. There was nothing wrong with it, but there was nothing right with it, either. "Somehow I expected something a little grander."

"Me too," Bernie remarked as they hurried up the walkway and rang the bell. It echoed inside, cutting through the voices.

"It's open," Sam called out. "Come on in."

Libby and Bernie did. They walked into a small hallway and took a left into the living room. Sam was standing in front of the fireplace while the rest of the cast members were sitting on a large sectional. Everyone nodded at Bernie and Libby, and they nodded back.

"By the way, my wife says to say hello. She and the twins are visiting her mom," Sam informed them as he told the sisters to sit in the two folding chairs. They were the only empty seats in the room. "I want to thank everyone for coming," he said as Libby and Bernie settled themselves down. He cleared his throat and continued. "I suppose you're wondering why I called this meeting."

Mike put his cup of coffee down on the end table next to the sofa. "You're kidding, right? The only thing I'm wondering is, why did it take you so long?"

Sam frowned. "Okay, Mike. Point taken. I guess I was hoping this would go away, but it hasn't."

"Obviously," Adam said.

Sam started pacing. "So we have some decisions to make now."

Nell frowned. "You think?"

Doug leaned forward. "Is the show being canceled?"

"God, I hope not," Lori said, thinking of all the work she and her partner, Nell, had put in getting ready for it.

"Not if I have anything to do with it," Sam said grimly as he removed an envelope from his shirt's breast pocket. "But you may feel different after you hear this."

"Don't forget about mine," Adam reminded him.

"Believe me, I'm not," Sam replied.

Nell's eyes widened fractionally. "You're kidding, right?"

"No. I'm not. It's simple. I want you to tell me what you want to do after you've heard what I'm about to read you. I thought you were entitled to know."

"Know what?" Doug demanded.

"He'll tell us, if you'll let him," Mike said.

"I don't believe I was talking to you, Mickey," Doug snapped.

"I prefer to be called Mike, as you well know," Mike said.

Doug shrugged. "Sorry, Mickey. Oops. Mike."

Sam clapped his hands. "People, please listen. It's getting late."

60   *Isis Crawford*

"Sorry," both Doug and Mike muttered.

Everyone watched as Sam opened the envelope, took a piece of paper out, and put on his reading glasses. He cleared his throat. "This note was slipped under my door this morning."

"Like Nell's and mine," Lori said.

Sam nodded. "This one, however, is a lot more explicit and a lot less amusing." He stopped and looked around, making sure he had everyone's attention. When he was satisfied that he had, he read out loud: " 'To Whom it May Concern, If you go ahead with the program, you, the contestants, and everyone on the set will suffer. Punishment comes to those who have transgressed. You all know what you have done. And don't think I don't mean this, because I do. You've been warned. What happened at the run-throughs was just the beginning.' "

Everyone looked at each other.

"I don't suppose it was signed?" Nell asked.

"I wish," Sam replied.

"I liked the nursery rhymes better," Mike observed.

"Me too," Sam agreed. Then he turned to Adam. "Why don't you read the note you got," he suggested.

"With pleasure." And Adam took a note out of his pocket, smoothed it out with the edge of his palm, and read: " 'Don't do it. You'll be sorry if you do. Punishment comes to those who transgress.' "

"Looks like we have a theme going here," Bernie observed.

Nell pursed her lips. "Don't do what?" she asked.

Mike answered before Adam could. "Duh. Compete in the bake-off, obviously."

"You don't know that," Nell protested.

"Well, given the note that Sam read us, what the hell else could it be referring to?" Mike asked her.

A CATERED BAKE-OFF   61

"Mike's right," Ellen said.

Sam turned to Adam. "Did your note come in a plain white envelope?"

"Yup," Adam replied.

"Did it have a stamp or an address?" Sam continued.

"It didn't have anything on it," Adam told him.

Lori twisted a lock of her hair around her finger. "I don't understand," Lori said.

"What's to understand?" Sam countered. "I think it's fairly obvious that someone doesn't want us to go ahead with the contest. If this isn't a threat, I don't know what is."

"Why? I mean, it's a bake-off, for God's sake," Nell said as she rebuttoned the button on her blouse that had popped open.

"It sounds as if whoever wrote this thinks that you guys did something terrible and need to be punished for it," Libby observed.

"Speak for yourself," Nell said.

"Maybe the person who wrote it has something against reality TV," Ellen suggested.

"That's absurd," Doug said.

Before Ellen could reply, Adam turned to Sam. "Did you do something bad?"

"Not that I'm aware of," Sam replied. He put his hand over his heart. "I have led a life as pure as the drifting snow."

Bernie smiled. "The phrase is *as pure as the driven snow.*"

Adam leaned over and rested his mug on the coffee table. "Ditto—whatever kind of snow we're talking about."

Mike snorted. "More like the snow that's on the ground at the end of the season, if you ask me."

Everyone laughed at that.

62   *Isis Crawford*

"Maybe whoever wrote the notes was upset they didn't get picked to be on TV," Libby suggested.

"I find that hard to believe," Sam told her. "This is a local show. It's not prime time."

"I don't know," Nell said. "People these days are nuts."

Bernie took a deep breath and let it out. Then she asked Sam if he'd shown the letter to the police.

"I did," he replied.

"And what did they say?" Libby asked, remembering her dad's comments.

"What you said before," Sam told her. "It's probably someone we didn't pick for the contest and that usually stuff like this turns out to be nothing."

"Given what happened in the last two run-throughs, I find that difficult to believe," Libby commented.

"I don't suppose the police dusted the envelope and the note for fingerprints?" Bernie asked Sam.

"As a matter of fact, they did. The only prints were mine," Sam informed her as he folded the note up and put it in his pocket.

"So, what do you think?" Bernie asked Sam.

He shook his head. "Honestly, I don't know what to think anymore."

Adam pointed to his note. "Did anyone else here get one of these?"

"We got a nursery rhyme," Bernie said.

"We did, too," Lori replied.

"Ditto," Mike answered.

"I wish I hadn't read it," Nell told them.

"How about you guys?" Bernie asked the two judges. They shook their heads.

Adam frowned. "You mean Sam, Bernie, Libby, Lori, Nell, Mike, and I are the only ones that got these notes?"

"So it would appear," Bernie observed.

"I guess we're special," Lori remarked.

Adam made a face. "Terrific. I'm so excited."

Bernie finished the coffee she'd poured herself from the jug sitting on the sideboard. Before turning her attention back to Sam, she briefly thought about the implications of what Adam had just said.

Sam cleared his throat and began to speak. "I just wanted to make sure that everyone knew about this." He looked around the room. "Does anyone want to pull out?"

"Because of the note?" Lori asked. She corrected herself. "Excuse me, *notes*. Hell no."

"Don't be ridiculous," Nell said.

"Of course not," Mike said.

"Screw whoever wrote these," Adam said in a turnabout. "I'm not giving up my fifteen minutes of fame."

Nell laughed. "You wish. Lori and I are going to whomp your ass."

"Very elegant," Adam told her. "Also, very unlikely. Mike and I are going to make French toast out of you."

"I think that's for the judges to decide," Sam said as he looked around the room.

The two judges nodded in agreement.

Sam continued speaking. "It sounds as if everyone wants to go on with the contest."

A chorus of *you bet* and *of course, we do* greeted him.

"Are you sure?" Sam asked. "Because if you're not, if you have doubts, now would be the time to pull out. No one will blame you if you do."

"I'll blame you," Mike said.

Everyone laughed again.

"Last chance," Sam said.

"We're all in," Bernie said.

64   *Isis Crawford*

Sam smiled and rubbed his hands together. "Okay, then. That's that." And he went into the kitchen. A moment later, he came out holding a tray bearing nine glasses and two bottles of champagne.

"I'm impressed," Bernie said, looking at the label on the bottle. "You got the good stuff."

Sam grinned. "Only the best for my contestants. Certain things are not worth drinking if they're cheap." Then he set the tray down on the coffee table, picked up the first bottle of champagne, and began loosening its cork until it popped, and the champagne began pouring out.

Sam filled up Nell, Lori, Adam, and Mike's glasses. Then he opened the second bottle and filled up everybody else's.

"To us," he said, raising his glass.

"To flaky piecrusts and tender cakes," Nell said.

"And smooth buttercreams," Mike added.

"Good ratings," Adam said.

"And satisfied customers," Bernie said, continuing the list.

"Not to mention, the ten-thousand-dollar prize," Lori commented.

Everyone clinked their glasses together and drank.

"This is going to be interesting," Bernie observed.

"I hope not," Libby told her sister. "We've had enough of interesting to last for a while. I'm not a big fan." And she wasn't. In her mind, *interesting* meant *trouble*. "I like boring."

"I guess we'll find out," Bernie said.

"I guess we will," Libby agreed. She finished off the last of her champagne and put her glass down. "I mean we've been invaded by a herd of goats, the tent collapsed, and the oven exploded. What else could go wrong?"

"Well, the hand of God could come down and smite us," suggested Sam.

"The way we're going, I wouldn't be surprised," Lori observed.

"That would definitely increase our ratings," Doug joked as Bernie looked around the room.

For some reason she couldn't name, she was beginning to get a bad feeling in the pit of her stomach, and it wasn't indigestion.

Chapter 10

"Here we go again," Bernie said to Libby on Saturday as they paused at the gate to give the security guard their names. The rest of the week had been quiet, and Libby and Bernie were praying that it would stay that way. "Let's hope this time there are no interruptions."

"It's showtime," Libby sang out as they drove by the flock of goats peacefully grazing near a white birch tree. The goatherd waved at them, and they waved back as they watched the Aussies go after a kid that was wandering off in the direction of the stream that ran through the estate.

"I would think a lawn mower would be easier than the goats," Bernie commented as she drove down the road to where she was supposed to park her van. "Less work."

Libby laughed. "But not as ecologically correct. On the other hand, lawn mowers don't eat T-shirts," she observed as she looked at the tent. It was back up. It looked a little worse for wear, with a few grass stains here and there, but the important thing was that it was still standing, even if it was tilting to the left. You'd have to look closely to see the patches where the goats had nibbled on the fabric. Sam had done a good job, Libby decided.

A CATERED BAKE-OFF 67

"I hope the tent stays up," Bernie commented as she parked Mathilda next to the other cars. "It doesn't look very stable to me."

Then she and her sister walked down the hill toward everyone else. The sisters were the last ones to arrive. In the distance, Bernie could see that Nell had toned down her outfit, opting for gray pants and a white shirt, instead of her usual bright clothes, as opposed to Lori, who had gone in the opposite direction and was wearing a red top and purple skirt.

"She looks like a clown," Libby said, commenting on Lori's pink-and-green hair.

"Well, you certainly can't miss her," Bernie commented.

"I wish we could have gotten through one rehearsal in the tent," Libby replied, changing the topic.

"Me too," Bernie agreed. "A little practice would have been nice."

They'd practiced their first and third assignments in the shop, and Bernie felt good about those, but it would have been nice to have a little more practice in situ. That way, they would have gone into the show knowing what the ovens' and mixers' quirks were. Bernie was thinking that this was a little like being in a traveling band and setting up in a strange venue. You never knew where the dead spots were—like you never knew where the cold and hot spots in an oven were, if you hadn't used it.

During Bernie's ruminating, her sister said something.

"What?" Bernie said, turning to her. "I'm sorry, I missed what you were saying."

"I was telling you that I wish I knew what the technical challenge was going to be."

"Me too," Bernie replied.

Unfortunately, there was no way to know, because the judges announced that when the contest was under way;

68   *Isis Crawford*

and although both she and Libby had looked through some of the old *Great British Bake Off* shows on YouTube, trying to see if there was some sort of pattern they could discern, they hadn't been able to spot one.

"I hope we don't have to do puff pastry," Libby confided to her sister.

"I'd rather do that than strudel," Bernie replied as she and her sister hurried down the hill.

"Now that you mention it, I would too," Libby reflected. While her mom had been able to roll out the dough so thin you could read a newspaper through it—literally—neither sister had ever acquired the knack.

On the other hand, Libby was fairly confident about the other two assignments. She thought about their signature bake again. She still liked the cake they'd named Tropical Paradise. The three layers of genoise should work, because the three layers would bake and cool off faster than two layers. And the rest of it, the mango and pineapple puree, flavored with a pinch of ginger, and the rum drizzle were almost foolproof, as was the coconut-flavored buttercream. She was just a bit worried that the cake decorations—a sprinkle of toasted pistachio nuts, glacé mint leaves, and pineapple bits—might be too much.

But she had full confidence in their showstopper. Tasked with building an architectural icon out of pastry, she and Bernie had chosen the Golden Gate Bridge, and she was still glad they had. Even though, Libby admitted, two hours wasn't a lot of time to construct their edifice out of pastry, fill it with chocolate-raspberry–custard filling, then paint it with a raspberry glaze and dot the bridge with vehicles made from dark and milk chocolate and toasted walnuts.

The vehicles were the problem. They were extremely fiddly, meaning they took a lot of time and attention to construct. On the other hand, they really brought the bridge to life. Hopefully, they'd be able to manage everything. It had worked out when they'd done it in the prep room, and Libby supposed that they could omit the vehicles if they ran out of time.

Bernie was thinking the same thing as her sister as she watched one of the cameras being rolled into place. Things should be fine, she was telling herself, *should* being the operative word here. That was the thing with baking, the thing that made this kind of contest so nerve-wracking. You could bake something ten times over and it would come out perfectly, but the eleventh time could turn into a disaster.

First of all, there were the time restrictions. Those didn't help. They were designed to up the pressure. Basically, there was no room for mistakes. And then there was the weather, since they were, for all intents and purposes, baking outside. No air-conditioning in a tent! Which mattered because humidity and temperature affected how things were going to turn out, especially with baking. For example, if it was too hot out, the buttercream would melt; and if it was raining, the flour would absorb moisture and turn tough. Fortunately, the day was dry and sunny, although showers were predicted for seven that evening.

They couldn't have asked for a better day weather-wise, Bernie decided as she studied the other contestants and judges. As she did, she realized that something seemed off. Lori was nibbling on her thumbnail; Nell was twisting a lock of hair around one of her fingers; Mike and Adam were pacing back and forth. Meanwhile, Doug and Ellen were huddled a little way away, talking to Sam. Bernie thought it looked like a serious conversation. When Sam saw Bernie and Libby, he waved them over.

"What's up?" Bernie asked as they approached.

70   *Isis Crawford*

"This," Doug said, and handed Bernie a note. "This was waiting for me on the set when I got in this morning," he explained as Bernie opened it.

The contents were short and sweet. She read the message out loud: " 'Roses are red/Violets are blue/Don't worry/ You'll be dead soon, too.' "

"And it came with this," Doug said, pointing to a small white box on the table, the kind of box you would put a piece of jewelry in.

Bernie and Libby peered inside. A dead mouse lay on its back, feet up, nestled on a little cotton square.

"Poor baby," Libby said.

"Well, there's one thing you can say about whoever is doing this," Bernie remarked. "They're persistent."

"And not very subtle," Ellen remarked. "They've definitely upped their game."

"That's for sure," Bernie said, turning to Ellen. "Did you get anything?"

"You mean like a note?" Ellen answered.

"Yes. Or something dead," Bernie replied.

Ellen shuddered. "No, thank God."

"This time, the note was on the desk in the office," Sam explained to Bernie and Libby. "And before you ask, the door was opened, and everyone here had access to it."

"I take it, you called the cops?" Bernie asked Sam.

He nodded.

"What did they say?"

"Not much, Bernie," Sam replied. "They said they'd send someone over to pick up the letter and the mouse when they had a minute."

"So they're not exactly treating this as urgent," Bernie observed.

"Nope," Sam said. "They are not."

"What about doing that whole DNA thing they do on TV?" Doug asked.

A CATERED BAKE-OFF 71

"What about it?" Sam said.

"Maybe they could get an ID off the box or the note or the mouse."

"I wouldn't hold my breath," Bernie told him. "That's expensive and there's a long turnaround time. Like maybe six months, the last time I heard." Then she asked Doug if he'd gotten a note before.

Doug shook his head. "No, I haven't."

"Lucky you," Lori said.

"Must be my sterling personality," Doug cracked.

"Anybody show up on the security cameras?" Libby inquired.

Sam shook his head. "Nope."

Bernie stifled a sneeze. She hoped she wasn't getting sick. "What did the guard say?"

"He didn't see anything, either," Sam told her.

"Well, anyone could climb over the wall around the estate," Bernie pointed out. It was constructed out of rocks and measured four feet high. "Even Libby could."

"Ha. Ha," Libby said. "Very funny."

"But true," Bernie said.

"So, now what?" Doug turned to Sam and asked.

"Now we hire extra security. I don't see any other choice." Sam made a face. "Another unanticipated expense. Just what I don't need."

Bernie gestured to the property. "The owner won't cover it?"

Sam frowned. "Nope. It's my problem according to his lawyers."

"Funny how the rich guys are always so cheap," Ellen noted.

"How do you think the rich guys get rich?" Nell asked.

"How come you're talking to the lawyers, Sam?" Doug asked.

72   *Isis Crawford*

"They've been my point of contact. I haven't actually talked to the owner," he replied.

"That's because he's probably too busy keeping track of his multimillion-dollar mansions, yachts, and private planes to be bothered," Mike observed.

Sam laughed. "No. That was the first owner."

"Yeah, Mike," Bernie said. "Although the second owner was no piker, either, in the money department. Local gossip says he lost the estate in a poker game, something like eighteen, twenty years ago. At least that's what my dad told me."

"That must have been some poker game," Ellen observed.

"I guess when you have that much money, it doesn't really matter," Doug said. "This place would be like a house in the burbs to him. It's all economy of scale."

"I wouldn't know," Lori commented. "I'm still counting pennies."

Sam checked the time on his phone. "Okay, ladies and gentlemen, we really need to start filming. Otherwise, we're going to end up behind schedule."

"Okay, then," Bernie said. "Let's bake."

Sam grinned. "Works for me."

Chapter 11

"It's showtime," Libby said to Bernie as everyone headed toward the tent.

When they were inside and had found their marks, the director signaled for the cameras to start rolling. Once they'd gone live, the next ten minutes were spent introducing the contestants to the audience at home. After that, Doug gave everyone their assignment.

"You have exactly one hour to bake and decorate your signature cake," he told the assembled teams standing in front of him. "I expect perfection in your creations, nothing less is acceptable." There was a nervous titter. "I'm serious," he told everyone. Then he clapped his hands and said the magic words: "On your mark, get set, bake."

On Doug's last syllable, the teams sprinted to the pantry to collect their supplies. When they'd gotten everything they needed, they hurried back to their workstations, trying not to trip on the cables snaking across the floor. The three stations had been set up in a triangle so everyone could see what the other teams were doing.

"Good luck," Nell called to Bernie and Libby as she studied the controls on her cooktop.

74   *Isis Crawford*

"Good luck to you, too," Libby replied as she and her sister got down to work. An hour wasn't a lot of time, she reflected, feeling a flash of panic creep up her spine. At least it wasn't when they had to decorate the cake, as well as bake it. That was because the cake layers had to be cool to the touch—otherwise, the frosting would melt. But then, Libby reminded herself, that was one of the reasons they were using three layers, not two. That way, the cake would both bake and cool faster because there was less surface area.

Libby turned on the oven and set the temperature to 350 degrees, while Bernie filled a saucepan with five inches of water and set it on the stove on low heat. She needed the water to be hot, but not boiling. When that was done, Bernie took a bowl out of the cabinet and started cracking the eggs into it, one after another. When she was through, she fished a small piece of shell out of the mixture with a fork and began stirring the six eggs together. After that, she carefully put the bowl in the water bath.

This was the trickiest part of the operation. You had to warm up the eggs so they would expand when you added the sugar to them—the cake didn't have any kind of leavening agent in it, except the eggs—but you had to be very careful. If the eggs got too hot, they'd scramble, and you'd have to throw them out and start all over again. It was impossible to rescue them. On the other hand, if the eggs were too cold, the cake would be tough and flat. It was a difficult balancing act to walk.

While the eggs were warming, Bernie melted a stick of butter and sifted two cups of cake flour into a glass bowl. It was important to use cake flour, because cake flour had less protein in it—about 7 to 9 percent, as opposed to 10 to 12 percent for regular flour. It was also milled into a finer consistency, all of which made for a tenderer crumb.

When Bernie was through with those tasks, she measured out a cup of sugar and thought about what she was going to do after the eggs had warmed up. The trick was to slowly incorporate the sugar into the eggs, continuing to beat the mixture until a thick yellow ribbon formed.

After that, she had to fold the sifted cake flour into the egg mixture in three parts with a spatula, taking care to properly incorporate everything so that no streaks of flour showed. The last step in the process consisted of carefully adding the melted butter and the teaspoon of vanilla into the batter, a little bit at a time.

Six ingredients. That's all the cake was made from. It sounded simple, but Bernie reflected that a genoise bore out the adage that the fewer the ingredients, the harder the dish was to do correctly. A genoise was all about technique, which was one of the reasons why she and Libby had chosen it. Although it sounded easy enough to make, a good genoise was difficult to properly execute, and Bernie reflected that she wouldn't be surprised if they were the only ones electing to pursue this option.

"So, what do you think?" Libby asked Bernie as she started cutting the rind off the pineapple. She'd decided to tackle that first and the mango second.

"About what?" Bernie asked while dipping the tip of her forefinger into the egg mixture to see if it had reached the right temperature. Nope. Not yet. It was still a little too cool.

"About the dead mouse," Libby replied.

"What about it?" Bernie replied.

"You think whoever did this found the mouse like that, or they killed it?"

Bernie looked at her sister quizzically. "Does it matter?" she asked.

"Yeah, I think it does. One shows intent, while the other is more casual," Libby replied. "I mean, think about

76   *Isis Crawford*

it," she continued. "You have to admit there's a big difference between finding a dead mouse in the pantry and capturing and killing one."

"I suppose," Bernie absentmindedly told her sister, all her attention focused on the water bath. She tested the eggs again. Still not warm enough. She cursed under her breath and raised the heat on the burner ever so slightly. While it was true that haste made waste, it was also true that the clock was ticking. She had to speed the process up; otherwise, they'd never be done in time.

"There's no *suppose* about it," Libby replied as she cored the pineapple, then roughly chopped three-quarters of the fruit into chunks and pushed them off to the side. Next she took the remaining slices and cut them into small slivers. Then she washed the mint leaves, patted them dry, and began to make the sugar syrup she would use to candy both the mint leaves and the pineapple slivers. After they dried, she would use them to decorate the cake. "We're talking a qualitative difference here."

"The mouse was white, Libby," Bernie noted as she tested the eggs again. Finally they were warm to the touch. She took the bowl off the stove, turned the heat off, and picked up the hand mixer.

"Meaning?" Libby replied

"Meaning that it was either someone's pet or used in a lab. Field mice are brown."

"That's a fact?" Libby asked.

Bernie laughed. "Yes, that's a fact."

"So, it's more likely that someone killed the poor thing?" Libby mused.

"I'd say," Bernie agreed. "And you're right. Somehow that makes it worse." She was about to say why she thought that, but Nell tapped her on the shoulder.

"I don't suppose you guys have an extra couple of eggs

we can borrow," Nell asked. "Our custard isn't looking so good."

"You scrambled it?" Bernie asked.

Nell frowned. "Yup. This is what happens when you rush."

"Tell me about it," Bernie said, thinking of her eggs in the water bath. "Once that happens, you can't go back."

"Well?" Nell said when Bernie didn't say anything else. "Is that a yes or a no?"

Bernie shrugged. "It's okay with me if it's okay with my sister," Bernie told her, deciding to forget about the incident at the first run-through and be the bigger person.

Nell turned and repeated her question to Libby. "Please," she added. "I asked Mike. He said yes, but Adam turned me down."

"I did," Adam said, having overheard Nell's request. "That's because I don't believe in rewarding carelessness."

"Like you've never done something like that," Nell told him.

"Actually, I haven't," Adam shot back.

"Well, I have," Libby said. "Take the eggs."

"Thank you. It's refreshing to deal with nice people for a change," Nell said, grabbing two eggs.

"What does that mean?" Adam demanded.

"It means you've always been a putz," Nell told him as she hurried back to her station.

Libby watched her go. Then she took a nibble of one of the pineapple slices. While it was juicer than the fruit she'd used last week when she and her sister were testing out the recipe, this pineapple had a lot less flavor. She was thinking she'd have to strain some of the juice out, and then boil it down to concentrate it, when the two judges appeared in front of her and Bernie.

"So, tell me what you're doing?" Ellen asked her.

78   *Isis Crawford*

Libby explained while Doug nodded his head.

"Very nice," Doug said. "You just want to make sure you don't have too much liquid in the mix. That will make the cake soggy, and no one likes a soggy cake. Or a soggy bottom, for that matter." He smiled, pleased with himself.

Then Ellen moved on to Nell and Lori, who were working at top speed to make up the time they'd lost when their eggs had curdled, while Doug went to make himself an espresso.

"Do you think Ellen and Doug liked what we were doing?" Libby asked Bernie.

"I don't see why they shouldn't," Bernie replied as she went back to combining the egg yolks and the sugar. By now, the mixture was thick and glossy. She turned off the portable mixer, put the mixer back where it belonged, returned to the workstation with the bowl full of eggs, grabbed a silicon spatula from a drawer, and prepared to slowly and gently fold the flour into the egg mixture. Doing it by hand was much safer. She'd just sifted a third of the flour into the bowl, when she heard a loud hiss followed by a shriek. Then there was another hiss. And another shriek.

Startled, Bernie dropped the bowl she'd been holding. "What the hell!" she cried out as the eggs made a bright yellow puddle on the floor.

Nell screamed and pointed. Bernie whirled around. At first, she couldn't see anything. Then she did and wished she hadn't. Doug lay crumpled on the floor in front of the espresso machine. He was partially enveloped in a cloud of steam. His hands were lobster red, his face and chest were covered in blood, and he was making a high keening noise.

For a moment, no one moved. They were stunned. Frozen in place. Then Ellen yelled, "Oh my God," and everyone in the tent dropped what they were doing and ran toward Doug.

"Someone call 911!" Sam yelled.

"I will," Adam said, reaching in his back pocket for his phone.

"What happened?" Libby asked Ellen as she and Bernie neared Doug.

"The espresso machine exploded," Ellen replied.

"Exploded?"

Ellen stifled a sob. "Yes. *Exploded.* I saw it. I was standing on the other side of the table when it happened." She pointed at Doug, who was writhing in agony. "That poor man." She started to sob as Bernie rushed to wet a towel with cool water and place it over Doug's burns.

After what seemed like an eternity, but was only five minutes, the ambulance came.

Chapter 12

The next day was another day of bright blue skies and puffy white clouds. It was a little after ten in the morning when Sean sat back in his chair, held up the front section of the Sunday *New York Times,* coughed, and pointed to a small item on page 12. The lead line above the body of the story read: THE SHOW GOES ON. FREAK ACCIDENT HELD RESPONSIBLE FOR JUDGE'S CRITICAL INJURY.

"Hey, we made the national news," he said.

Libby frowned. "Oh, goody. What I want to know is how come Longely is only in the news when something bad happens here?"

"Good question," Bernie replied as she plopped down next to her sister on the sofa. "What else does the story say, Dad?"

"Not much." And Sean cleared his throat and read the rest of the piece out loud: " 'Police are investigating an unfortunate event that occurred on the set of *The Longely Bake-Off.* Questions have been raised about the proper operation of the piece of equipment deemed responsible for Mr. LaForte's accident and subsequent heart attack. A onetime resident of Longely, Mr. LaForte has lived in several places, but had recently relocated to this area. He was the owner of The Potted Pig in Seattle, and, according to Sam Levine, the producer of the show, Mr. LaForte was acting as a judge for the baking competition, *The Longely Bake-Off*. At this time, another judge has not been named."

Bernie put down her glass of iced coffee, which she'd just taken a sip of, on the coffee table and turned to her dad. "Well, that doesn't say much, does it?"

"No, it doesn't," Sean agreed. "Not that the paper would, since this is the beginning stage of an ongoing investigation."

"The article gives the impression that the police are thinking the thing with the espresso machine was an accident," Libby observed.

"Given the notes and the dead mouse, I don't see how they can come to that conclusion, let alone everything else that's been occurring, do you?" Bernie said to Libby. Then she added, "I bet it's why Sam wants to hire us."

Sean frowned. "He does?" This was news to him.

Libby shrugged. "That's what he said when he called earlier this morning."

Bernie turned to her dad. "What do you think?"

Sean folded his paper and put it on the coffee table before answering; then he said, "Well, I have to say using an espresso machine to try and kill someone is a little . . ." he paused, searching for the right word.

"*Odd?*" Libby suggested.

Sean nodded. "I was going to say *inefficient*, but *odd* works as well." He paused again as he reconsidered his word choice. "No. I take that back. The word I'm looking for is *opportunistic.*"

Libby shifted her position and took a sip of her chai tea latte. "I wonder what Lucy is going to say now?"

82   *Isis Crawford*

"You mean how is he going to cover his ass, after blowing off the notes you guys got?" Sean inquired after he took a bite of the cheesecake Bernie had made earlier that morning. For a moment, he savored the smooth feel of the cheese on his tongue and the sweet, tart flavors of the sugar and the lemon. "Very good," he observed, lifting his empty fork for emphasis.

"It always is," Bernie replied. The recipe was bulletproof. An old recipe from her mom, it was a customer and family favorite, and A Little Taste of Heaven featured it on the menu at least three times a week. In fact, Bernie was thinking of serving it for breakfast, along with their muffins and Danish. *I mean, why not? It has calcium, right?* She was going to ask her sister what she thought of the idea, when she heard the downstairs door open and close. "That must be Sam," she said as she listened to the footsteps coming up the steps.

A moment later, Sam walked through the door of the Simmons flat. Libby reflected that he looked exhausted. The phrase *aged overnight* came to mind. He had deep circles under his eyes, a five-o'clock shadow on his cheeks and chin, and stains on his pants and shirt.

"Hey, Sammy, you're not looking too good," Sean told him.

Sam smiled. "Neither are you," he replied.

Sean laughed and patted his potbelly. "Too many sweets." Then he stopped laughing and got serious. "I understand you've got a bit of a problem on your hands."

"That's why I'm here," Sam told him.

Bernie and Libby looked from one man to the other and back again.

"I didn't know you two know each other," Bernie said.

Both men nodded at the same time.

"Your dad and I go way back," Sam said. "He was my Big Brother. We used to play pickup games over at the basketball court back in the day in Barry Park."

Sean laughed and nodded his head in Sam's direction. "He had a lot to learn."

"That was true, but I could shoot better than your sorry ass," Sam told Sean. "That's for sure."

Sean snorted. "Hang on to that if it makes you feel better."

"It's the truth," Sam declared. "You wanna go back to the park? Call up Teeny?"

"Teeny?" Libby repeated the name. "Who's Teeny?"

"Clyde," Sean replied. "He was another Big Brother."

Libby's eyes widened. "Your friend Clyde?" she asked.

"That's the person," Sean said.

Bernie choked on her iced coffee. "You're kidding."

"Teeny?" Libby asked Sean.

Her dad laughed. "I know," Sean told her. "He's huge. That's why we called him Teeny."

"Makes sense to me," Bernie commented.

"He was the one who called me up and suggested I get in touch with you guys," Sam said to Bernie and Libby. He frowned. "Not that I wasn't planning on doing that anyway."

"I'm surprised Lucy hasn't tagged you for this," Sean told him.

"He has," Sam told him. "That's one of the reasons I'm here. According to Clyde, I'm a person of interest, never mind that anyone could have screwed around with the espresso machine."

Libby frowned. "It looks as if Lucy definitely has it in for you," she said.

"I already told them about you and Lucy's wife," Sean said.

"First wife, and they were on the way out already," Sam corrected him. "I just helped things along."

Bernie raised an eyebrow. "How many times has Lucy been married anyway?" she asked.

"Four. No. Five," Sean said after he'd thought for a minute.

Sam sighed. "There's also the fact that I got into a little trouble when I was younger."

"What kind of trouble?" Bernie inquired.

Sam hesitated for a moment. Then he said, "Doug and I got into a fight. I beat him up pretty bad, but that was a long time ago."

"Define *pretty bad*," Bernie said.

"He broke his arm," Sean explained.

"Actually, it was his wrist," Sam clarified.

Sean snorted. "Doesn't matter. In Lucy's mind, you add both things together . . ." Sean shrugged, and his voice trailed off for a moment as he rubbed the tips of Cindy's ears. Her purring filled the room.

Sam nodded. "But that was then, and this is now. I mean, why would I do anything to Doug at this juncture? Putting this on me makes no sense, but then logic isn't something that Lucy traffics in," he told her. "I mean think about it." His voice rose. It quavered with indignation. "It's no secret that I'm out on a limb, financially speaking, with this show. So, why would I do something to jeopardize it? I wouldn't. Which is why I'm here now, asking for your help." He shook his head. "I thought I could go it alone, but that's not working too well." Then he pointed to the coffee table. "Do you think you could spare a slice of that cheesecake?"

"Not a problem," Libby said as she patted the sofa cushion, motioning for Sam to sit down next to her. "You

A CATERED BAKE-OFF 85

look as if you haven't been getting your beauty sleep," she observed, changing the subject.

Sam laughed and ran his hand over his cheeks. "Is it my five-o'clock shadow at ten in the morning or the dark rings under my eyes that gives it away?"

"Both," Bernie promptly replied as Sam sat down.

"I got maybe an hour of sleep time. If that," he told them. "I couldn't seem to get what happened on the set out of my head."

"Neither could I," Libby told him, commiserating. She shuddered as Bernie cut Sam a large slice of cheesecake and poured him a cup of coffee.

"Here you go," Bernie said, placing the items in front of him. "This will make you feel better, too." Then she watched Sam devour the slice of cake.

"God, that was good," Sam commented as he reached for his cup of coffee after finishing the slice.

"Have some more," Bernie suggested, cutting him another even larger piece.

Sam devoured that piece, too. "Thanks," he said when he was done. "I feel a little better," he allowed, sitting back on the sofa.

"Never underestimate the healing power of sugar and fat," Libby cracked.

Sam smiled briefly. "And the fact that this is the first solid food I've had since *it* happened," he said, putting the emphasis on *it*. "That might have something to do with it as well."

"You're probably in shock," Sean told him.

"You're probably right," Sam agreed. He took a deep breath and let it out. "I still can't believe it," he said. He bit his lower lip. "I keep on hearing Doug scream. I just can't get the sound out of my mind."

"It'll take a while," Sean told him.

"You should know," Sam said.

"Unfortunately, I do," Sean replied, thinking back to some of the things he'd witnessed over his years on the Longely police force.

For a moment, everyone was silent; then Sean readjusted his chair to give himself a better view of the street. "So, what you're telling me is that the Longely PD is pursuing an investigation and you're the low hanging fruit—"

"*Low hanging fruit?*" Libby interrupted.

"Easy pickings," Sean explained.

Sam sighed and scratched a mosquito bite on his neck. "That's exactly what I'm telling you, Sean."

"Is the show still airing?" Libby asked.

Sam nodded. "Fingers crossed." Everyone was silent for another moment as they watched two squirrels chase each other around the birch tree outside the window.

Then Sean asked if the police had gone over the espresso machine yet.

"They did, but they couldn't find anything," Sam replied. "The explosion erased any evidence of tampering. I did look up stats on this kind of thing happening. And they were pretty much nil. This was a once-in-a-bluemoon event. A point-zero-zero chance."

"And when it has happened?" Bernie asked.

"It's usually due to operator's error," Sam told her.

"Doug could have made a mistake, then," Bernie pointed out.

"He could have," Sam agreed, "although it seems unlikely. It's not as if he hasn't used this kind of machine before."

"The other option is that someone jerry-rigged the espresso machine," Libby stated.

Sam nodded. "Exactly." Then his phone buzzed. He

took it out of his pocket and looked at it. "Sorry, folks, I have to take this." And he stood up and went outside.

"So, what do you think?" Bernie asked her dad while Sean watched Sam pacing back and forth, gesticulating, as he talked to someone on his phone in front of A Little Taste of Heaven.

After a minute, Sean turned to her and said, "What I think is that Sammy needs our help."

Chapter 13

"It's amazing how something can happen right in front of your face, and you don't see it," Sean mused as he and his daughters waited for Sam to come back upstairs.

"Like when that guy around the corner killed his girlfriend and buried her in his flower bed and no one saw anything, never mind it happened during the neighborhood block party," Bernie recalled.

"Like that," Sean confirmed. "If it hadn't been for Mrs. Clark's beagle digging up the lady ferns, Lila probably would never have been found."

Libby sighed. "We certainly wouldn't have noticed anyone doing anything unusual yesterday, unless they were jumping up and down in front of us. We were too busy concentrating on what we were doing. Right, Bernie?"

Bernie nodded. "Right. In fact, we were facing away from the espresso machine when the explosion happened."

Sean took another bite of cheesecake, then put a little dab of the cake on his finger and held it out for their cat. "I see," he said as he watched Cindy lick it off. Her tongue felt like warm sandpaper on his skin. "Who was facing toward the machine?"

A CATERED BAKE-OFF 89

"No one," Bernie promptly answered.

"At least, not the contestants," Libby added. "The espresso machine was off to the side by the tent flap."

"So, what you're saying is, anyone could have come in and booby-trapped the espresso machine without being noticed," Sean observed. "That's certainly a possibility. One thing is for sure, though. Sam needs even more security " Out of curiosity, he'd taken a walk around the estate by himself that morning. Just to see. Old habits die hard.

"Unless whoever jerry-rigged it, did it before the machine arrived at the site," Libby said.

"That seems unlikely, in the general scheme of things," Sean replied, sitting back in his seat.

"But still a possibility," Libby insisted.

"Yes, still a possibility, if you like the far-fetched," Sean conceded.

"Dad, aren't you the one who said you have to consider every angle when solving a crime?" Libby asked.

Sean didn't answer, because he had said that.

"What are you thinking?" Bernie asked her dad as she watched the expression on his face.

"Oh, I was just wondering if what happened was meant for Doug LaForte, or someone else," her dad replied. "Was this a random event? A threat gone wrong? A practical joke that got out of hand? Was it meant to scare people away from participating in the show, or was Doug LaForte the intended target?"

"Which would mean that the notes and the oven and the goats were window dressing. They were all done to misdirect, to hide the fact that Doug was the intended victim," Libby hypothesized. Then she added, "On the other hand, maybe there were two people involved. One person wrote the notes and let the goats out, while the other person was responsible for the oven exploding, and the espresso machine."

"Definitely an embarrassment of riches," Bernie noted.

Sean nodded. "Indeed, it is. Too much so."

Bernie stifled a yawn. She was still tired from yesterday. "But why LaForte, assuming he was the intended victim?" Bernie asked.

Sean resettled himself in his seat, then answered his daughter's question. "A lot of people around here didn't like Doug LaForte very much back in the day. If I remember correctly, there was talk of indicting him on . . ." Sean wrinkled his forehead while he thought. "Stealing a car? Setting his backyard on fire? I can't remember, but what I do know is that's why his family left the area. They were afraid he was going to get himself in real trouble."

"But that was a long time ago, right?" Bernie protested.

Sean nodded. "Fifteen years ago." He corrected himself. "No. More," he said after he recalculated the number in his head. "Scary how time flies," he commented as he went back to feeding the cheesecake to his cat.

"That's a long time for someone to hold a grudge," Bernie reflected. "I mean, you might not want to talk to them, but doing what they did to him?" She scratched her nose. "That's pretty bad."

"You'd be surprised," Sean said, waving his fork in the air for emphasis as he thought of his wife and her sister. They hadn't forgiven each other for something that had happened when one was seven and the other ten years old. They'd still been arguing about who had lost a Barbie doll forty years later. Of course, they hadn't seriously injured each other, either. "Some people's memories go back a long, long way."

"Like Libby's," Bernie said.

"Ha. Ha," Libby replied. "Look who's talking!"

Bernie snorted. "Hey, I'm not the one still bringing up the fact that you had to walk to school, and I got driven," she told her sister as she watched her dad finish off the rest of his slice of cheesecake and offer the plate to Cindy to clean.

"She's getting fat," she observed.

"I like to call it *pleasingly plump*," Sean replied, "and isn't that word a no-no these days?"

"You mean *fat*?" Bernie asked.

Sean nodded.

"I don't think the cat is going to care," Bernie pointed out.

"She might," Sean told her as Cindy turned around three times and resettled herself in his lap.

"I think one thing we can all get together on," Bernie said, "is the method of execution."

"Bad joke," Libby chided.

"Okay, we're all agreed that someone most likely blocked the steam valve on the espresso machine, which allowed the steam to build up until it exploded?" Sean theorized.

"That seems like the best explanation," Libby replied as Cindy jumped off Sean's lap and onto the window ledge to surveil the squirrels chasing each other up and down a tree. "Do you think whoever did this was trying to kill Doug or injure him?" Libby asked her dad.

"Good question," Sean remarked. "Either is a possibility. Frankly, I don't think whoever did it cared. Maybe, if they have a good lawyer, they can plead it down to manslaughter."

"Well," Libby continued, "I don't think something like this is something you come up with at the last minute. If what Sam says is correct, someone had to have planned this in advance."

"I disagree," Bernie told her. "I can see someone acting

92   *Isis Crawford*

on impulse, taking something like . . . like . . . a piece of plastic and putting it in the valve."

"If that were true, it would mean whoever did it is part of the cast," Libby said.

Bernie nodded. "Exactly. Or a judge."

"Why not the crew?" Sean inquired.

"Because none of them were near the table the espresso machine was on," Bernie answered.

Libby shuddered again. She could still hear Doug's screams echoing in her head. She wondered if she'd ever *un*hear them. "Not a nice way to go," she said. "I think I'd rather be shot. Or jump out of a plane without a parachute."

"Me too," Bernie agreed.

"It was also very public," Libby added, continuing with her train of thought. "Why?"

"Maybe that was the point of the exercise," Sean observed. "Maybe whoever did this wanted everyone to know what they'd done. Maybe they wanted to send a message."

"Which would mean that someone was there to receive the message," Libby pointed out.

"As in, if someone pitches, there has to be someone catching on the other end?" Sean asked.

"Exactly," Libby said. She was tucking a lock of hair behind her ear when Sam walked back into the room. "Everything okay?" Libby asked him.

Sam nodded. "That was Jeff Grasso."

Bernie clicked her tongue against her teeth. "I'm sure he's happy about the recent turn of events," she said. He owned the business that was sponsoring the show.

"Ecstatic," Sam replied, sitting back down on the sofa.

"Do I denote the smell of sarcasm in the air?" Sean asked.

A CATERED BAKE-OFF 93

Sam laughed. "You could say that."

"So, what did he want?" Sean inquired. "Is he pulling out?"

"I wouldn't be surprised if he was. Fortunately, he isn't. He wanted to tell me something about the explosion that he thought I should know."

"Are you planning to tell us or is this a secret?" Sean prodded after a minute had gone by and Sam didn't say anything else.

"I am planning to," Sam responded. He leaned forward. "But I'm telling you this in strict confidence," he said, lowering his voice for dramatic effect.

"Meaning?" Libby asked.

"Meaning it's off the record."

"Seriously?" Bernie asked. "We don't have records. We don't even have files."

"I thought they were the same thing," Libby said.

Bernie was reaching for her phone to look it up, but Sam interrupted her. "Nevertheless, I need your word," Sam replied, referring to the previous subject of their conversation.

The sisters looked at one another. "Okay," Bernie said after a moment had gone by. "You have it."

Sam smiled and turned to Sean. "Yours too?"

"Mine too," Sean replied.

"Although," Sam continued, "I don't think that what I'm going to tell you is going to come as any big surprise."

Sean nodded. "Probably not, but let's hear what you have to say anyway."

Sam began to talk. "Jeff has a nephew named Dennis. He . . . he's been in some trouble and Jeff is trying to give him a fresh start."

"Wasn't he the one who stole a car a while back and

crashed it into one of the stores at the mall?" Sean asked, remembering the story now.

"That's him," Sam said. "He's out on parole."

"Hence the reason for keeping this on the down-low," Bernie guessed.

Sam nodded. "Yeah. The cops are already looking at him. You know how they are."

"Dennis was on the set yesterday?" Bernie asked.

Sam nodded. "He was the guy in the porkpie hat and the Scooby-Doo sunglasses."

"He's a runner, right?" Libby inquired. "Skinny jeans? Anime T-shirt?"

"That's him," Sam replied.

"And?" Bernie said.

"He got there a little bit on the early side, and since he hadn't had any breakfast, he decided to make himself a latte." He looked around. Sam had everyone's attention. "Which he successfully did."

Bernie smiled. "Interesting."

"So now we have a timeline as to when the espresso machine was tampered with," Sean observed. "We know that it happened on the estate."

"Exactly," Sam replied.

"Was anyone else on the set?" Libby asked.

"According to Dennis, he was the first one to arrive. Two of the engineers came in about ten minutes later, followed by the rest of the crew," Sam answered. "According to the police, none of them used the machine to make themselves a coffee. They all did takeout."

"Someone could have hopped over the wall and tinkered with it," Bernie said, repeating an earlier suggestion.

"If they did, the new security cameras didn't pick it up," Sean said.

"Maybe because whoever did this knew where the security cameras were located and avoided them," Libby observed.

"Maybe," Sean agreed. "Which means we're talking cast as the perpetrators again."

Bernie gave a little shiver. "God, I hope not."

"There's more," Sam said.

"I figured," Sean remarked.

"Dennis and Doug had a little spat the day before," Sam replied.

"How bad a spat?" Bernie asked.

"Bad enough," Sam replied.

"I could see why the kid might not want to speak to the police," Libby noted.

"Also," Sam continued, "he went to see Doug at the hospital. He was there with him when he went into cardiac arrest."

Bernie raised an eyebrow. "I didn't know that."

"Do you know why Dennis went?" Sean asked Sam.

Sam nodded. "He said he felt guilty about some of the things he said to him."

"More to the point, I don't suppose Dennis said anything to him about what happened?" Libby inquired.

"As in, *so-and-so wanted to kill me*?" Sean asked. "Something along those lines?"

"Yes," Bernie said. "Something like that."

Sam laughed. "If he did, Dennis didn't tell me."

"We should talk to Dennis," Bernie suggested.

Sam stretched. "Good. That's what I was hoping you would say. And, as it so happens, I know where Dennis is now."

"Timing is everything," Bernie said, repeating one of her dad's favorite mantras.

"It certainly is," Libby said, thinking of the cinnamon

rolls that were ready to be popped into the oven. Then she looked at Sam and said, "You're a really nice guy."

Sam blushed. "Why do you say that?"

"Helping this kid out when you're on the line," Libby told him.

"I'm really not, you know," he replied.

"He's telling you the truth," Sean verified. "He really is a son of a bitch."

"And proud of it," Sam answered as Sean laughed.

Chapter 14

It was a little after eleven in the morning when the cinnamon rolls had finished baking, Mrs. Startz had come by to pick them up, and Libby had fixed the paper jam in their computer.

"Time to go," Libby said as she and Bernie left the shop, jumped into their van, and drove over to the Longely skate park. Located in an old, abandoned parking lot at the tip of the promenade bordering the Hudson River, the skate park had been the focus of protests when it had been built ten years ago, but the bad things its opponents had predicted would occur—a plethora of drug deals and gang fights—had never materialized.

"Sounds as if everyone is having a good time," Libby noted as she eased Mathilda into the last parking spot at the back of the lot. The seagulls she'd displaced wheeled and squawked above her and her sister's heads.

The place was full and the screeches of excitement and the thump of wheels on the half-pipes got louder as Bernie and Libby got closer. When they'd woven their way through the mass of helmeted kids, they stopped and surveyed the scene in front of them. Teens were racing dirt

98   *Isis Crawford*

bikes up and down the half-pipes, boys and girls were doing tricks on their skateboards, while younger kids were climbing on the jungle gym off to the side, and parents were sitting on benches gossiping with one another.

"There he is. That's Dennis," Bernie said, recalling him from the set as she pointed to a skinny kid who had just wiped out trying to do an ollie. "He looks like his uncle," she observed. "Same color eyes and hair, same cleft chin."

"Just a lot shorter and younger," Libby added as she watched him climb up the half-pipe. She noticed he was limping a little as she and Bernie headed toward him, dodging skaters and bikers as they went.

"Yes?" Dennis said when the sisters reached him. He'd taken off one of his kneepads and was inspecting his knee. It was red, but there wasn't any blood.

"Glad you didn't get hurt," Libby told him.

"Me too," Dennis Grasso said. He put his kneepad back on, straightened up, and loosened the strap on his helmet.

Libby started to introduce herself, but Dennis interrupted her midsentence. "No need. I know who you are from the show. So, what are you guys doing here? Shouldn't you be back in the kitchen working on your recipe?"

"We're looking for you," Bernie told him.

"How come?" Dennis asked.

"Your uncle Jeff told Sam Levine, who told us, that you have some information you want to share about what happened on the set on Saturday," Bernie told him. "We'd like to nail down what you told him. Make sure nothing gets lost in the translation, so to speak."

Dennis frowned. "He did, did he?"

"Yes, he did," Libby said. "You can call him if you don't believe me."

"Oh, I believe you," Dennis said. He scratched under his helmet. "You're doing your PI thing?"

A CATERED BAKE-OFF 99

"I wouldn't put it that way, but yes we are," Libby said.

"Then you could have saved yourself a trip, because I don't have anything to say," Dennis said, turning to go.

"Your uncle already told us about the spat you had with Doug and about your hospital visit with him," Libby said.

"Then you know everything already," Dennis said. "There's no need to talk."

"I think there is," Bernie replied. "What did you guys fight about? Your uncle didn't say."

"Because I didn't tell him," Dennis replied.

"Then how about telling us," Libby said.

Bernie chimed in with, "Yeah. It won't go any further." She raised her hand. "I promise."

"And I should believe you, why?" Dennis asked.

Libby answered him. "Two reasons: Number one, we keep our word."

Bernie lifted her right hand. "Pinky swear," she said.

Dennis couldn't help it. He laughed and Libby continued.

"And number two, the sooner this is wrapped up, the less chance there is that your name will come to the police's attention, and that's the last thing you want, right?"

"I guess," Dennis said after a moment's thought. He laced his hands together and cracked his knuckles. Bernie winced at the sound. "Okay," he began. "I don't know what Sam told you, but the whole thing with Doug wasn't a big deal. Doug owed me some money and he told me he couldn't pay me back till next week and I got pissed. That's it."

"Is that why you went to the hospital to see him?" Bernie guessed.

"In a way," Dennis said. He studied two geese flying overhead for a moment, then looked back at Bernie. "Actually, I felt bad for some of the things I said and I wanted to apologize."

He's lying, Bernie thought, watching him, but she didn't say that. "Somehow I think there's more to the story than that," Bernie told him, instead.

"If you say so," Dennis told her.

"How about telling us what's really going on," Libby coaxed.

"I already have," Dennis replied.

"I don't think so," Libby told him.

"I do," Dennis said.

This time, it was Bernie's turn to respond. "How about telling us because you're a good citizen and you believe in truth, honor, beauty, and the American way?" she asked.

Dennis laughed again. "Does that line work for you?"

"Not usually," Bernie admitted. "But I keep on trying."

"Well, good luck with that, but I have to get going," Dennis told Bernie, and he turned to leave.

"How about you help out your uncle," Libby said, trying one last tactic.

Dennis turned back to listen.

"After all," Libby continued, "I'm guessing he got you your job."

"So, what if he did?"

"This would be a way of thanking him. He is paying for the show," Libby told him.

"He can afford it," Dennis said, reaching up and tightening his helmet. "Anyway, what is it they say about there being no such thing as bad publicity?" He gave a quick salute. "Well, it's been fun talking to you guys. See you next Saturday."

"Wait!" Bernie cried out.

He turned back to the sisters. "What now?"

"Are you a betting man?" Bernie asked, the words coming out of her mouth before she realized what she was saying.

Dennis raised an eyebrow. "I could be. What do you have in mind?"

Bernie smiled. "How about you talk to us if I skate down this half-pipe on your skateboard," she said, nodding to the one in front of them.

"Bernie!" Libby shrieked at the same time that Dennis said, "You're kidding, right?"

"Nope," Bernie told him. "I'm dead serious."

"The operative word here is *dead*," Libby said.

Dennis and Bernie both ignored her.

"Ever skated before?" Dennis asked.

Bernie nodded. "Out in Cali."

"She's kidding," Libby told Dennis.

"I'm not, Libby," Bernie told her sister. "I did. Actually, I was pretty good."

"He doesn't know anything," Libby told her. "Don't risk a broken bone. It's not worth it. Especially with the bake-off coming up."

Dennis put his hand on his hips. He frowned. "Hey, I do know things."

"Like what?" Libby challenged.

"Like . . ." Dennis stopped himself and laughed. "Good one. You almost got me. But you want to know what I know? Your sister has to pony up. I want to see this."

"So, are we on, or what?" Bernie asked him.

"We're on," Dennis said, and then before Libby could say anything else, Dennis handed Bernie his skateboard.

He pointed to his helmet. "Want this?"

"Please," she said.

"This is a very bad idea, a very bad idea," Libby told Bernie as Dennis took off his helmet and gave it to her sister.

"So, you just said," Bernie replied. "Don't worry. I'll be fine."

102   *Isis Crawford*

"No, you won't be," Libby insisted.

"A little positive energy here, if you don't mind," Bernie replied as she put Dennis's helmet on and fastened the strap. "It's a little big," she noted.

"That's because I've got a big head," Dennis told her.

Bernie laughed. "That's supposed to be my line," she said.

"Still want to do this?" Dennis asked.

"Absolutely," Bernie replied, although she was having second, third, fourth, fifth, and sixth thoughts about what she was about to do. But it was too late now.

Meanwhile, Libby had closed her eyes. She couldn't bear to look at what was going to happen next.

Chapter 15

Bernie took a deep breath and looked down the half-pipe. She estimated the slant to be at a ninety-degree angle. *Well, maybe not that steep, but close enough. Libby is right. I am nuts. What was I thinking?*

It had been twenty years since she'd been on a board. She was about to turn back, when she remembered the time she'd been skateboarding in Oakland. She'd been going down a steep hill, probably as steep as this half-pipe, and she'd gotten the wobbles. She'd thought she was done for, but she'd managed to get off with just a rolled ankle. *If I could do it then, I can do it now,* she told herself. *I've got this.* And with that, she took another deep breath, said a silent prayer to the skateboard gods, and pushed off.

She'd forgotten how much she loved this as she started down the half-pipe, gathering speed as she went. At least she was wearing sneakers with a good tread, she thought as she concentrated on getting her footing and her balance right. And suddenly there it was. It was true—there are certain things you never forget how to do.

She leaned forward, arms out, everything forgotten in the sensation of the moment. She could feel the rush of the wind prickling the skin on her arms, taste summer in her mouth, hear the yells around her. Then she felt the rhythmic *thump, thump* of the board's wheels on the wood moving up through her body until it encased her. She leaned forward a little bit more, angling her body slightly to the left to avoid a collision. She was flying. And then, all of a sudden, she wasn't.

Before she knew what had happened, she'd pitched forward and landed with a crash midway down the half-pipe. Stunned, she watched Dennis's board roll to the bottom. Miraculously, everyone managed to avoid it. For a moment, she couldn't breathe. *I've literally had the breath knocked out of me,* she thought. Then before she could think of getting up, Libby and Dennis were at her side.

"I told you," Libby chided.

Bernie wanted to answer, but it hurt too much to talk.

"That was some wipeout," Dennis said, a hint of admiration in his voice.

"Are you okay?" Libby asked in a softer tone.

Bernie wanted to say *I'm fine,* but when she started to move her shoulder, a stab of pain ran down her side. She wondered if she'd broken her shoulder or cracked a rib. She took two more breaths. Then Libby and Dennis helped her up. She could stand, so that was good. She put weight first on one foot and then on the other. *Also, good.* Next she moved her hands and made a circle with her wrists. Nothing broken there. She started to raise her left arm and stopped as another stab of pain shot through her. *Yup.* She'd definitely done something to her shoulder. Hopefully, she'd just bruised, not broken, it. She was thinking about what it would mean if she had, and how unbearable Libby would be, when Dennis spoke.

"Here, Bernie, let's get you to the bench," he said.

Bernie nodded and the three of them slowly made their way back up the ramp and to the nearest seat.

"How are you doing?" Libby asked as Bernie carefully lowered herself onto the wooden seat.

"Outside of my shoulder hurting, I think I'm okay," Bernie replied, hoping that what she said was true. "I just need a minute or two to recover."

"What you need is a trip to an urgent care," Libby said. Then because she couldn't help herself, she added, "I told you."

"Yes, you did," Bernie allowed. She started to raise both arms to take off her helmet and felt another sharp pain. *Okay.* She put her left arm down and just used her right hand to unclip the helmet. "Here," she said, handing the helmet back to Dennis. "Good thing that I had this on."

"Definitely," Dennis agreed, taking it from her.

"Yeah," Libby said, "you can't afford to lose any more brain cells."

"I still have more than you," Bernie shot back.

"I guess you want me to honor our bet," Dennis said before Libby could reply.

"What do you think?" Bernie replied.

"I would say that would be a yes." Dennis sat down on the bench next to her and crossed his right leg over his left while Libby sat next to him. "Okay. What do you want to know—unless, that is, you want to do this later," he said as he watched a ten-year-old girl skate down the ramp.

"No, now is good," Bernie said.

Then Libby asked Dennis to go over when he'd made himself a latte. "So, then, you were the first person on the set," Libby asked, recapping what Sam had told her.

Dennis nodded.

Libby continued her questions. "When did the rest of the crew arrive?"

Dennis thought for a moment, then said, "They started trickling in about ten minutes later. We were there setting up about an hour before you guys."

"And the guy at the gate checking passes was there when you arrived?"

Dennis nodded again. "He was there. I had to sign in."

"Did anyone else use the espresso machine?" Libby inquired.

Dennis shook his head. "Not to my knowledge. Except for Doug, of course."

"And the espresso machine looked okay?" Bernie asked.

"As far as I could tell, it did," Dennis answered.

Libby put up her hand to shade her eyes from the sun. "You didn't have any trouble with it?"

"Nope," Dennis replied. "Everything worked the way it was supposed to work."

"And no one used the machine after you did?" Libby asked, reconfirming what she'd been told by Sam.

"Not to my knowledge," Dennis replied. "Doug and I were pretty much the only ones on the set that did. The machine was kinda fiddly," he explained as he scratched behind his ear. "Most people didn't want to be bothered." Then he added, "But I was in and out of the greenroom doing errands, so I'm not one hundred percent sure."

Libby nodded. At least they had a timeline now. "Okay. Now, moving on to topics two and three—"

"Which are?" Dennis asked, interrupting.

"Your spat with Doug and your visit to him in the hospital," Libby replied.

Dennis frowned. "What about them?"

"We just want to hear what happened," Libby told him.

"I already told you," Dennis protested. "Nothing happened."

"Tell us again," Bernie told him.

"Why?" Dennis demanded. "I already did. It's not like I have anything to add."

"Somehow I think you do," Bernie said. Then she

winced, because she'd turned slightly to look Dennis in the eye.

"Well, I don't," Dennis told her.

Libby leaned forward. "Hey, are you backing out of your bet?"

Dennis got all indignant. "No. Of course not."

Bernie put on her most winning smile, which was hard to do with her shoulder throbbing the way it was, and repeated what she'd said about not informing the police and keeping everything on the down-low.

"Your uncle wouldn't have told us if he didn't trust us," Libby added.

Dennis waved at a gangly kid with a purple mohawk walking by them. "Like I said before, Doug owed me money and I was pissed he didn't have it. I need it to pay my bills and the fine the judge laid on me."

"How much did he owe you?" Libby asked.

Dennis frowned. "About one thou, give or take."

"Wow," Bernie said. Surprised, she'd been about to turn and look at Dennis, but she stopped herself in time. "That's a fair chunk of change," she commented, instead.

"I'll say," Libby agreed. "I thought he would owe you something like twenty bucks."

"No, not quite," Dennis replied.

Bernie raised an eyebrow. "Somehow I don't see you having that kind of money to lend him in the first place."

"You'd be surprised," Dennis said.

"Yes, I would be," Bernie replied.

"Okay," Dennis allowed as he fiddled with the strap on his helmet.

"Okay what?" Bernie asked.

"It's a little more complicated than that," Dennis said.

"No kidding," Libby replied.

Dennis swallowed. Bernie and Libby waited.

108   *Isis Crawford*

"You can't tell my uncle," Dennis said after a minute had passed. "He doesn't know about this."

"We won't," Bernie and Libby both promised.

Another minute went by; then Dennis started to talk. "I have this friend . . . who takes bets."

"You mean they're a bookie?" Libby asked.

"Kinda," Dennis said. Then he fell silent again.

"And?" Bernie nudged.

Dennis took a deep breath and let it out. "Doug lost a bet, and I was collecting, only he told me he didn't have it, so I got pissed and kinda threatened him with some bad stuff, and he told me to go to hell."

"What was he betting on?" Bernie asked.

Dennis mumbled an answer.

"Sorry, I didn't hear you," Libby said.

"He likes to play poker," Dennis said. "That's all I know."

"Okay," Libby said, changing the subject and asking Dennis about the hospital. "How come you went to see Doug?"

"I guess I just felt bad," Dennis replied. "Like I said, I mouthed off pretty bad, and after what happened . . . I wanted to . . ."

"Get your money before he croaked?" Bernie guessed.

"No, I wanted to say I'm sorry for being a jerk."

Chastened, Bernie apologized to him. "Did Doug say anything?"

"Like who did it?" Dennis asked.

Bernie nodded. "Yeah."

Dennis shook his head. "It was hard to understand him," Dennis reflected. "He said that he was sorry he'd come back. At least I think that's what he said. He was talking really low, and I had to lean over close to hear him."

"You sure that's what he said?" Bernie asked.

"Yeah, I'm positive," Dennis replied.

"Did he say anything else?" Libby asked him.

"Like what?" Dennis asked.

"Anything at all?"

Dennis shook his head. "He stopped talking after that. He was really drugged up and he had this plastic thing over his mouth to help him breathe." Dennis cracked his knuckles again. "Then the nurse came in and told me I had to get out of there. Guess they don't allow people who aren't family in the ICU." Dennis grimaced. "Poor guy. What happened to him is just bottom-line bad."

Libby and Bernie both shuddered, remembering what Doug had looked like.

"I'll say," Bernie observed. "I'll take being run over by a bus any day of the week."

"He'd probably never would have looked . . . like he did before, if he'd lived," Dennis observed, carrying on with the conversation.

"Do you have any idea why he said he should never have come back to Longely?" Libby asked.

Dennis shook his head again.

"Do you know if he had a fight with anyone on the set? Besides you, that is," Bernie persisted.

Dennis scrunched up his eyes while he thought. "Not really. At least, not when I was around, but this I can tell you—he was nice to me."

"How was he nice to you?" Bernie asked.

"Well, for openers, he shared his breakfast with me when I told him I hadn't had any because I overslept. Of course, that was before I asked him for the money," Dennis reflected.

"But he wasn't nice to the others on the set?" Libby wanted to know.

Dennis shook his head. "He was kinda an asshole, actually. Real sarcastic. Whenever anyone said anything, he'd make these snotty comments, like he knew everything and no one else knew anything. It was like he was playing king of the castle. Also, I just got this feeling that there was something going on."

"Like what?" Libby pressed.

Dennis shook his head for the third time. "I don't know. I mean, everyone shut up whenever I came over. But there was this weird vibe in the air. Like people wanted to say things, but were holding back." Dennis sighed. "I guess I visited him because I figured he needed some company. You know, like for moral support."

"That was very nice of you," Libby commented.

Embarrassed, Dennis looked down at the floor. "Thanks," he muttered. "Actually . . ." He stopped.

"Actually, what?" Libby asked.

"Nothing," Dennis replied.

"You think what happened was your fault, don't you?" Bernie guessed, correctly interpreting the expression on Dennis's face.

Dennis shrugged, leaned over, and retied his sneakers. "Yeah. I guess," he said after a moment. "I mean, what if I did something to the machine to make it explode?"

"But you didn't," Libby said.

Dennis shook his head. "I know that. I know I didn't. My brain tells me that. But I just can't help thinking . . . I mean, it would be horrible if . . ." And his voice dropped off.

"You didn't," Libby repeated, more firmly this time.

Dennis swallowed. "But I'm not going to know that, right?"

Bernie decided it was time to change the subject.

"Did you see anyone around, other than the cast and crew, before the filming started?" she asked Dennis.

Dennis thought for a minute; then he told them he hadn't. "Anything else you want to know?"

"Yes," Bernie said. "When was the espresso machine delivered?"

Dennis named the time.

"Are you sure?" Bernie asked.

Dennis nodded. "I know, because I had to run down and open the gate for them."

"I thought you said the guard let you in," Libby said.

"He did," Dennis answered, "but he was in the bathroom when the delivery guy wanted in."

Libby smiled. "I don't suppose you happen to know where the machine was rented from?" she asked, even though she knew the answer already. She just wanted to hear what Dennis had to say.

When Dennis answered, he named Libby's first choice, Central Restaurant Supply. "At least," he said, "that was the name on the truck."

Bernie reached over and patted Dennis on the back. "Thanks."

"Did what I say help?" Dennis asked.

"It helped a lot," Bernie assured him.

"Absolutely," Libby said at the same time.

Dennis smiled and stood a little straighter. "Good. I'm glad. If there's anything else I can do . . ."

"Don't worry, we'll be in touch," Bernie said. Then she gave him their business card and told him to call if he remembered anything else. "Even if it doesn't seem important," she added. "At this point, any little detail will help."

"Will do," Dennis replied, taking the card and slipping it into the pocket of his cargo shorts. Then he stood up, put his helmet on, and tightened the chin strap. "See ya next week," he told them as he walked over to the nearest half-pipe.

112   *Isis Crawford*

"Not if I see you first," Bernie called after him.

"You think he's telling the truth," Libby asked her sister as she watched Dennis speed down the ramp.

"I think he's telling most of the truth, but not all of it," Bernie replied, wincing at the pain running down her left side as she stood up. She felt fine until she moved.

"That's what I figure, too," Libby replied, studying her sister's face. "And now I think it's time to get your shoulder looked at. I just hope you haven't broken anything."

Bernie grunted. She hoped so, too.

Chapter 16

"What the hell happened to you?" Brandon asked Bernie when she and Libby walked into RJ's later that evening. He had to raise his voice to be heard over the sound of the baseball game on the television set above the bar.

Bernie pointed to her sling. "I assume you're talking about this?"

Brandon wiped his hands on the towel he had slung over his shoulder and frowned. "No. I'm talking about the blond streak in your hair." Then he added, "That should make cooking a bit difficult."

"Tell me about it," Libby replied as her boyfriend, Marvin, walked through the door. He was dressed for the heat in a polo shirt, khaki shorts, and sandals.

"Hey, what happened to you?" he asked Bernie as he walked over to where Libby, Bernie, and Brandon were talking.

"Funny, I just asked her that same question," Brandon said.

"I slipped," Bernie replied, omitting the most salient fact.

114 *Isis Crawford*

Brandon grinned. "Morally? Ethically? Comically?"

Libby snorted. "She fell off a skateboard when she was going down a half-pipe at the skate park."

Marvin's eyes widened. "She did *what*?" he demanded of Libby.

Bernie turned toward her sister before she could answer and said, "Thanks for telling them, Libby."

Libby gave her a quick salute. "Anytime, Bernie. Anytime."

"A half-pipe?" Marvin echoed.

Brandon leaned forward. "I hate to say this, but aren't you a little—"

"Out of shape for that? A little old for that?" Bernie asked.

"You said it, I didn't," Brandon replied.

Bernie drew herself up. "It could have been worse. I could have broken something."

"It can always be worse. You could be dead or in a coma," Brandon noted as a woman came over and told Bernie and Libby that she hoped they'd win the bake-off.

"So, what did you do?" Marvin asked Bernie after the woman had joined her friends at the other end of the bar.

"I bruised my shoulder and one of my ribs," Bernie replied.

Brandon shook his head in disbelief. "What were you thinking?"

"My very words," Libby replied.

"Obviously, I wasn't thinking," Bernie answered at the same time as her sister laughed. "I've been saying that for years," Libby told her.

"Cute," Bernie said.

"I think so," Libby replied.

Bernie made a face. "Here I'm mortally wounded, and you're making fun of me."

A CATERED BAKE-OFF 115

"Poor baby." Brandon reached over and patted Bernie on the head. "Sorry, but we're one violin short today," he told her.

"That's just mean," Bernie replied.

Brandon laughed. "So sensitive."

"But I'll forgive you," Bernie continued.

"Forgive me for what?" Brandon inquired.

"Being rude," Bernie told him.

Brandon snorted, but Bernie ignored him and went on with what she'd been saying. "I'll tell you what—I'll forget about this if you buy me a couple of shots of that." Bernie pointed to the bottle of Macallan Double Cask 15, a fifteen-year-old single malt scotch sitting on the top shelf.

"You're expensive, you know that?" Brandon asked as he glanced around the bar to make sure everyone had what they needed.

"But worth it," Bernie answered.

As Brandon got everyone their drinks, Marvin turned to Bernie and Libby and handed Libby an envelope.

"Here," he said. "This was under your van's windshield wiper."

Libby studied the envelope. It looked like the kind you'd find in any drug or stationery store. In the middle of it, someone had typed TO THE SIMMONS SISTERS in caps.

"It looks as if someone used a typewriter to do this," Libby said, noting the slight imperfections in the type.

"You sure don't see those anymore," Marvin observed.

"No, you don't," Libby agreed as she opened the envelope, took out the piece of paper, unfolded it, and read the message.

"Bad news?" Marvin asked, seeing the expression on Libby's face.

116   *Isis Crawford*

"That's one way of putting it," she replied, handing the piece of paper over to him. "Take a look."

He did. Then he read the four-word sentence out loud: "'I'm not through yet.'" Marvin looked up from the note. "I assume this has to do with what happened at the bake-off."

"That would be my thought," Bernie replied.

"Sounds like a threat to me," Marvin observed.

"Well, it's not an invitation to the prom," Brandon commented as he handed Marvin his beer, poured a white wine for Libby, and got Bernie her scotch.

"Just in case anyone thought Doug's death was an accident," Bernie said.

"I wonder if everyone else got something like this as well," Libby mused. She was reaching for her phone to call Sam and find out, when he beat her to it.

"And?" Bernie asked Libby after she'd hung up.

"Everyone else got one, too," Libby told her. "Evidently, Nell and Lori are talking about quitting. Sam's holding a meeting on Wednesday, down at the estate, to reassure everyone that it's safe to continue. He's hoping we'll have some answers by then."

"That's not a lot of time to get any," Bernie pointed out.

"I know," Libby agreed. She drummed her fingers on the bar. "That note wasn't on the van when we parked at our place."

"No, it wasn't," Bernie agreed. "One of us would have noticed if it had been." She ran her finger around the rim of her glass while she thought. "Which means someone must have followed us to RJ's from the shop and waited for us to walk in here"—she indicated the bar with a wave of her hand—"before slipping that note under Mathilda's windshield wiper."

"I didn't notice anyone hanging around the flat when we came out, did you?" Libby asked her sister.

Bernie shook her head. She hadn't, either. Then she added, "Except for Old Miss Randall weeding her flower boxes, and I hardly think she qualifies as a threat."

"Or," Brandon suggested, "whoever did this could have put an Apple AirTag on Mathilda. They could be keeping tabs on you that way."

"Good point," Bernie said. "I keep forgetting about those things."

"Welcome to the surveillance age," Marvin said as Bernie put her glass down.

"You going to take a look?" Brandon asked.

Bernie nodded.

"I'll go with you," Libby told her.

"Include me in," Marvin added.

"Don't let anyone touch our drinks," Bernie said to Brandon as the three of them trooped toward the door.

"Make sure you look inside the engine block," Brandon called after them.

Marvin, Libby, and Bernie came back half an hour later after having conducted a thorough search of the van. They'd checked out Mathilda's wheel wells, felt in and around the fenders, and opened the hood and scrutinized the engine, per Brandon's suggestion. Then they'd gone through the inside of the van, but all they'd found in there were old coffee cups, candy wrappers, coffee cake crumbs, one of Libby's sweaters, and the ring Bernie had thought she'd lost two months ago.

Finally they walked around the parking lot before going down the street half a block in either direction to see if they could spot anyone hanging out in their cars. They didn't. If they had been there, Bernie and Libby reckoned, they'd have skedaddled when they'd seen Bernie, Libby, and Marvin coming out of the bar.

"Any luck?" Brandon asked once they'd come back in and sat down.

118 *Isis Crawford*

Bernie shook her head. "Nope. No Apple tag. Or if there is one, we can't find it."

"Which means someone followed us," Libby inferred.

Bernie thought about the vehicles parked on their block again. She hadn't noticed any vehicles that didn't belong there, but then she hadn't been looking very carefully, either. She closed her eyes and tried to visualize the cars that had been parked on either side of the block before they'd left. There'd been Otto's Hyundai, Mrs. Silverman's Toyota, the Diggersons' minivan, Bob's Vespa, and the Simpsons' Volvo.

Of course, Bernie thought, whoever was following them could have parked at the far end of the street, in which case neither she nor Libby would have seen them anyway. Also, they hadn't seen anyone pulling out after them.

"This seems like overkill," Marvin pointed out.

"Well, whoever is doing this does seem a tad obsessed," Brandon agreed.

"Don't they, though," Libby observed.

"They're certainly putting in a lot of time trying to scare everyone off," Marvin observed.

Bernie took another sip of her scotch. "I don't get it. Why this obsession with the bake-off? Why would anyone care? It's just a TV show. A local one at that."

"God only knows," Marvin said as he pulled a bowl of pretzels on the bar closer to him. "People are nuts these days. Who knows what anyone is thinking?"

"There must be something else going on, something that we're not seeing," Libby observed after everyone had spent a moment contemplating the state of humanity.

"Yeah. But what?" Brandon inquired as he looked around to see if anyone else wanted a drink. It was slow tonight, but then summer usually was, even on the weekends. Most

A CATERED BAKE-OFF   119

people were outside enjoying the nice weather at this time of year.

"I might have an idea, even if it is far-fetched," Bernie allowed after another minute had gone by. At which point, she told Brandon and Marvin about her and Libby's chat with Dennis.

Brandon rubbed his chin with the knuckles of his right hand while he listened. "Dennis. Dennis Grasso," he said, repeating the name, when Bernie had stopped talking.

"What about him?" Bernie asked.

"He used to work for Eva D."

"She runs an after-hours poker game, doesn't she?" Bernie asked.

Brandon nodded. "Among other things." He paused for a minute, then said, "Here's another thought. What if she's making book on the bake-off?"

"That seems like a stretch," Bernie said.

"So does an espresso machine blowing up," Brandon noted.

"This is true," Bernie conceded.

"I wonder who the favorite would be if that were the case?" Marvin mused.

"Us naturally," Libby said. "I'm insulted you could think it would be anyone else." Then she laughed, took another sip of wine, and asked Marvin about Doug's funeral.

"Our company isn't handling it," Marvin said. "Len is. Evidently, LaForte has an aunt in Akron, Ohio. She's having him cremated here and sent out there. Len told me she has some sort of problem getting around."

"You can do that?" Libby asked.

"Absolutely," Marvin said. "It's the cheapest way to go. Putting him in a coffin and having him shipped out would cost about thirty thou. Probably more these days with in-

120   *Isis Crawford*

flation," he reflected after he'd taken another sip of his beer and eaten another pretzel.

Bernie turned to Brandon. "What do you know about Doug LaForte?" she asked.

"I heard rumors that he was getting himself in a lot of trouble when he was in Longely," Brandon said. "That's why his family left town and went to Oxford. He didn't stay too long there, either, from what I heard."

"That's what Dad said," Bernie told him. She added, "According to him, he wasn't liked too well in Oxford, either, for that matter. Anything else?"

"He's a lousy tipper," Brandon replied.

"Besides that," Bernie replied.

"Why ask me?" Brandon said.

"Because you're the gossip king of Longely," Bernie told him.

Brandon put his hand on his chest. "I'm insulted."

"No, you're not," Bernie told him. "Seriously," she said a moment later.

"Oh, seriously? Well, that changes everything," Brandon mocked. Then he relented. "I don't know much really, but I know someone who might know a little more. He was assistant principal at the Longely elementary school, and he still comes in here occasionally for a game of pool." Brandon gave Bernie his name and number.

Bernie went outside and phoned him, but her call went straight to voicemail. Bernie left a message and went back inside. Kevin Cohen called Bernie back a half an hour later, but he didn't have a lot to say, other than he remembered Doug as the kid who had squeezed a tube of toothpaste into his ear in kindergarten, and had fallen off the jungle gym later that year and broken his arm in two places.

"*Toothpaste?*" Marvin repeated when Bernie hung up.

Bernie laughed. "My cousin did that with a stick of butter when he was two."

"What happened?" Marvin asked.

"Nothing. Amazingly, he was fine," Libby told him while Bernie frowned and contemplated her drink.

"I think we need to talk to Eva. And maybe have another talk with Dennis," Bernie said a moment later.

"As well as find out a little more about how espresso machines work," Libby added.

"Such as how hard is it to jerry-rig one of them," Marvin suggested.

"Exactly," Libby replied, holding up her glass for some more wine.

Chapter 17

It was a little before eight o'clock on Monday morning when Sam walked through the prep room door. Bernie was attempting to fold egg whites into the batter for an angel food cake, just using her right hand, while Libby was taking two trays of raspberry corn muffins out of the oven.

Oh, no, Libby thought when she saw him. *Something else has happened.*

At this point, she wished that Bernie had never gotten them involved in the show. She stifled a yawn and thought about how tired she was and how much she had to do. In truth, she hadn't slept well. She'd tossed and turned all night long. Every time she'd started to fall asleep, she ended up rehashing her conversation with her dad and Bernie.

Had Doug been the target, or was his death a result of a malfunction? Was the killer trying to get everyone to quit the bake-off and scuttle the show? Did someone have a betting pool going on? Were they trying to fix the odds? Highly unlikely, but people have been known to bet on pretty much anything.

She felt like a hamster on a wheel, going round and

round. There were too many possibilities and none of them added up to anything logical. For example, her gut told her that whoever had written the verses probably hadn't rigged the oven or the espresso machine. On the other hand, her gut had been wrong before. Or was this simply a case of an espresso machine gone bad? Libby didn't know. She didn't have enough information to come to a conclusion.

One thing was clear to her, however. It was becoming indisputable that there was a good chance one of the people in the cast was responsible for what was going on, and that was a scary prospect.

She remembered reciting the names of the contestants and judges to herself in her dream as she tried to figure out who was the guilty party. The name had popped into her head, and she recalled telling herself to get up and write it down; but the next thing she knew, it was five-thirty in the morning and her alarm was going off. She had tried to remember the name she'd come up with, but it was gone. And it hadn't come back.

At that point, with a great deal of effort, she'd pulled herself out of bed, gotten dressed, and started on the day's chores: There'd been cinnamon rolls, scones, and muffins to bake; opening up the store; running to the bank to get change; not to mention trying out a new recipe for carrot cake, one that incorporated mango chunks; making a chocolate cake with mocha frosting and a rum filling for Mr. Cooper's birthday party; trying to fix a problem with the credit card machine.

She'd been just about to call the credit card company— the damned machine still wasn't doing what it was supposed to do—when Sam had walked through the door.

"How's it going?" he asked as he headed toward the sisters.

Bernie pointed to her sling. "I'm feeling a little better."

"You think you'll be ready for the weekend?" he asked.

"Definitely," Bernie said, although she wasn't sure at all that would be the case. "Good thing I'm a righty. And how are things going with you?"

Sam sighed. "The saga continues. Someone wrote *Bakers Go Home,* on the door of my house."

"Maybe whoever did it is anti-carb and pro-keto," Libby suggested.

"Maybe," Sam said, laughing. "I bet you wonder why I'm here." Then before Libby could answer, he handed Libby a torn-off piece of paper. "That's where Doug was staying," he said, pointing to the address he'd scribbled down. "It's an Airbnb around the corner from the old strip mall on Cumberland. I don't know if looking at his place will help or not," Sam continued. "It may turn out to be a waste of time, but at this point, I figured any little bit of information you can get . . ."

". . . will be a good thing," Libby said, finishing Sam's sentence. "Maybe Doug left something behind that will shed some light on the situation."

"Hopefully," Bernie said as she put the spatula she was holding down on the prep table and asked Sam if they were getting a new judge for the contest.

"We are," Sam replied. "May I?" he asked, pointing to the tray of fresh-baked lemon bars sitting on the far end of the stainless-steel prep table.

"By all means, take one," Libby replied.

"Who is it?" Bernie wanted to know.

Sam grinned. "That's for me to know and you to find out," he replied as he took a bite.

"Seriously," Bernie said.

Sam pointed to himself. "Me. I'm going to step in," he said as he bit into the bar he'd taken. "Very nice," he said,

A CATERED BAKE-OFF   125

savoring the flavors. "Very nice, indeed. Just the right balance of sweet and tart. And I like the crust. It's a little different. What's in it?"

"The usual suspects. Graham crackers, sugar, and I added coarsely chopped, toasted walnuts for a little extra flavor," Libby replied. Then she got a bakery box down from one of the shelves and filled it with a selection of pastries from the front of the shop. "For you and the wife," she said, handing the box to him when she came back in. "I put in a couple of cupcakes for the stepkids as well. They're the ones with the sprinkles on top."

"Is this a bribe?" Sam asked.

Libby laughed. "It's whatever you want it to be."

"Good," Sam said. He raised the box. "The children thank you, as do I." He started to leave, but stopped and turned at the door. "You'll let me know what you find, if you find anything, that is," he said.

"Most definitely," Bernie said.

"If we do," Libby amended.

"So, what do you think?" Bernie asked Libby after Sam left.

"I think going out there is probably going to be a waste of time," Libby said.

"Agreed," Bernie replied. "But on the other hand . . ."

"Yes, we won't know until we've looked," Libby answered, articulating the obvious. "And as long as we're out, we should stop at Central Restaurant Supply on our way back to the shop and have a chat about espresso machines."

"Always an interesting topic," Bernie observed.

"That's what I'm thinking. Great minds and all that," Libby quipped.

"Well, I wouldn't go that far," Bernie said.

Libby laughed. "Neither would I," she replied.

126   *Isis Crawford*

And with that, Bernie went upstairs to take some more Advil, and discuss their plan of attack with their dad, while Libby finished the angel food cake for her sister, put it in the oven, and told Amber, their counter girl, when it needed to come out.

Ten minutes later, she and Bernie were out the door and on their way to their destination. There was a PGA golf tournament in progress, so traffic was heavier than usual, and the drive over to where Doug was staying took longer than they had anticipated.

They were just pulling up to the mint-green-colored colonial when a car shot out of the driveway of 197 Avalon Drive.

"Wasn't that Steve . . . Steve . . . ?" Libby asked Bernie as she watched the car put on another burst of speed as it rounded the corner.

". . . Steve Gardner," Bernie said, supplying the man's last name. "He's one of the camera guys on the *Bake-Off* crew."

"That's right," Libby said.

Then she looked at Bernie, and Bernie looked at Libby.

"Fortune favors the bold, Libby," Bernie noted as Libby put her foot on the gas and followed Steve Gardner down the block. By the time she got to the corner, though, he was gone.

"You should have gone faster," Bernie admonished Libby.

"I was going as fast as Mathilda will let me," Libby retorted. "It's not as if I'm driving a Porsche, you know. She only goes fifty miles an hour, and that's if she has a tailwind."

"Sixty," Bernie said, wishing that she were doing the driving.

"In your dreams," Libby snapped. "Anyway, we know where to find him."

"Yes, we do," Bernie said.

In addition to working behind the camera on the *Bake-Off*, he had a part-time gig at a camera chop over on Hawley. She looked up and down Avalon Drive. The only thing moving that she could see was a garbage truck lumbering down the road, followed by a man on a riding mower.

"He was going the kind of fast that you go when you've done something wrong," Libby observed.

Bernie clicked her tongue against her teeth. "Or you're late to an appointment."

Libby laughed. "Now you're beginning to sound like me."

"And vice versa," Bernie told her sister as Libby made a U-turn and headed back to 197 Avalon.

"I wonder what he was doing here?" Bernie said as she tightened her sling again. The damn thing kept on slipping.

"Only one way to find out," Libby said as she parked by the curb and she and her sister walked up to the house. She reflected that the place looked old, but well cared for, as she rang the doorbell.

Chapter 18

A moment later, a heavyset middle-aged lady in lilac sweats opened the door. "Yes," she said, looking Bernie and Libby up and down. "Can I help you?" Then her expression changed. "I recognize you," she squealed. "You're competing on *The Longely Bake-Off.*"

"That's us," Bernie said.

The woman put her hand to her mouth. "Wasn't what happened just terrible?"

"It certainly was Mrs. . . . ." Here Libby paused, because she didn't know the woman's name.

"Roberts," the woman said, "but you can call me Beth."

Bernie put on her best smile and stepped forward. "Nice to meet you, Beth," she said.

"So, is the contest still going on?" Beth asked.

"I hope so," Bernie said, thinking of what Sam had said about Nell. "I think so. We're supposed to be doing it all again next week, barring any other unforeseen events, that is."

Beth pointed to Bernie's sling. She looked concerned. "Are you sure you'll be able to do it with that, hon?"

"It's just a sprain," Bernie informed her. "It should be better by then."

Beth smiled. "Good." She leaned forward. "Because I'm rooting for you."

"Why, thank you," Libby said, unexpectedly touched by Beth's comment.

"So, how can I help you two?" Beth asked.

Libby told Beth why she and Bernie were there.

Beth frowned. "How odd. That's what the man who was just here said. He told me his name was Howard Deitz—"

Libby interrupted. "Is that what he said?"

"Yes? Why?" Beth asked.

"Because his name is Steve Gardner."

Beth raised an eyebrow. "It looks like we have a regular mystery going on here."

"What did he want?" Bernie said to Beth.

"He wanted to take a look at Doug's stuff. But I didn't let him."

"Can I ask why?" Bernie inquired.

Beth sniffed. "Because he also told me he was Doug's half brother. Well, I happen to know that Doug was an only child."

"Interesting," Bernie remarked. "I wonder why he said that?"

Beth sniffed again. "Obviously, so I would let him into the house. He said Doug had something of his he needed to get back."

"Did he say what it was?" Libby asked.

Beth shook her head. "No, he didn't, and I didn't ask. I mean, what was the point? He would only have lied to me again."

"I wouldn't have let him in, either," Libby observed to keep Beth talking.

"I think he was surprised that I wouldn't let him," Beth told her. "He got really nasty when I said no. He told me I'd better let him in or else I'd be sorry." She put her hands on her hips and scowled. "I mean, really? When I asked him what he was planning on doing, he called me a *controlling bitch*. I had to threaten him with calling the police unless he got off my porch." Beth's voice rose in indignation. She pointed to herself. "I'm a pretty good judge of character. Have to be, renting out space in my house and all. Over the years I've learned, once a liar, always a liar."

"I suppose you do have to be able to tell the good guys from the bad ones," Bernie said, all thoughts of spinning a tale about needing to get into Doug's room gone.

"Damn right I do," Beth told her as she waved to a neighbor driving by. "Poor Doug. What a terrible accident. You know," she confided, leaning forward again, "Doug told me he was afraid something bad was going to happen to him."

"Did he now," Bernie said.

Beth nodded. "He did, indeed."

"I guess he was right," Libby observed.

Beth frowned. "He asked me to do a reading for him."

"A reading?" Libby squinched up her face in puzzlement.

"I think she means tarot, Libby," Bernie said.

Beth nodded. She fluffed out her hair. "I'm pretty good at it, if I do say so myself. You know what the cards said?" she asked the sisters.

"No. What?" Bernie replied.

Beth looked from one sister to the other and back again. "The first card that came up was the tower," she confided.

"Meaning?" Libby asked.

Beth leaned in again. "Death. Imminent catastrophe," she whispered, as if even saying those words out loud was putting their energy out into the universe. Then she straightened up. "In my experience, the cards never lie." Beth shook her head sadly. "Unfortunately, or fortunately, people are either born under a lucky star, or they aren't. Doug wasn't. Poor thing. May he have better luck in his next life."

A mourning dove cooed, and the three women were quiet for a moment contemplating the vagaries of the universe. Then Bernie said, "You sound as if you knew Doug."

Beth nodded. "I did. It had been a while, though, since I'd seen him. It's more like we exchange Christmas cards and follow each other on Instagram."

"Did he say anything else about feeling threatened?" Libby asked Beth. "Like who was threatening him and why?"

Beth shrugged her shoulders. "Not really. No." She rubbed the pendant hanging around her neck with her fingers. "I guess I should have asked. Mostly, we just chatted about stuff. You know, made small talk."

"About what," Bernie inquired.

"We talked about baking stuff. We discussed recipes, and different kinds of flours; when you should use cake flour and when you shouldn't; how to make powdered sugar when you don't have any in the house; how bad most boxed cake mixes are and how you can make your own. But mainly, he told me stories about things that had happened on the different baking shows he was on. Like the time that a contestant on a bake-off show in Toledo, Ohio, mistook salt for sugar and added it to the Bundt cake she was making."

"I remember that," Bernie said, laughing at the memory.

"I do, too," Beth replied as she swatted at a bee buzzing around her. "Then he told me about the time a contestant in Portland, Oregon, sabotaged his neighbor's crème brûlée by changing the oven temperature, or about how

132   *Isis Crawford*

another contestant in Duluth hid the vanilla extract so no one else in the contest could use it." She shook her head. "He really was a very good storyteller. Very entertaining. I didn't realize he had hosted so many shows. I guess most of the reality shows don't last that long."

"Did he say anything about anyone he was having trouble with now?" Libby asked.

Beth shook her head. "Sorry, I'm afraid not."

Libby tried again. "Did he say anything about the show?"

"He said he thought there should be another couple of teams competing," Beth replied, "but that was as far as it went."

"How about the cast and crew?" Bernie asked Beth. "Did he say anything about them?"

"He did mention a kid called Dennis. Said he owed him some money and that he was good for it, but that the kid was nagging him, and that Dennis was getting to be a pain in the butt," Beth answered.

"Did Doug say how much he owed Dennis?" Libby asked.

"I got the impression it wasn't a lot," Beth replied. "But," she added, "not a lot is a relative term. These days, not a lot could mean five bucks, ten thousand, or a million." She frowned. "It all depends on your frame of reference."

Libby nodded. "True."

"Do you think we could see where Doug was staying?" Bernie asked Beth.

Beth looked at her watch. "Ordinarily, it wouldn't be a problem, but I have to be out of here in an hour. I have a doctor's appointment over by Twelve Corners, which I've rescheduled twice. Can you come by later?"

"We won't take long," Libby promised.

"I don't know," Beth told her. "I still have stuff to do before we go."

"Please," Bernie begged. "There may be something in there that will help us figure out what happened to Doug."

"I doubt it," Beth informed her. "It's mostly clothes."

"Can we take a quick look anyway?" Bernie asked. "Please."

"What are you going to do with his stuff?" Libby asked.

Beth shrugged. "Send it back to his aunt tomorrow. She's already been in touch. There isn't that much."

"Listen, you're probably right. There's probably nothing there that will help us. On the other hand . . ." Bernie made a what-if gesture with her hands. Then she posed a rhetorical question. "After all, why did Steve Gardner want to take a look?" Bernie pointed out. "Why did he get so pissed when you wouldn't let him? To me, that suggests that something in there is of interest." She could see from the expression on Beth's face that what she said had gotten her thinking.

Beth stooped down and picked up a piece of paper that was lying under the laurel bush. "Let me get this straight, then. You're saying this Gardner guy had something to do with what happened to Doug?" Beth asked.

"It's a real possibility," Libby replied. "One I think that we need to consider."

"We'll be quick," Bernie added. She raised her hand. "Scout's honor," she promised, even though she'd never been a Boy, a Girl, or an Eagle Scout.

Beth thought for another moment. Then she said, "Okay." Libby was about to thank her when Beth held up a finger and said, "I don't suppose you could give me one of your bake-off recipes when the contest is over." She explained, "I'm on the board of directors of Homeless Hounds and we're holding a bake sale the first weekend in

September to raise money for the shelter. I was thinking it might be fun if—"

Bernie interrupted before Beth could finish her sentence. "We can't give you the recipe, but what we can do is bake the cakes and donate them to the sale."

Beth grinned. "Even better." She held out her hand; she, Bernie, and Libby shook on the deal. Then Beth turned and stepped inside her house. "Well, come on," she said, motioning them in from the other side of the doorway. "I haven't got all day."

Chapter 19

Bernie and Libby followed Beth over her house's threshold. Built in the 1950s, the Colonial smelled of cleaning products, lavender, and fried food. The three women trooped down the narrow hallway hung with family photographs and took a right at the corner. Then they walked through a neatly furnished living and dining room, into a well-used kitchen, and from there into the mudroom.

"This way," Beth said, opening a door across from the entrance to the garage and beckoning them to follow her down the short flight of stairs that led to what had once been an in-law apartment. "We built this for my husband's mom ten years ago," Beth explained. "She's been gone two years now. No. Three." Beth sighed. She blinked tears away. "Cancer is a terrible thing," she reflected as Bernie and Libby looked around the bright, cheerful three-room apartment. There was a living/dining area, a bedroom, a small galley kitchen, and a full bathroom with a steam shower.

"This is really nice," Libby commented.

Beth beamed, but her smile vanished when she noticed

136   *Isis Crawford*

one of Doug's suitcases. It was lying open, its contents spilled out onto the floor. "Oh, dear," she said as she rushed to pick things up. "I don't know what happened. Everything was packed."

"I'd say that's what happened," Bernie told her, and pointed to the window facing the backyard. Someone had broken it. Shards of glass littered the floor. "Be careful," she warned Beth. "You don't want to cut yourself."

Beth turned to the sisters, outrage written on her face. "That son of a bitch," she cried, her voice quavering with anger. "I told whatever he calls himself . . ."

Bernie supplied the name again. "Steve Gardner."

Beth continued: ". . . that he couldn't come in, and this is what he does! I can't believe he was doing this when I was making myself another cup of coffee and I didn't hear a thing. You would have thought I would have heard the glass breaking."

Bernie made a clicking noise with her tongue. "Well, at least now we know why Steve Gardner was in such a hurry to get out of here." And she told Beth what she and Libby had seen as they'd been pulling up to the house.

Beth bit her lip and shook her head. "I don't know what's happening around here these days," she lamented. "Between the car thefts and the shootings, no one is safe here anymore." She took a deep breath and let it out. "That guy must have circled around the block and cut through Fred Allen's yard. Talk about nerve. And now I gotta get the window fixed before tomorrow. I have another guest coming here tomorrow afternoon," she explained. "I don't seem heartless, do I?" she asked Libby anxiously. "This lady called, and since I had an opening . . ." Her voice trailed off. "I mean, it's not like Doug is coming back here."

"It's fine," Libby reassured her.

A CATERED BAKE-OFF   137

Bernie studied the broken window for a moment. Whoever did it hadn't used any finesse, that was for sure. Next she went over to the window, leaned out, and took a closer look at what was below. From where she was standing, she could make out trampled laurel leaves and a small shovel half hidden by the plants. "Yours?" she asked Beth.

Beth nodded.

"He must have used this to break the glass," Bernie continued. "I wonder what was so important here that Gardner felt he had to break in?"

"That is, if it was him," Libby said.

Beth turned to her. "Of course, it was him! Who else could it be?" she demanded. "The window was fine this morning when I was in here getting everything together."

Neither Libby nor Bernie responded. The answer seemed self-evident.

Beth shook her head. "What the hell could he have wanted? There was nothing worth taking that I could see when I packed up Doug's possessions," she said.

Bernie noted that spots of color had blossomed on Beth's cheeks. She started to pick up the things on the floor, but Bernie put out her hand to stop her.

"We'll do it," she said. 'You get ready for your appointment."

Beth thanked her. Then she shook her head again. "If there's one thing I've learned after doing this for a while is that some people have no regard for other people."

"What exactly did Steve Gardner say to you?" Bernie asked as she contemplated the two wheelies. They were a set. One larger, one smaller. Both made of canvas. There was certainly nothing special about them. They looked like the kind you'd buy in Marshalls for fifty-nine dollars and thirty cents.

"Just what I already told you," Beth replied. "That there

138 *Isis Crawford*

was something Doug had borrowed from him, and he needed it back."

"Like money," Bernie said, thinking of what Dennis had told them.

Beth shook her head. "He didn't say that, and I didn't see any when I was packing Doug's things up."

"That's all Gardner said?" Bernie asked again, hoping that Beth had left something out.

"Pretty much," Beth replied. "He asked if he could get something from Doug's things and I told him I didn't feel comfortable doing that and he'd have to talk to Doug's aunt. I offered to give him the number, but he didn't want it. At that point, he just got really insistent. That's when I told him I was going to call the cops if he didn't get off the porch. I think he'd been drinking," she confided. "He had alcohol on his breath." She swallowed. "Poor soul," she murmured.

"I take it you're talking about Doug LaForte?" Libby asked.

"Who else?" Beth said. "It's all so sad."

"Yes, it truly is," Bernie agreed.

"You don't think it was an accident, do you?" Beth asked.

"Unfortunately, I don't," Bernie replied.

"The police don't, either," Libby added.

Beth shook her head. "Who would do something like that?" she demanded.

"That is the question, isn't it," Libby replied.

"According to my dad," Bernie said, continuing the conversation, "most people didn't like Doug when he was growing up here."

"That's true," Beth said. "Doug wasn't really popular. People said bad things about him. In fact, I think one of the reasons his aunt and uncle moved was to give him a

A CATERED BAKE-OFF 139

fresh start in a new school. Truth be told, he wasn't very nice to most folks, but I don't think Doug ever got over the deaths of his parents. I think that hit him very hard. It changed him. And even if he wasn't very nice, even if he played some mean practical jokes, that was a long time ago. People change."

"They certainly do," Bernie agreed.

"How well did you know him?" Libby asked.

"Pretty well. We lived on the same block before he moved," Beth responded.

"This one?" Bernie asked.

"No. Over on Scottholm Lane." Scottholm Lane was on the other side of Longely, five blocks away from a Wegmans supermarket. "Bad luck just seems to follow certain people around," Beth mused.

"What do you mean?" Libby inquired.

"Well, first Doug's parents dying like that—"

Libby interrupted. "Like how?"

"In an automobile crash with a drunken driver. It was in the newspaper."

"Oh, yes," Libby said. She remembered reading about it. "Anything else?"

"Well, his house caught fire. Electric short. I mean, even his dog died, and he loved that thing more than anything. He took to his bed for three days after that happened."

"I'm curious. How come he's staying with you?" Bernie asked, changing the subject. "I know he has his own place."

Beth explained. "He does, but it's undergoing a major reno. He's adding a room and redoing his kitchen and bathrooms," Beth told her. She corrected herself. "Or was. I guess that's over now."

"Sounds expensive," Libby said, thinking of the money Dennis said Doug owed him.

"It sure is these days," Beth agreed. "Anyway, I ran into

140 *Isis Crawford*

him one day at Home Depot while he was picking out paint colors and we got to chatting. When I heard about what was happening with his house, I told him he could stay with me if he needed to." She scratched behind her ear. "I was surprised when he called and took me up on my offer. But I'm glad that he did. I have to say, he's definitely a lot nicer than he used to be. It was fun talking about the old days." She fluffed out her hair again. "Who's the new judge going to be?"

"Possibly our producer," Libby answered.

"Sam Levine?" Beth asked.

Both Bernie and Libby nodded.

Beth shook her head. "He should get someone else. He has no sense of taste," she confided. "His sister told me he lost it when he got Covid. Of course," she reflected, "Ruby doesn't like Sam and she lies." Then she added, "Even if Sam does choose himself, they're going to need someone else anyway. What if there's a tie?"

"Good point," Libby said. "I have no idea who that would be, though. The management doesn't share information with us."

Bernie chimed in. "Yeah. We're just the peasants. No one tells us anything."

"You're not peasants, you're the talent," Beth blurted out. "Without you, there wouldn't be a show."

Bernie grinned. "Libby and I would like to think so."

Beth was quiet for a minute; then she repeated what she'd said earlier. "But they are going to get someone else, aren't they? I mean, you can't have just one judge. That wouldn't be fair."

"No, it wouldn't," Bernie replied, having mentioned that to Libby earlier in the day.

Then Beth left to get ready for her appointment, and Libby and Bernie turned their attention to the suitcases

Doug had left behind. It was time to go through them. Unfortunately, neither one provided any jaw-dropping revelations. In the first suitcase, Libby and Bernie found pretty much what they had expected.

Doug had brought several shirts, three pairs of shoes, five pairs of slacks, three pairs of jeans, a sweater, underwear, pj's, two hoodies, and enough toiletry items to supply a small cruise ship. The second smaller suitcase contained a multitude of cookbooks, as well as pens, pads, several packs of yellow legal pads, and a Timex Snoopy watch.

"Now, there's something I didn't expect to see," Bernie said, pointing to it. "I figured him for something a little more upscale."

"Is anything missing?" Libby asked Beth when she reappeared fifteen minutes later. She and Bernie had spread the suitcases' contents out on the bed.

"Not that I can see," Beth responded after she'd studied the items on the bed for a couple of minutes. "But then, I really wasn't paying much attention. I just shoveled everything in and closed the suitcases up."

Libby started going through Doug's pants' and shirts' pockets. "You didn't see a phone or a laptop when you packed everything up, did you?"

Beth shook her head. "I assume he took his phone with him. He was wedded to the damn thing. I wouldn't be surprised if he went to bed with it at night—you know, slept with it on his pillow. And as for his laptop—now that you mention it—I thought he took it with him to the estate. He mentioned something about using it to keep track of the judging. Maybe it's still up there."

"I wonder if that's what Gardner was looking for?" Libby mused.

"We need to call Sam and find out if he has it," Bernie

said. "Although I'm pretty sure he would have mentioned it if he had."

"Or Clyde would have let us know," Libby said. She was just about to suggest that Bernie make the call, when she looked down and saw something sticking out from underneath the bed. When she knelt down to get a better look, she realized the thing she was looking at was a handle of some sort. She pulled. The thing turned out to be an old-fashioned, battered, brown leather briefcase.

"Looks like something an old-time lawyer would use," she observed after she put it on the bed. Bernie and Beth crowded around while she opened it up. The first thing she took out was a laptop computer sleeve, the second thing she took out was a small notebook, and the third thing she took out were four old Polaroid photographs. The first photo was of a house, the second was of a beagle, the third was of a football field, and the fourth was of two high school kids.

"Is that Doug and Nell when they were younger?" Bernie asked, looking at the picture. "Yeah, it is," Libby said after she'd studied it. The two teens were standing in front of an old hot dog stand. Nell was smiling and Doug was holding up a foot-long hot dog.

"She's gotten a lot thinner, and he's gotten a lot balder," Bernie observed.

Libby laughed. "That's for sure. It looks like they were good friends," she noted. She clicked her tongue against the front of her teeth while she thought. "Why do you think Doug had these?" Libby wondered after a minute had gone by.

"I don't know. To remind him of old times or maybe to show them to Nell," Bernie hypothesized.

"You're probably right," Libby agreed. She couldn't

think of another reason, either. Then she pointed to the empty laptop sleeve. "Well, he definitely had a laptop."

"That's probably what Steve was after," Bernie suggested as Libby thumbed through the notebook she and her sister had found in the briefcase. "Unless it was the notebook."

Libby grunted as she continued looking through it. The notebook was divided into two sections: phone numbers and random notes about food that Doug had eaten at various restaurants.

"I guess Doug wasn't a big fan of Selena's," Libby observed as she scanned his notes. Selena's was a Mexican restaurant two towns over. "He thinks their Vietnamese tacos are, and here I'm quoting, 'an abomination.'"

"Well, he's right. They are," Bernie replied. "Anything else of interest?"

Libby nodded. "Eva D's phone number." And she showed the entry to Bernie.

"Maybe there is a betting pool going on for the bake-off, after all," Bernie said.

"Someone's betting on your show?" Beth asked, her voice rising in disbelief. "That's ridiculous."

"That's what I thought," Bernie said. "But maybe it isn't so ridiculous, after all." And she took pictures of the notebook's pages before returning it to the briefcase. Because, as her dad had taught them: You never know what is relevant and what is not.

After Beth left to check on the mail, Bernie and Libby spent the next ten minutes examining Doug's suitcases, looking under the bed he'd slept in, and going through the chest of drawers, the closet, and the bathroom. It turned out to be a waste of time. If there was anything else there of interest, the sisters didn't find it.

144   *Isis Crawford*

As she and Libby were driving away from the house, Bernie called Brandon and asked him to arrange a meetup with Eva D. Half an hour later, Brandon called back and told Bernie he'd set the meeting up. It turned out that Eva D had some questions she wanted to ask Bernie and Libby as well. But before they met with her, they had another stop to make. Two stops, actually.

Chapter 20

"Marty, my man, how are you doing?" Bernie asked the co-owner of Central Restaurant Supply when she and Libby walked into the shop a half hour after leaving Beth Roberts's house. Looking around, she couldn't help thinking that the shop seemed even more crowded than it usually did. Normally, it was crammed with merchandise stacked up in no discernable order, but there were still rows. Now it was just a jumble of stuff. There was so much stuff that Bernie and Libby had to walk sideways between the towering aisles of stoves, refrigerators, coolers, and pizza ovens to reach the front counter.

"Someone go out of business?" Libby inquired, pointing to the mass of equipment in the front of the shop.

"Mario's Pizza," Marty replied, looking up from his phone. "Along with the Riverside Diner. It has not been a good month for small restaurants."

"What happened?" Bernie asked. "Those guys have both been in business for thirteen years."

"Fourteen," Marty said, correcting her. He put his phone on the counter. "What happened is, some venture capitalist company bought out both sites and doubled their rents. The vultures are circling again."

146 *Isis Crawford*

"That's terrible," Libby cried.

"Yes, it is," Marty agreed. "But it seems to be the thing to do these days. Goodbye, mom-and-pop; hello, venture capitalists. They're buying up all the land they can—at least they are here. Anyway, Mario told the company to go screw themselves. He's going down to North Carolina to open a business there."

"I thought Tony owned that building and the one next to it," Libby said. She frowned. She knew things were getting bad; but from the pile of equipment in the store, they were even worse than she had imagined.

Marty shook his head. "He did, but ABC bought Tony out. They made him a cash offer he couldn't refuse. I hear they're looking for a spot to put up a mixed-use residential complex. Like we need another one around here."

"And Moe?" Bernie asked.

"Same thing, only he's closing the diner and retiring," Marty replied. "Decided he doesn't want to start all over again. Just be glad you own the building your business is in."

"Believe me, we are," Bernie replied, gesturing to herself and her sister.

"And speaking of business," Marty continued, "the answer is no."

"No," Bernie repeated. "What do you mean *no*? I haven't even asked you anything yet."

"But you were going to," Marty said. He was in his mid-forties, six-four, and skinny. A former basketball player, he had always reminded Bernie of Ichabod Crane. "That's what the moron," also known as Joe, the co-owner of the shop, "said you were going to do, and he was right. For once. Amazing. Truly amazing."

"So, now Joe's gifted with second sight?" Bernie asked. "I mean he's not even gifted with first sight. Or third sight, for that matter."

A CATERED BAKE-OFF   147

"There's no such thing as first sight," Marty declared.

"There's no such thing as second sight, either, as long as we're on the subject," Bernie told him.

"You don't know that," Marty said.

"And you don't *not* know that," Bernie snapped back as her sister clapped her hands. Bernie and Marty stopped bickering and looked at her.

"Actually, Marty, we're here to ask you if you have any more of those silicone muffin trays," Libby lied. "We need four more."

"Yes, I have them, and no, you weren't going to ask me that," Marty countered.

Libby raised an eyebrow. "I wasn't?"

"No, you weren't," Marty said.

"How do you know that?" Libby demanded.

"My superior ESP skills," Marty told her.

Libby snorted. "Oh, so now you've become a mind reader, as well as a purveyor of baking supplies?"

Marty grunted. "It doesn't take much to figure things out in this situation. And by the way, as long as we're talking about baking, I don't think the cake you're making on the show is going to work. Not that you asked me for my opinion," he added hastily.

"You're right, I didn't," Libby told him.

"But I'd like to hear it," Bernie said, stepping forward. "Why are you saying that, Marty?"

"Because the cake is going to be soggy," Marty told her. "You need to reduce the amount of liquid in it. You're using too much."

Bernie nodded. She'd been thinking the same thing. That's also what the judges had said as well. "Yeah. I didn't expect the pineapple to be so juicy. We probably need to press more liquid out of it."

Marty shook his head. "I would cook the pulp down if

148   *Isis Crawford*

I were you. Concentrate it. That way, you won't lose any of the flavor."

"Maybe we should," Libby allowed after a moment of thought.

"If we can," Bernie said.

"Why can't you?" Marty asked.

"Because we're supposed to replicate exactly what we were doing before the . . ."

"*Accident,*" Marty said, supplying the word when Bernie paused.

"That's not the word I was going to use," Bernie said.

"Obviously," Marty said. "Otherwise, you wouldn't be here."

"Maybe we just dropped by to say hello," Bernie said. "Maybe we miss your scintillating conversation. Have you ever thought of that?" she asked Marty.

He snorted. "Nope! And while we're on the subject, what's going to happen to the show?"

"Meaning?" Libby replied.

"Meaning," Marty answered, "that Doug isn't going to be judging anything, and neither is Sam if he's arrested. No judges, no contest."

Bernie leaned forward. "Who told you they were going to arrest Sam?"

Marty corrected himself. "I misspoke. I heard he's a *person of interest.*"

"From whom?" Bernie asked once more.

Marty smiled. "Longely is a small town. Word gets around. That's why you're here, aren't you? Because Sam hired you to find out who did it." He spread his arms out. "Tell me, am I wrong?"

"No. You're not," Bernie admitted.

"Well," Marty continued, "I also heard that Doug and Sam got into a fight about the show. Something about free advertising for Doug's new place."

A CATERED BAKE-OFF 149

Libby perked up. "I didn't know he was planning on opening one," she said.

Marty nodded. "That's what I heard. It was going to be some kind of Mexican joint. Fusion." He made a face, then rubbed the top of his head. "But I can't believe Sam would try and kill Doug over something like that."

"I can't, either," Libby agreed.

"Make that three of us," Bernie said, and she pointed to a row of espresso machines on the far wall. It was time to ask the question she'd come to ask. "So, how could one of those explode?"

"Anything can explode, given the right circumstances," Marty told her.

"And what would those be?" Libby inquired.

Marty rubbed his nose with his knuckle. "I take it that this isn't a hypothetical question?"

"No," Libby replied at the same time that Bernie answered, "Yes, it is."

"So, which is it?" Marty inquired, looking from one woman to the other and back again. Then he watched Bernie turn to Libby and say to her, "I have one word for you, Libby. No, three words. *Liability and lawsuits.*"

"Oh," Libby said, understanding spreading across her face.

"Exactly," Bernie replied. She held out her hand, palm facing the ceiling. "So, Libby, tell the man what he needs to hear."

"No need to make such a big deal out of it, Bernie," Libby groused as she turned to Marty and told him the question was hypothetical.

"Excellent," Marty said. "Now that's settled, I will answer it for you. Espresso machines can explode because they are essentially mini boilers that have valves attached to them. So, the answer is: Theoretically, they can explode, but in actuality, an explosion happens very rarely. When it

150   *Isis Crawford*

does happen—and I would estimate the odds are about a million to one—it's usually for two reasons: one, operator error, or two, because the machine was improperly maintained."

"Or because someone fiddled around with it and did something they shouldn't have." Libby couldn't help herself from adding that.

"Well, there is that, too," Marty allowed. He sneezed, then sneezed again. "Hay fever," he explained, before continuing with what he'd been saying. "Now, I happen to know for a fact that the machine you're asking about was in good working order when we delivered it to the set."

"Why are you so certain?" Bernie asked him.

"Because we rented it out to the Janeckos for their wedding reception and it was returned to us the night before you guys got it." Marty tapped a black leather notebook sitting on the counter next to him. "This is our equipment rental ledger." He opened it up, turned to the fifth page, and pointed to the top entry. "See, here's the machine." He pointed to the first column. "This is the date it went out of the shop." He moved his finger to the second column. "And this is the date it came back in." Then he pointed to the third column. "And this is my signature indicating I went over the machine myself, cleaned it, and did a trial run to make sure it was functioning properly. Which, by the way, is what I do with all pieces of rental equipment when they're returned."

He closed the ledger and pushed it away from him with the tips of his fingers. "That's how I know that whatever happened to the espresso machine wasn't on us. It was working fine when it left this building. Maybe what happened was an accident, maybe it wasn't, maybe it was a malfunction, but the only thing that I'm sure of is that whatever happened wasn't on us."

"A malfunction? Is that a possibility?" Libby wondered aloud.

Marty answered immediately. "Anything can malfunction. Several years ago, somewhere in the U.K., I forget where exactly, a large espresso machine exploded and injured several people. Five went to the hospital, although the injuries were minor. Evidently, there was a design flaw with the relief valve. It happens. It's rare, but things like that do occur."

"But not with the model at the estate, right?" Libby asked.

"No, not with this model. At least, not so far. We wouldn't be renting it out if there was an issue," Marty replied.

"Fair enough," Bernie said. She smiled her most charming smile and asked the second question she'd come here to ask. "How hard would it be to sabotage an espresso maker anyway? What would one do to achieve that end?"

Marty thought for a moment. Then he said, "Not hard at all if you know what you're doing."

"Someone would have to know?" Libby said. "They couldn't figure it out on their own?"

Marty laughed. "It wouldn't take an engineering degree from MIT, if that's what you mean. Actually, it wouldn't surprise me if there was a video on TikTok or one of the other streaming services that demonstrates how to accomplish that particular task."

"TikTok? Do you really think they have videos of that kind of stuff on there?" Libby asked.

"Like I said, it wouldn't surprise me," Marty replied. "God knows, they have all sorts of weird random videos there."

"It wouldn't surprise me, either," Bernie reflected gloomily as she thought back to the set and the fact that everyone in the cast and crew had access to the espresso machine.

"On second thought, though," Marty continued, "really all you need is half a brain to figure it out. It's simple. You just have to slip something in the valve and let the steam pressure build up . . ." He paused for dramatic effect. "And then boom!" He made an exploding gesture with his hands.

Libby thought for a moment. Then she said, "To recapitulate, basically what you're saying is that pretty much anyone could have jerry-rigged the machine."

Marty nodded. "Yes, that's exactly what I'm saying."

"How long would it take to do something like that?" Libby asked.

Marty thought for another moment and said, "Not long at all. All you'd need would be a piece of something, like a thin plastic wafer or Silly Putty."

"*Silly Putty?*" Libby repeated. "You're kidding."

"No, I am not," Marty remarked. "You could just jam it in there, and if you wanted to be extra sure, you'd put a piece of duct tape over the opening as well. Or you could superglue the release valve shut. That's another option. Of course, you'd have to make sure to get that glue into all the corners."

"Could you use paper?" Libby asked.

"No," Marty replied. He backtracked a moment later. "Well, maybe cardboard. No. That's porous, too." He thought for a bit. "Although cardboard might work if you cut it to size and taped it down with duct tape, but that would take longer and be more visible."

Bernie sighed. "I wonder if this was aimed at the group or at Doug?"

"I would guess the probability is that it was aimed at the group. At least that's my thought from what I read," Marty replied. "For the opposite to be the case, to have

A CATERED BAKE-OFF 153

planned and executed this in advance, you would have to know what Doug's schedule was to the minute."

"Like at three forty-five, he was planning on making himself a cappuccino," Libby said.

"Well, he was a man of regular habits," Bernie pointed out.

"How regular?" Marty asked.

"Very regular," Bernie replied. "Or you could be right, and Doug could have just been collateral damage."

"Not a great thing to put on one's tombstone," Libby observed.

"No, it's not," Marty agreed.

"Or," Libby said, continuing the conversation, "maybe someone in the cast heard Doug say that he was going to make himself a cappuccino and got there before him and sabotaged the machine."

"That's also a possibility," Bernie admitted glumly.

"On the other hand," Libby continued, "if we go back to the first possibility and assume that the attack—"

"Attack?" Bernie raised an eyebrow.

"Well, it was, wasn't it?" Libby demanded. "What else would you call it?"

"I suppose you're right," Bernie conceded reluctantly.

"So, as I was saying," Libby continued, "if the *attack*"—here she raised her voice to emphasize the word—"was directed at the cast and crew in general, then the motive would be different."

"And what would that be?" Marty asked.

"Obviously, someone doesn't want the show to go on," Libby responded.

"So we're back to that again," Bernie noted.

"I mean, why else let the goats loose or screw with the oven?" Libby asked as she hitched up her Bermuda shorts. "Those resulted in minor inconveniences. They cost Sam time and money, but no one got hurt."

"Like with the notes," Bernie reminded Libby.

154   *Isis Crawford*

Marty sighed. "All I know is that the espresso machine was working properly when it left the store. I would swear to it."

"God, what a mess," Libby observed as she absent-mindedly picked up a soup ladle that was lying on the counter, then put it back down. "Basically, we're no better off than we were when we started making inquiries."

"Well, we're a little better off," Bernie countered.

"But not by much," Libby replied.

Bernie allowed that her sister was correct again. She looked at her phone. It was time to go. They still had to talk to Steve Gardner.

Chapter 21

Bernie and Libby sat in their van, studying Steve Gardner's car. It was parked under an old ginkgo tree, kitty-corner to the camera shop where he worked part-time. The shop itself was located in the town center of Chili, a small suburban town located three miles away to the north of Longely.

Except for a steady stream of customers going in and out of Dunkin' Donuts, the street the sisters had parked on was quiet at this time of day. Day camps were still in session and people were still at work. Bernie and Libby watched as a flock of pigeons squabbled over a spilled bag of popcorn in the middle of the road. The pigeons scattered briefly when a woman, struggling with a load of packages, walked through them into a UPS Store; then the birds quickly reformed, only to scatter again when a hawk swooped down on them.

Libby fanned herself with the flat of her hand, then pointed to the car. "What do you think?" she asked Bernie.

"I think that's the car we saw tearing out of Beth's driveway," her sister replied.

"I think so, too," Libby said as a man got into the Tesla parked in front of their van and took off.

156   *Isis Crawford*

"Yup. Same color, its license plate begins with the letters *CS*, it's got a dent in its rear fender, and a Six Flags decal on the right side, so I would say, it's the same one," Bernie replied as she blinked a drop of sweat out of her eye.

It has to be at least ninety out, she reckoned.

"Okay." Libby took a drink from her water bottle. "So, what now?"

"Now we go talk to Steve," Bernie said, and she undid her seat belt and stepped out of the van.

Libby followed, but instead of heading directly for the camera store, Bernie stopped at Steve's vehicle.

"What are you doing?" Libby asked.

Bernie shrugged. "Just taking a quick peek," she replied, looking inside. The back seat was stacked with bins of clothes that appeared to be destined for Goodwill, black garbage bags, and cartons full of kitchen supplies.

"I wonder if Gardner is moving?" Bernie mused as she tried the door handle. It wasn't locked. She opened the door and stuck her head inside. She was thinking that maybe whatever Steve had taken from Doug was in the car, but she didn't get a chance to find out. Before she could take a look, Libby tapped her sister on her shoulder.

"Bernie," she said.

"I just need a minute," Bernie told her in an annoyed voice.

"I don't think you have a minute," Libby replied.

"Why not?" Bernie asked, turning.

"That's why not," Libby replied, and pointed to Steve Gardner bearing down on them. Bernie reflected that he didn't look happy.

"What are you doing in my car?" he demanded when he got closer.

"*Your* car?" Bernie said, straightening up and putting her hand to her mouth. "I'm so sorry. I thought it was my friend's. And anyway, I'm not in it, technically speaking.

You know," she continued, "you should lock this puppy up. Especially with all the stuff you have in here. Unless, of course, you want it to get stolen."

Steve took a step toward her. "I'm calling the police," he said.

"Good," Bernie told him. "Go ahead. It'll save me the trouble."

"Really?" Steve said.

"Yes, really," Bernie told him.

"Aren't you going to ask me why my sister said what she did?" Libby inquired.

"No, I'm not, because I don't really care," Steve replied.

"I bet Beth Roberts does," Bernie said. "What was that name you were using when you were at her house?"

Steve shook his head. "I don't know what you're talking about."

"I think you do," Libby replied.

"Are you calling me a liar?" Steve demanded, his face turning ugly.

"How about a fabulist? Is that any better?" Libby asked.

"What the hell is a *fabulist*?" Steve cried.

"It's a fancy name for a *liar*," Bernie said before continuing with what she'd been saying. "Breaking a window, entering Beth Roberts's house, stealing something. Tsk-tsk. You could do some serious jail time for that."

"I repeat. I don't know what you're talking about," Steve insisted.

Bernie ignored him, took her cell out of her bag, and turned to Libby. "I think Beth must be through with her appointment by now, don't you think so, Libby?"

"Absolutely," Libby replied.

Steve looked from one woman to the other and back again. "Who?"

"Beth Roberts, of course," Bernie replied. She waved

158   *Isis Crawford*

her phone in the air. "I know she'll be willing to come down and collect whatever it is you stole out of Doug's room, so she can send it back to his aunt." She took a step toward him.

"You're nuts," Steve said. "The heat must be getting to you."

"I don't think so," Bernie told him. "We saw you. Tell me, did you fool around with the espresso machine, too? You know, make it explode."

Steve took a step back. "You're crazy! I had nothing to do with that."

"So, you did break into Doug LaForte's room?" Libby asked.

"I didn't say that," Steve said.

"Yeah, you did." Libby pointed to a Band-Aid on the side of Steve's left hand. "Cut yourself on the window you broke?" she asked.

"No," Steve said, putting his hand in his pocket. "I cut myself slicing an apple, if you must know."

Libby snorted as Bernie began to dial.

"Who are you calling?" Steve demanded.

"I told you," Bernie answered. "The police."

"Unless you want to tell us what you were after," Libby said, "then we won't."

"I wasn't after anything," Steve replied.

Bernie laughed. "You're telling me you just broke in for the hell of it?"

Steve bit his lip. "No. Yes."

"Which is it?" Libby demanded.

Steve didn't say anything.

"Look," Bernie said. "This will just be between us." She softened her tone. "I'm sure you had a reason to do what you did."

"I did."

A CATERED BAKE-OFF   159

"Then how about telling us," Libby said. "We're just interested in figuring out who is behind what happened to Doug. That's all. Honest."

Steve was silent for a minute. Then he said, "I got nervous, okay?"

"Nervous about what?" Libby asked.

Steve blushed and looked away. "I was afraid the police would go through Doug's belongings and find it."

"Find what?" Bernie inquired.

Steve wet his lips. "The video."

Bernie frowned. "What video?"

Steve coughed. "We had a thing going," he mumbled. "I didn't want the guys in the department to see it."

"You and Doug had a thing?" Libby asked, making sure she'd heard correctly.

Steve nodded. "It wasn't serious. At least it wasn't for me." He bit his lip. "I guess Doug thought it was."

"And you made a video?" Bernie asked.

"I just said I did," Steve answered. "I wanted him to throw it out, but he said he wanted to keep it to remember me by, and I told him I didn't want him to."

"And you guys had a fight over that?" Libby guessed.

Steve nodded and studied the cracks on the sidewalk. "He was really upset."

"Did anyone hear you fight?" Bernie asked.

"I don't think so, but I'm not sure," Steve answered. "It gives me a motive," he added.

"Yes, it does," Bernie agreed.

"Which is why I took it," Steve declared. "But I didn't make the espresso machine explode." He grabbed Bernie's hand. "I would never do something like that, I swear. You have to believe me."

"I do," Bernie said. "So, where's the video now?"

"Doug's laptop is down at the bottom of the Hudson."

160   Isis Crawford

Steve grimaced and shook his head. "I knew I shouldn't have taken it, but sometimes my therapist says I make bad choices."

"I think we can take that as a given," Bernie commented.

Steve pointed to her phone. She was still holding it. "Are you still going to call the police?"

Bernie shook her head. "No, I don't think so. I don't think this piece of information is going to help the police with their inquiries."

Steve hugged her and turned to leave.

"So much for that line of inquiry," Libby said to Bernie as she watched Steve hurry back to the camera shop.

"And the laptop," Bernie said.

"Hopefully, we'll do better on our third stop," Libby opined as she climbed back into the van.

Chapter 22

Bernie and Libby walked into Larry's Hole in the Wall at three that afternoon. Located in a rundown strip mall on the far side of town, the bar was the last dive bar in the area. All the others had been pushed out by higher real estate prices and an influx of people from New York City. There were no twelve-dollar locally brewed bottles of organic beer or twenty-dollar cocktails with fancy names here. Just Bud Light, rotgut whiskey, and cheap gin. The bar was one of those places where the customers arrived at eleven in the morning and left at two in the morning, when the bar closed, and the bartender called cabs to take them home.

The scent of stale beer and cigarettes—even though smoking was outlawed in bars these days—hit Bernie and Libby when they walked inside. They stood in the entrance for a moment blinking as their eyes and their noses became accustomed to the gloom and the smell. Looking around, Bernie decided that the wallpaper, the wrestling trophies on the shelves, and the signed pictures on the wall hadn't changed since the place had opened in 1954. For that matter, the customers probably hadn't, either—what there were of them.

162 *Isis Crawford*

The bar was practically empty, the four customers who were there were spaced several bar stools apart from each other, each person hunched over the counter, sipping their drink. It was as quiet as Marvin's father's funeral home. Quieter actually. The only sound was the yells from a baseball game airing on the old TV hanging on the wall. None of the customers looked up when Bernie and Libby walked in, as if the effort of lifting their heads and turning them was too much work to bear.

"What about those Mets," Bernie said to the bartender, referring to the game on the television as she watched the dust beams dancing in the ray of sunlight coming through the window.

The bartender didn't reply. He was a small guy, with an oddly prominent Adam's apple, purplish bags under his eyes, and what looked like a haircut he'd done himself with a pair of pruning shears. Bernie decided he'd probably been working at the bar for as long as the customers had been coming in.

"Not into conversation?" Bernie asked.

The bartender scowled. "Not unless you want to talk about the vibrations of cantilever beams in the universe."

"Personally, I prefer to talk about the theory of relativity myself," Bernie responded.

Libby stepped in front of her sister. "We're here to see Eva," she told the bartender before he could reply.

"Then why didn't you say that in the first place?" he demanded as he picked up his cell and dialed. "Got two females here to see you, Eva," he said, his voice raspy from years of smoking a pack a day. He looked them up and down and described them ending with, "They look like civilians to me. Will do," he said after he'd listened to what Eva had said. Then he hung up, laid his phone back on the bar, and pointed to the door on the far side of the room.

A CATERED BAKE-OFF 163

"Through there," he told the sisters, after which he went back to watching the game.

"Brandon said to say hello," Bernie told him, remembering the message she was supposed to deliver from her boyfriend.

The bartender grunted again. "Tell him the next time he sees me, he'd better give me the twenty he owes me. Tell him I haven't forgotten our bet," he said to Bernie without taking his eyes off the set.

"Will do," Bernie replied as she walked over to the door the bartender had indicated, opened it, and stepped inside. Libby followed her sister into the room. Eva was sitting at a round table, which looked as if it seated eight. She was waiting for them.

"You're on time," she noted, turning her head slightly as she continued shuffling the deck of cards she was holding in her hand. "I like punctuality."

"Thanks. We try," Bernie replied as she assessed the woman in front of her.

"Good," Eva told her. "I like that. It seems to be a vanishing virtue these days." And she nodded for the sisters to sit down.

Eva was definitely not what Bernie had been expecting. For some reason, she'd imagined she'd look like someone from the cast of *The Real Housewives of New Jersey*—too much makeup and jewelry, pointed fingernails, a tight dress, and lots of hair, but that wasn't the case. Eva looked like the kind of woman you would see picking her kid up from an elementary school in the suburbs.

There was nothing remarkable about her, certainly nothing that hinted at her running a large-scale gambling operation. Eva's eyes and hair were nondescript brown. Her hair was done up with a scrunchy and her makeup was minimal. Just a touch of lip gloss and a light wash of blue

164   *Isis Crawford*

on her eyelids. She was wearing tiny diamond studs on her earlobes, and an Apple watch on her wrist. A slightly stretched-out white boatneck T-shirt and a pair of khaki pants completed her outfit.

As Bernie and Libby got comfortable, they looked around the room. In contrast to the bar outside, which would have looked right at home in a 1940s grade-B movie, this room had all the personality of a hotel chain lobby. The pale blue walls looked freshly painted and were hung with cheerful landscapes. There was a faux Oriental rug on the floor, and a black-leather-and-metal sofa and two matching armchairs off to the side. A glass coffee table sat in the middle of the arrangement.

"Nice," Bernie said as she noticed there was another door behind Eva and wondered where it led.

Eva nodded to indicate she'd heard the compliment. "I like to think so," she said.

"Thank you for seeing us," Libby stated.

Eva gathered the cards in front of her, shuffled them, and began dealing out a solitaire hand. "What can I do for you?" she asked.

"We have some questions that we're looking to have answered," Libby began.

"That's what Brandon said," Eva told her, cutting Libby off before she had a chance to finish her response. "Which is why I agreed to meet with you. I thought I'd speed the process up."

Bernie was about to say how nice that was, but Eva went on talking before she could get her words out.

"Here's the thing," Eva said, her voice turning serious. She stopped dealing out her cards and concentrated all of her attention on Bernie and Libby. "I have a happy clientele and I would hate to have them inconvenienced by any . . . disruptions . . . which is why I'm talking to you now." Eva took a sip from the bottle of Perrier sitting on the table next to her and continued to talk. "To be clear, I am not making book on the results of *The Longely Bake-Off*. I am not trying to influence the result. Whatever happened to Doug was unfortunate, but has nothing to do with me."

"So, you know him?" Bernie said.

"What makes you say that?" Eva asked.

"Because you referred to him by his first name," Bernie told her.

Eva smiled. "Observant. But what if I do?" she countered, concluding with, "I know lots of people."

"Dennis Grasso said Doug owed you money," Libby told her.

Eva snorted.

Bernie leaned forward. "He didn't? You're saying Dennis was lying to us?"

"Let's just say Dennis has a vivid imagination," Eva replied.

"Does he work for you?" Libby asked.

Eva replied, "If he did—and I'm not saying he did—he doesn't anymore. I don't tolerate side hustles."

Eva's tone sent a chill up Libby's spine.

"So, you didn't have someone booby-trap the espresso machine?" Libby asked.

"Don't be a moron," Eva snapped, her eyes narrowing. "Why the hell would I do something like that?"

"Why am I being an idiot?" Libby inquired.

"I said moron," Eva told her.

"What's the difference?" Libby wanted to know.

"There is no difference," Eva said. "I just like being quoted correctly, that's all. And to answer your question, if I wanted Doug dead, I would hardly do it in a manner that would attract public attention and bring the authorities crawling

166   *Isis Crawford*

all over this place. Right now, we have an"—Eva paused for a moment searching for the right words—"ongoing understanding, one that benefits both of us. Why would I want to do something that disrupts that?"

"Maybe you wanted to send a message?" Bernie suggested.

Eva snorted. "To whom? You've been watching too many gangster movies." She took a card off the top of the deck and tapped its edge on the table while she considered her next words. "Out of curiosity, to whom would I be sending this so-called message to anyway?" she asked.

Bernie picked a name out of the proverbial hat. "How about Sam or Jeff?"

"Sam and Jeff who?" Eva asked, although Bernie strongly suspected that Eva was playing with her and Libby, and that Eva knew exactly to whom she was referring.

"Sam Levine or Jeff Grasso," Bernie answered.

"And why would I do that?" Eva challenged.

"I don't know. My guess would be that one or both of them owed you money and you decided that disrupting their production would be a way to get their attention," Bernie suggested.

Eva laughed. "One of the reasons my business is successful is precisely because I don't let my . . . clientele . . . get in over their heads. I don't issue credit. I don't do loans. All debts must be settled at the end of the evening. I would rather have a smaller steady clientele, who know their limits, than a few high rollers for an evening."

"Okay," Libby said, unsure of where to go from here.

Eva looked at her and said, "You really don't have a clue about what's going on, do you?" Then before Libby had a chance to answer, she said, "I agreed to see you as a favor. Well, you can go back and tell Brandon that we're even."

"We are?" Bernie asked.

"Yes, we are," Eva said. She began playing solitaire again. "You know, it sounds as if you two aren't making much headway with your investigation. Maybe you should stick to your baking and leave the detecting to the police."

"Thanks for the advice," Bernie said.

Eva looked up from studying her cards. "No need for sarcasm. I'm just telling you, it seems to me you're out of your league here."

"And why would you say that?" Libby asked.

Eva laughed. "Because, like I just said, you two obviously don't have a clue about what's going on."

"And you do?" Bernie asked.

Instead of answering the question, Eva raised her hand and pointed to the clock on the wall. "And now I believe it's time for you two to go." At which point, as if on cue, the door behind Eva opened and a large, muscular guy walked out.

"This is Nestor," Eva said. "Nestor will be seeing you out."

"One last thing," Libby said as she and her sister stood up. "Do you think Doug LaForte was the intended target or collateral damage?"

Eva frowned and put her finger to her lips. "I said no more questions," she replied as Nestor took a step toward them. "When I say it's time for you to leave, I mean it's time for you to leave."

Libby and Bernie headed for the door, with Nestor following behind them. Evidently, they'd gone about as far as they could go here.

"Well, what do you think?" Bernie asked Libby as she got in the van.

"Aside from the fact we're in the wrong business?" her sister said as she started up the van.

"Yes, aside from that," Bernie replied.

168   *Isis Crawford*

"I think we need to find out more about Dennis Grasso," Libby said. "Evidently, he wasn't telling us everything."

"That's what I call an understatement," Bernie commented as she watched Libby back out of the van's parking space.

When they were on the road, she called Jeff Grasso to ask him if he knew where Dennis was. As it turned out, he did. Or thought he did. Libby and Bernie spent the next half an hour chasing Dennis down.

Chapter 23

Bernie and Libby started looking for Dennis where Dennis's uncle had told them his nephew was going to be. The estate. According to Jeff, Dennis was supposed to be in the office, helping with preparations for the upcoming show. But the office door was locked when Bernie and Libby arrived, so they went around to the side entrance and rang the bell, but no one answered there, either. Bernie rang the bell again.

"Maybe Dennis is somewhere else in the house," Bernie suggested. The house was large, a little under six thousand feet, so it was possible that if you were at the other end of it, you might not hear the bell going off.

"Maybe," Libby agreed as Bernie turned and followed the footpath back to the office. Libby went with her. "What do you think?" Libby asked her sister as Bernie peered in the window.

"I think we're striking out," Bernie remarked as she studied the scene in front of her.

The office looked even messier than the last time she'd been in it, and that was saying a lot. The piles of paper on the rolltop desk had grown even taller, and there were

170   *Isis Crawford*

even more cartons shoved up against the wall. Bernie was wondering how Sam could work in a mess like that, when she heard footsteps behind her and turned. It was the goatherd and one of his Aussies.

"Can I help you?" he asked.

Bernie explained that they were looking for Dennis Grasso.

"You just missed him," the goatherd informed her.

"I don't suppose you know where he went?" Libby asked as she patted the Aussie on his head.

The goatherd tugged on his beard while he considered the question. Then he said, "I think I overheard him say something on his phone about going over to Lori's place to get something, but I'm not really sure."

"If he comes back—" Libby began, but the goatherd interrupted before she could finish her sentence.

"Sam?" he asked.

Libby corrected him. "Dennis."

"Right," the goatherd replied.

"Just tell him we're looking for him," Libby told him.

The goatherd lifted a hand to indicate that he'd heard her. "Sure thing," he told her as a van, with CV'S MEDICAL SUPPLIES written along its side, came up the driveway.

"Is everyone okay?" Bernie asked, pointing to it.

The goatherd laughed. "Oh, that. Everything's fine. Well, as fine as can be, given the circumstances. Ben needs oxygen on the regular."

Bernie frowned. "I thought he was on a trip somewhere."

"That's Duncan. I'm talking about his brother Ben," the goatherd replied. "He got mugged a long time ago. Unfortunately, that left him unable to walk or pretty much do anything for himself without help. That includes breathing."

"That's awful," Libby remarked.

The goatherd sighed and scratched at his elbow. "Yeah, it definitely sucks to be him," he said.

"What happened to the person who did it?" Bernie asked.

"Nothing as far as I know," the goatherd replied. "They never got 'em." He shook his head at the injustice of it all. "People like that deserve a place in hell," he said. "They really deserve to suffer the way their victims do." He was going to say something else, but before he could, the goatherd's phone rang. "Sorry, gotta take this," he said as the caller's name flashed across the screen.

Bernie and Libby watched him go.

"What do you think?" Bernie asked her sister. "Are you up for a quick trip to Lori's?"

Libby nodded. "Sure. Why not?" It was only a fifteen-minute drive, but then most things in Longely were. This time, though, it took twenty minutes because of a backup due to construction on Dell and Avondale.

Lori was in the middle of mixing up a batch of cupcakes when the sisters rang her doorbell.

Her face crumpled when she answered the door and saw who was standing there. "Oh my God," she cried. "What else has happened?"

"Nothing," Libby said. "Absolutely nothing."

Bernie laughed. "I can understand why you would think that, given the circumstances, Lori," she said. "But everything is fine. Really."

"Whew." Lori put her hand over her heart and let out a deep breath. "You had me worried for a second."

Libby apologized. "Sorry, we didn't mean to scare you," she told her. "We're just looking for Dennis. Dennis Grasso," Libby elucidated when she saw the puzzled look on Lori's face.

Lori shook her head. "Why would he be here?"

172   *Isis Crawford*

"The goatherd at the estate said he heard him say he was going over to your place," Libby answered.

Lori shook her head again. "He must have misheard. He isn't here."

Bernie stepped forward. "So, you haven't seen him? He hasn't been around?"

Lori shook her head for the third time. "Can't think of any reason why he would be, actually."

"So, he's not your BFF?" Bernie asked.

This time, it was Lori's turn to laugh. "Hardly. I mean, I recognize him from the set, I know him to say hello to, but that's about it." She tucked a strand of bright green hair behind her ear, then invited them in to see what she was working on. "You might as well, as long as you're here. I could use your opinion."

"Our pleasure," Bernie said.

The sisters followed her into her kitchen. "I'm in the middle of experimenting with a recipe for gluten-free cupcakes," Lori explained. "Something that tastes good on the second day."

"Good luck with that," Libby said.

"That's the problem with gluten, or rather its lack," Bernie observed as Lori walked over to the kitchen island and peered into the mixer bowl. "Things that are baked with gluten-free flour tend to have a rubbery texture. I mean, they're fine the first day, but after that, forget it."

"Tell me about it," Lori said. "These are for a family picnic," she explained. "I thought I'd do a riff on a Spanish olive oil cake, using cornmeal and regular Italian flour."

"That should work," Bernie told her. "We've tried Italian flour in some of our muffins, and so far, so good."

"I guess we'll see how my cousin does with it," Lori said.

"Any icing?" Libby asked.

A CATERED BAKE-OFF   173

"I was thinking of something fudgy to balance out the cornmeal. Maybe dark chocolate, with a hint of orange in it, because I'm thinking of adding orange zest to the batter," Lori replied.

Libby nodded. "That should work. Sounds good."

"Or you could use ginger," Bernie suggested. "Ginger marries well with chocolate."

"Yes, it does," Lori agreed.

"Or lavender," Bernie said. Then she thought about it and took the suggestion back.

"I think I'll stick with the orange, but thanks for the suggestions," Lori told her. She rubbed her hands together. "Ready for this coming weekend? I'm surprised we're going forward with the contest, considering what's happened."

"Me too," Bernie said.

"Well, I'll say one thing for Sam," Libby added. "He's persistent."

"Or nuts," Bernie said.

"That too," Lori agreed as Bernie and Libby turned to leave.

Once the sisters were in their van, Bernie called Sam and got Dennis's home address. Then they headed off to 145 Dell Street.

"Wow," Libby said when they arrived at the house ten minutes later.

"It definitely stands out," Bernie commented sarcastically.

"I'm sure the neighbors are pleased," Libby observed.

Bernie laughed. "I know I would be."

The house Dennis was living in definitely needed a paint job. The paint was flaking off in spots, leaving barren patches of wood in its wake, making the walls of the house look as if they had a bad case of the measles. In addition, the front

174   *Isis Crawford*

yard was overgrown with weeds, and the driveway was cracked in a dozen different places. Now purslane, milk-weed, and dandelions poked their heads through the as-phalt, making interesting designs. A big FOR RENT sign was tacked to the door.

Libby pulled onto the driveway and the sisters got out and climbed the five wobbly steps to the sagging porch. Bernie studied the three mailboxes mounted on the wall next to the door. According to them, Dennis was living in the first-floor apartment, while the apartments on the sec-ond and third floors were vacant.

Bernie rang Dennis's bell and waited. There was no an-swer. She tried a second time. Still, no answer. Then she rang the bells for the second- and third-story flats, for the hell of it. No one answered those, either. Next she looked in Dennis's mailbox. Aside from two skateboard maga-zines, the box was empty.

Bernie turned to her sister. "So much for that," she said. She was about to turn back and head for the van, but she thought she heard a noise. "Do you hear anything?" she asked her sister.

"I'm not sure," Libby said.

"I thought I did," Bernie told her. Then Bernie heard the noise again. It sounded as if something had fallen.

The sisters looked at each other and headed toward the backyard. When they got there, they saw a dish on the ground. Libby pointed to a line of coleslaw on top of a round plastic table, and a black cat on the ground next to the dish. "I believe that's our culprit," she observed as the cat scurried away.

Bernie nodded and walked over to the small outbuilding that served as a garage and peeked through the window. "Take a look," she said, motioning to Libby.

"Not what I would have expected," Libby said when

A CATERED BAKE-OFF   175

she saw a scooter and an e-bike sitting in the garage. Both of them looked brand-new.

Libby and Bernie exchanged another glance. "Do you think those are Dennis's?" Libby asked her sister.

"Probably," Bernie said. "There isn't anyone else around."

She tried the door. It wasn't locked. She slid it open, stepped inside, and looked. Libby followed. The garage was empty, except for the scooter, the e-bike, a rusty-looking push mower, a couple of dented metal garbage cans, a plastic rake, and two skateboards. Bernie bent over and picked up one of the skateboards. It looked brand-new. She picked up the other one. That looked new, too.

"I wonder where Dennis got the money for these?" Libby mused, indicating the skateboards, the scooter, and the e-bike with a nod of her head.

"Good question," Bernie said as she straightened up.

Both sisters stepped back into the yard and Libby closed the door to the garage. Bernie nodded toward the house. "I think we should take a look inside."

"Why?" Libby asked.

"All the new stuff, and then there's the lock on the back door."

"What about it?" Libby asked.

"Look at it," Bernie said.

Libby did. It was a brand-new, shiny police lock.

"Given the condition of the house, do you think the landlord put it on?" Bernie asked her sister.

"Probably not," Libby allowed after a moment of thought.

"Which means that Dennis did," Bernie continued. "Why would he do that—unless he has something in there of value."

"That he recently acquired, given that the lock looks brand-new," Libby added, following her sister's train of thought.

176   *Isis Crawford*

"Exactly," Bernie replied.

"But what about the neighbors?" Libby asked.

"What about them?" Bernie wanted to know as she walked around a torn-up wicker chair. The postage stamp–sized backyard was in even worse shape than the front yard, she decided.

"They can see into this backyard. What if they call the police?" Libby asked.

"I don't think they're home," Bernie pointed out. She stifled a sneeze. "There are no cars in the driveways."

"And if they are?" Libby asked.

Bernie shrugged. "You know what they say. Nothing ventured, nothing gained."

Libby grunted. "Is that what they say?" Over the years, she'd found that sometimes things didn't work out that way.

"As a matter of fact, it is," Bernie responded, although she wasn't sure that was the case here. At least it hadn't been so far.

Chapter 24

The two ginger tabby cats sitting on top of a wooden stockade fence meowed as they watched Bernie walk up to Dennis's back door.

"Did you do this?" she asked them, pointing to a half-eaten piece of chicken lying in the grass.

The tabby on the right meowed, while the tabby on the left turned and began to clean its hindquarters.

"Not talking, hunh? I'll take that as an admission of guilt," Bernie told them as she rubbed her shoulder. She wasn't wearing her sling anymore, but her shoulder still ached. She probably should have taken some aspirin before she left, she reflected as she studied the back door.

Like everything else on the property, it was old and dilapidated and needed a paint job. Bernie reached over and tried turning the doorknob. It didn't move. Then she tried again, just for the hell of it. Nope. No motion. Not that she'd expected there would be. She swatted at a wasp buzzing around her head while she looked through her bag for her lockpicks.

"Got them," she said, setting to work. Five minutes later, she was no further along.

178 *Isis Crawford*

For a moment, she thought about kicking the door in, like they did in the movies. "What do you think?" she asked the cats.

The cat on the right meowed as she studied a robin perched on the limb of a birch tree, one house over, while the cat on the left continued cleaning himself.

"Yeah, probably not a good idea," Bernie told the cat on the right. "Especially since the door is solid wood."

This time the tabby on the left meowed, while the one on the right yawned and began licking its front paws. Bernie blinked as a drop of sweat ran into her eye. It felt hotter outside than the weather forecaster had predicted. A moment later, Libby joined her. She'd been checking to make sure she'd put Mathilda's parking brake on.

"How's it going?" Libby asked as she swatted at another wasp. It was getting to be the time of year when they were beginning to get more aggressive.

"Slowly," Bernie said, and she started working on the door again. A moment later, she heard a click. She turned the doorknob. "We're in," she said, opening the door. She and Libby stepped into the back hallway.

"I think it's time to empty the garbage," Libby observed as she breathed in the odors of old beer, spoiled milk, and dirty clothes. She looked around. The hallway was filled with empty cardboard cartons, recyclables, lawn chairs stacked against the wall, and an old desk that was minus its two bottom drawers. Next Bernie and Libby moved on to the living and dining rooms. Bernie started looking through the living room, while Libby took the dining room.

The living room was empty, except for a large beanbag chair/sofa combo, a table lamp, a packing carton, which was doubling as a coffee table, three skateboards leaning against the wall, and two big posters of the skateboarder gods Tony Hawk and Nyjah Huston taped to the wall with masking tape.

"Well, I'll tell you one thing, Dennis is definitely not into home decorating," Bernie said as she stopped and glanced at a bunch of bills scattered on the table. All of them were marked second and third notice. They were opened and Bernie took a look. Evidently, the powers that be were about to turn off Dennis's power and water. He also owed money to the IRS.

Then Bernie picked up a page that had been torn out of *Thrasher*. The magazine listed the top ten skate park destinations in the United States. Dennis had circled Hawaii and San Francisco. Bernie put that page down and picked up another one. Dennis had listed airline fares to Hawaii and San Francisco on top of the page. In the middle, he'd written, *August 22?* and he'd scrawled *Time to go.* The last sentence on the page was: *Borrow Arlo's van?* Bernie was wondering who Arlo was, when Libby called her into the dining room.

When she got there, her sister was holding up packaging that had once contained a pair of Bluetooth earbuds and a new iPhone.

"Dennis has definitely come into some cash," Bernie said, and she told Libby what she'd found in the other room. "The earbuds, phone, scooter. We're talking thousands, and that's not counting the trip it looks like he's planning. That would add quite a bit more to the final tally."

"He could have won the lottery," Libby suggested.

"Somehow I don't think so," Bernie said. "We would have heard."

"So, what do you think he did to earn the money?" Libby asked.

Bernie shook her head. "Well, he certainly didn't get it working for Sam, that's for sure." Then she told Libby when Dennis was planning on leaving.

"Isn't he on probation?" Libby asked.

Bernie nodded. "That's what I remember hearing," she

180 *Isis Crawford*

told Libby as she and her sister walked into the kitchen. The first thing she noticed was a water stain on the wall, where water had leaked in from the roof. The kitchen sink had three dirty dishes and a couple of take-out containers in it, while the stove looked as if it could use a scrubdown with Lysol.

There was a small round table, with two chairs, in the corner, and Bernie and Libby went over to check it out. An empty bottle of Diet Coke sat on the table next to a piece of paper lying on top of an Oxford high school yearbook. Bernie picked up the piece of paper first. It had a list of names scrawled on it, including hers and Libby's. The names were the names of the contestants and the judges. Each had a check mark next to it.

Bernie wondered what that meant as she took a picture of the paper and began paging through the yearbook. It was twenty years old and showed its age. Some of the pages had begun to yellow and there were smudge marks on others. As she paged through the yearbook, she thought about the pictures she'd found in Doug's briefcase. Then she realized that in addition to Nell and Doug, there were pictures of the judges and the four other contestants in the bake-off as well. This was further confirmation of what they already knew: Everyone involved in the production, except for her and Libby, had gone to Ed Smith High School.

Bernie frowned. *What the hell is Dennis doing with this yearbook? Why does he have it? Had he lived in Oxford? And what is he doing with the yearbook of a class he'd been too young to attend?*

It looked as if Dennis might have more questions to answer, Bernie decided as she put the paper and the book back the way she'd found them. Then she and Libby started to go through the rest of the kitchen. They looked in the cabinet drawers, peeked in the refrigerator, and checked the inside of the oven. There was nothing in any of those

A CATERED BAKE-OFF   181

spaces, except a box of Honey Nut Cheerios and a pint of milk in the fridge.

Odd place for cereal, Bernie thought as she dumped the box's contents out onto the round kitchen table, just to make sure Dennis hadn't hidden anything in it. *Nope. It's just Cheerios.* She sighed and put the Cheerios back in the box and put the box back where she'd found it. *So much for that.*

Then she and Libby went through the bathroom. The only things in there were a toothbrush, toothpaste, some CBD gummies, and a bottle of Oxy. *For pleasure or pain?* Bernie wondered as she put the bottle back where she found it.

Dennis's bedroom didn't yield much, either. There was a mattress on the floor, with a sleeping bag laid out on it; a lamp next to the bed; a yellow legal pad full of scrawls; and an old chest of drawers, which looked as if it could have been lugged in from the street. Bernie went through the closet and the dresser quickly. The closet yielded five pairs of jeans and a couple of pairs of sneakers, which were half shoe goo and duct tape; while the dresser drawers held some ratty T-shirts, socks, underwear, two pairs of cargo shorts, and a yellow plastic piggy bank full of coins.

Bernie had just shut the drawers and was about to leave, but she spied an old backpack shoved behind a large, dying money tree plant. She opened the backpack up and a couple of crumpled-up Hershey's chocolate bar wrappers fell out. Bernie picked them up, to put back in Dennis's backpack, when she noticed there was writing on their undersides. She smoothed the wrappers out with her thumbnail and read the message. It was a nursery rhyme— or part of one.

"Look, Libby," she said, showing the wrapper to her sister.

182 *Isis Crawford*

Libby read the words out loud. "'Roses are red, violets are blue.'" And that was all. She raised an eyebrow. "Another coincidence?" she asked Bernie.

"Somehow I don't think so," Bernie replied.

"Are you thinking what I'm thinking?" Libby asked.

"That he got paid to write the nursery rhymes we got?" Bernie replied. "Maybe that's why he had that yearbook? For reference?"

"Maybe," Libby said. "Well, one thing we do know for sure—Dennis isn't returning to the straight and narrow."

Bernie tapped her fingers on her thigh. "I wonder who paid him."

"The same person who rigged the espresso machine?" Libby hypothesized.

"That would be my guess," Libby said. She looked at her watch. They had been in Dennis's house for a little over fifteen minutes. She signaled to Bernie that it was time to go. As she crossed the front hallway on her way to the back door, she stopped, and Bernie bumped into her.

"What the hell," Bernie said.

"You could say that." Libb pointed to the trip wire lying across the doorway. "Just imagine if we'd gone through the front door," Libby said as she studied the explosive device the trip wire was attached to. It was half hidden underneath a coatrack.

"It would not have been our best day, that's for sure," Bernie remarked.

"It would have been our last day," Libby commented as her sister squatted down to get a better look at it. Even though she was no expert, the device looked serious. "Someone could have gotten very badly hurt."

"Like dead," Bernie observed. "The question is who."

"Obviously, us," Libby replied.

"Besides us," Bernie said. She blinked another drop of

A CATERED BAKE-OFF 183

sweat out of her eye before continuing to speak. "Did Dennis do this to protect himself, or did someone else do this to blow Dennis up? If it was Dennis, was he protecting himself, something that he possessed, or both? If it was someone else, then that someone was serious about causing— what's that phrase?—*grievous bodily harm* to him. So, what has Dennis done to warrant this?"

Libby shook her head. She didn't know. "We should get out of here and figure it out later."

"You're right," Bernie agreed, standing up.

The sisters left via the back door. When they were outside, Bernie called Clyde to tell him what they'd found.

"What did he say?" Libby asked when Bernie had completed her call.

"He told us to get out of the area before the bomb squad arrives," Bernie told her.

Libby nodded. It made sense, since they weren't supposed to be there in the first place. While she climbed into Mathilda and started up the van, Bernie attempted to call Dennis, but the call went straight to voicemail. Then a message came on from the cell phone provider that said the person Bernie was seeking to talk to was unavailable.

"So much for leaving a message," she said, resting her phone on her lap. "Evidently, Dennis hasn't paid his bill."

"Great," Libby said as she finished backing out of the driveway and started heading down the street. Three blocks later, she asked Bernie if it struck her as odd that they were the only ones in the show that hadn't lived in Oxford.

"It certainly does," Bernie answered. She was thinking about the implications when Libby nudged her.

"Isn't that Dennis?" Libby asked, pointing to the car going by them in the opposite direction.

Bernie studied the driver of the beat-up Honda Civic

passing by them. The guy looked like Dennis. She squinted. Libby was right. It was Dennis. "Yes," she said, "it definitely is Dennis." Then she added, "It looks as if he's going home. Hurry!"

Libby made a U-turn in the middle of the street and sped up. Unfortunately, the next light turned red before she could make it through.

"Hurry!" Bernie urged again. By now, she was bouncing up and down in her seat, she was so anxious to get moving.

"I can't," Libby told her, pointing to the garbage truck lumbering across the road. "Not unless you want to be a squished pancake."

By the time the light had changed, Dennis was three-quarters of a block ahead of the van. Libby almost caught up with him then, but a UPS truck was partially blocking the street.

"Go around it," Bernie cried.

"I'm doing the best I can," Libby snapped as she zoomed around the truck, almost hitting an oncoming vehicle in the process.

By the time they reached Avalon, Dennis was on the porch standing in front of the main entrance to his home. Libby slammed on the brakes, while Bernie rolled the window down and stuck her head out.

"Dennis, stop!" she yelled.

Dennis heard her and turned around. He waved and grinned. "Be right there. Give me a minute," he said, lifting one of his hands up. Bernie could see he was holding a set of keys. "I take that back. Give me five. Just gotta go pee first."

"No. Don't go in there," Bernie cried.

Dennis laughed. "Sorry. When ya gotta go, ya gotta go," he yelled back. "This is what happens when you drink too many brews." He laughed again.

"No!" Bernie yelled. "Don't!"

But it was too late. Before Bernie could say anything else, Dennis turned, opened the front door to his apartment, and stepped inside. There was a loud boom and a rain of glass and wood.

As Libby and Bernie got out of the van and raced toward Dennis, they could hear sirens in the distance as she and Libby took the porch stairs two at a time.

When they reached Dennis, he was lying in a puddle of blood. There were flickers of flame near him. The curtains had caught on fire. Then they noticed the windowsill was burning as well.

Chapter 25

"One moment, you're fine," Libby reflected as she snapped her fingers, "and then it's *adios, muchacho*."

Brandon wiped his hands on the dishtowel he had slung over his shoulder. "I assume you're talking about Dennis."

Libby shuddered. "And us. There but for the grace of God."

"But we're still here," Bernie pointed out.

"But we might not have been," Libby said.

"I heard he died," Brandon said, interrupting the sisters.

"No, he's still hanging on," Bernie replied. She leaned forward to get closer to Brandon so she could hear what he was saying, because her ears were still ringing from the explosion. "Hopefully, he'll be all right."

"Unlike the house," Marvin said. "Not that it was worth much anyway."

Libby shook her head, remembering the ensuing blaze. "I can't believe the house went up as fast as it did."

"Old houses tend to do that," Brandon observed. "They're like tinderboxes waiting for a light."

A CATERED BAKE-OFF   187

It was nine at night, and Bernie and Libby were sitting at RJ's, having a drink. Actually, several drinks, if you wanted to be accurate. *Heaven only knows we need them,* Bernie thought. It had not been a good day.

Marvin took a sip of his wheat ale and put the glass down on the bar. "How bad is he?"

"Bad enough," Libby told him. She absentmindedly rubbed the palm of her hand. She'd cut it with a shard of glass from the explosion and it had required four stitches to close. "He's in the ICU with a concussion, several cracked ribs, second-degree burns on his hands, and internal injuries."

Marvin grimaced. "Poor guy."

"He looked like a porcupine, what with all the pieces of glass stuck in him," Bernie added. She couldn't get the picture of Dennis lying there, slivers of glass protruding from his cheeks and forehead, out of her mind. "Hopefully, he won't be needing your services anytime soon, Marvin."

"Hopefully not," Marvin answered. "We don't need any more business, that's for sure." With Covid rising again, it was busier at the funeral home than he would have liked. "Anyone with him now?"

"His uncle was at the hospital when we left," Bernie replied. "I think they're going to kick Jeff out in another hour." Visiting hours at Sinai West were over by ten.

"Is he talking?" Brandon asked.

"Dennis?" Libby asked.

"Who else?" Marvin responded.

Libby shook her head and took a sip of her bourbon. Normally, she stuck to wine, but she was making an exception in this case, even though the bourbon tasted like diesel fuel to her. "To answer your question: No. Dennis can't talk. They put him in a coma in the ICU. I think it's going to be a while before we can speak to him. I heard

188 *Isis Crawford*

one of the docs tell his uncle that if he wakes up—and he might not—he might have some cognitive problems. Of course," Libby continued, "it may not matter. We won't be able to talk to him anyway if we're in jail."

"We're not going to jail," Bernie reassured her sister as Marvin raised an eyebrow.

"You don't know that," Libby told her.

"Jail?" Marvin repeated. "How so?" he asked.

Libby answered. "Two words. *Breaking* and *entering.*" Then she downed the rest of her bourbon and held out her glass to Brandon for another one.

"Are you sure you want to do this?" Brandon asked her.

"I couldn't be more positive," Libby told him. "Fill 'er up."

Brandon shrugged. "Okay. But don't blame me when you wake up tomorrow feeling like crap."

"Which you will," Bernie told Libby.

"I don't care," Libby snapped.

Brandon shrugged. "Okay, I warned you. Why are they going to charge you anyway?" he asked as he got the bottle down from the shelf, poured Libby another shot, and put the bottle back where it belonged.

"They're not," Bernie said. "My sister is just being paranoid."

"I'm not," Libby said after she'd taken another sip of her bourbon.

"You are," Bernie countered. "The police have no reason to suspect we were in Dennis's flat."

"I'm not paranoid," Libby shot back. "One of Dennis's neighbors could have seen us going into the house. Our van isn't exactly inconspicuous."

"That's true," Brandon interjected. "Nothing like doing a B and E with the name of your business plastered on the side of your getaway car, I always say."

"Which we parked in the driveway," Libby added.

"Even better," Brandon said.

Bernie shook her head. "If the cops wanted to arrest us, they would have already."

Libby grimaced. "I hope you're right."

"Believe me, I am," Bernie said with more confidence than she felt.

"So, what *did* you tell the cops?" Marvin asked.

"That we were there five minutes before the explosion to talk to Dennis and he wasn't there, so we left," Bernie replied. "Then we saw him going by us, so we turned around. We'd just pulled into the driveway—and *boom*." She made a gesture with her hands. "I told the truth. I just left out a couple of details."

"And they believed you?" Marvin wanted to know.

"Well, there's no reason they shouldn't," Bernie answered.

"Unless Clyde tells them we'd just called to inform him about the explosive devices we found," Libby pointed out.

"Which he won't," Bernie said. "Dad already told us that."

Marvin took another sip of his beer. "And speaking of your father, what did your dad say about your latest adventure?"

Bernie thought for a moment, then said, "I think *livid* is the word I'd use to describe his reaction. The phrase *incandescent rage* also comes to mind."

"I can only imagine," Marvin replied while he watched Brandon move down the bar to wait on another customer. It was another quiet summer night at RJ's, and he reflected that he liked it this way. "He does tend to be a little—"

"Overprotective," Bernie said.

"That wasn't the word I was thinking of," Marvin told her. "But that will do, too."

190 *Isis Crawford*

Libby shook her head. "Who would have thought that a baking contest could lead to this kind of behavior? I mean, everyone is so nice on *The Great British Bake Off.* Why can't they be like that for *The Longely Bake-Off?*"

"I think the word you want is *polite,*" Bernie told her.

"Whatever," Libby said, making a face as she took another sip of bourbon. "All I know is, they don't go around trying to kill people there. At least they don't over something like an egg custard."

"Do you think the whole Dennis thing has anything to do with what's been happening at the bake-off?" Brandon asked the sisters when he got back.

"Probably," Libby answered as she shifted her position on the bar stool, trying to get comfortable. For some reason, her back was bothering her. She'd probably pulled a muscle helping move the store's forty-pound mixer so she and Amber could clean behind it. Of course, carrying Dennis outside and down the steps to the front lawn hadn't helped, either.

"Probably?" Bernie said, repeating her sister's comment. "Of course, it does, Libby. How could it not? Especially with what I found in there."

"Fine," Libby allowed. "Okay. You're right. There is a connection. But we were definitely wrong about one thing."

"What's that?" Brandon asked.

Libby fished a pretzel out of the bowl in front of her and ate it before replying. "We thought Dennis might have set up the explosive devices to keep people out, but that wasn't the case."

"To say the least. It was just the opposite, in fact," Bernie added. "I guess whoever rigged the explosive device was really gunning for Dennis—metaphorically speaking."

"So, what did you find in his house?" Marvin inquired, going back to the last topic of conversation. "Anything helpful?"

"As a matter of fact, we did," Bernie answered, and she told Marvin about the unpaid bills, the scooter, the earbuds, the skateboards, and his possible plans for a trip. "It looked as if Dennis was planning on skipping town."

"Maybe he knew that the doo-doo was about to hit the metaphorical fan," Brandon suggested.

"That would be my guess," Bernie agreed.

"Where do you think Dennis got the money to buy that stuff from?" Marvin asked.

Bernie told Brandon and Marvin about the Hershey wrapper she'd found. "He could have been paid to leave the notes we all found."

"Or his grandparents could have left him an inheritance," Marvin suggested.

Bernie shook her head. She'd called Dennis's uncle and had asked.

"I think it's more likely that he was blackmailing the person who paid him for leaving the notes," Brandon suggested.

"Also, a possibility," Bernie said. Then she tossed down the rest of her scotch and took out her phone. "And then there's this." And she showed Marvin and Brandon the shot of the piece of paper with the cast of *The Longely Bake-Off* written on it. "And this."

Marvin and Brandon both leaned in to get a better look at the photos Bernie was scrolling through.

"So, the cast went to the same high school?" Brandon asked.

Bernie nodded. "For various lengths of time. Except for us. Evidently, we're the odd people out."

"Oxford," Brandon said. He made a face as if the mere mention of the town left a bad taste in his mouth.

"I don't think I've ever been there," Marvin remarked.

"Me either," Libby said.

"Believe me, you're not missing anything," Brandon informed them. "There's nothing there to see." He took a drink from the bottle of water next to him. "The place probably doesn't even have cell service."

"Every place has cell service," Bernie protested.

"There are places in the Catskills that don't," Brandon pointed out.

"What were you doing in Oxford?" Bernie asked. "How come you were there?"

"I got a flat passing through," Brandon said. He put the cap back on the bottle and changed the subject. "The people there weren't very nice. I felt as if I was in the beginning of a grade-B horror movie. You know the kind where the family stops at a town fifty miles from nowhere and bad things happen."

Bernie laughed. She knew exactly what Brandon was talking about.

"And speaking of bad things," Marvin said, going back to their previous topic, "do you think Sam could have paid Dennis to leave the notes?"

This time, Libby was the one who shook her head. "No. Absolutely not! He has too much money riding on this."

Bernie tapped her fingernails on the counter while she thought. "What about Eva?" she posited, recalling the expression on Eva's face when she'd talked about Dennis. "She wasn't happy with him, that's for sure."

Brandon shook his head. "I'm not seeing it. No. Definitely not. No way."

"How come?" Libby asked.

A CATERED BAKE-OFF 193

"Simple," Brandon answered. "Because Eva's spent years keeping her operation out of the limelight. Why, then, do something that will bring the wrath of God down on her? The police would shut her down in a heartbeat. It would be the end of her business, a business she's spent a long time building up. Plus, that's not her style. If she wanted Dennis dead, she'd be a little more subtle. He'd be at the bottom of the Hudson River by now or buried in a landfill somewhere. This was too showy for her."

"There has to be a connection to the show or the people in it," Marvin observed.

"Well, we do know one thing for sure," Brandon said.

"Yeah, what's that?" Bernie asked.

"Whoever is behind this has a penchant for blowing things up," Brandon told her.

"This is true," Libby allowed, thinking back to the oven and the rigged doors at Dennis's apartment. "On that, we can all agree."

Brandon began tapping his fingers on the bar. "You should speak to Mike," he said after another minute had gone by.

"Who's Mike?" Bernie asked.

"Mike Goodman, of course," Brandon clarified.

"Oh. You mean contestant Mike," Bernie responded. "Why should we talk to him?" she asked, puzzled.

"Because not only is he in the bake-off, but he was in the army, too," Brandon informed her.

"So?" Bernie replied. "So were a lot of other people."

"Because if I remember correctly, he told me he did something with explosives," Brandon told her. "That's why."

"Good reason," Libby said.

"Isn't it, though," Bernie mused. She tossed back the rest of her drink, stood up, and beckoned to her sister. "Come on, Libby, we've got people to talk to."

194   *Isis Crawford*

"And miles to go before you sleep," Marvin couldn't resist adding.

"That too," Bernie agreed.

"Unfortunately," Libby replied as she thought about how nice it would be if she could tuck herself into bed right now.

Chapter 26

During the day, the road that led to the development Mike Goodman lived in was clogged with traffic, but because it was late and a weekday night, Route 52 was relatively empty. Everyone was tucked inside their houses for the evening. It took Libby and Bernie a little less than fifteen minutes to get to Glens Falls, and it would have taken even less time if Libby hadn't made the wrong turn at the Foxwoods Traffic Circle and ended up in Inwood by mistake.

"Why do they have to make things so complicated?" Libby complained as she looked for 73 Bonnie Brae Road.

"That was the idea with these kinds of developments," Bernie answered. "They were designed to keep the people who didn't live here out."

"Well, they've certainly done a good job," Libby commented as she slowed down to let a large raccoon waddle across the road.

The development, which had been built in the 1960s, had been planned around a small man-made lake, and the streets wound around the water feature—as real estate agents called it—like strands of spaghetti. The fact that there

196   *Isis Crawford*

were no streetlights made it difficult to navigate, what with the dead ends, double loops, and cutbacks. Then there was the difficulty of reading the street signs and the house numbers on a dark, moonless night. Finally, ten minutes later, after numerous wrong turns, Libby found Mike's house. It was situated on a slight hill on the development's outer loop. Here the greenery had been allowed to grow longer. It hadn't been pruned into boxy shapes, which gave the landscape a slightly less manicured, more natural feel.

Mike's house was painted white, with black shutters, and a bright red door. The house, with its attached garage, looked neat, tidy, and utterly unremarkable. The only thing that set it apart from its neighbors was the white picket fence enclosing the front yard.

Libby and Bernie were both a little surprised. Given Mike's taste in clothes, they'd expected something a little more flamboyant. Libby was thinking about that as she parked at the end of Mike's driveway. The rest of the space was taken up with Mike's vehicles: a van and an old Ford. As she and her sister got out of Mathilda, Mike's van made a loud, clunking noise.

Libby jumped and Bernie laughed.

"What was that?" Libby cried.

"Mike's van," Bernie replied. "I guess it needs an oil change," she commented as she opened the gate and she and her sister walked up the redbrick path to Mike's house.

Bernie rang the bell. They could hear a dog barking inside. When no one answered, Bernie rang the bell again. Mike stuck his head out of one of the windows upstairs.

"What do you want?" he yelled down. "It's late."

"I know it's late, but we need to talk!" Bernie yelled back up.

"About what?" Mike asked.

"The bake-off," Bernie told him.

"Not again," Mike groaned. "Give me a minute and I'll be down," he told her, after which he stuck his head back in and closed the window. Five minutes later, he opened the door. "Jeez, this better be good. Do you know what time it is?" he demanded. He was wearing boxers and a T-shirt, and had a serious case of bedhead going on. A small, gray-muzzled mutt of indeterminate age stood next to him, growling at them.

"As a matter of fact, I do," Bernie replied. She looked at her watch. "It's ten-thirty. Oops. Ten thirty-two."

"You think you're cute, don't you?" Mike said.

"So, I've been told," Bernie answered. "Guess you go to bed on the early side, hunh?"

"I have to be up at five to start baking," Mike growled.

"So do we," Libby told him.

Mike glared at her. "Is that supposed to make me feel better?"

Bernie did her best smile. "Actually, yes. It is."

"Well, it doesn't," Mike told her. "So, what the hell do you want?"

"To ask you a question," Libby replied.

"Haven't you heard of texting?" he demanded.

"We were in the neighborhood and thought we'd drop by," Bernie explained.

"No one is *just* in the neighborhood," Mike shot back. "At least, not this one."

"We were," Libby said.

"Right," Mike said.

"You don't believe us?" Bernie demanded.

"What I believe, or don't believe, isn't relevant," Mike told her. "Ask your question or I'm going back inside." He gave his dog a pat on the head. "Scooter and I need our beauty sleep."

"Don't we all," Libby said.

198 Isis Crawford

"You were in the army, right?" Bernie asked.

Mike looked even more annoyed. "That's your question?"

Bernie nodded. "It is."

"Yes, I was," Mike replied. "Why are you asking?"

"Do you know how to make bombs?" Libby asked.

"This is what you woke me up to ask about?" Mike demanded.

"Among other things," Bernie said.

Mike shook his head. "This is ridiculous. I shouldn't have even answered the door. You told me you were here about the bake-off."

"We are," Libby told him.

Mike looked from Bernie to Libby and back again. "And the two things connect, how?"

Bernie told him what had happened to Dennis.

Mike's eyes widened as he listened. "Tell me you're kidding," he said when Bernie was done talking.

Libby and Bernie shook their heads.

"I wish I were," Bernie said.

Then Libby chimed in. "Unfortunately, my sister isn't."

Mike rubbed his cheek with his hand as he digested this new piece of information. "Dennis, hunh?"

Bernie nodded.

"We're talking about Jeff's nephew, right?" Mike asked, just to make sure he was thinking of the right person.

"That's the one," Libby replied.

Mike frowned. "That's too bad. I don't know what's the matter with people these days. Everyone's gone nuts."

"That may be true," Bernie told him. "But that doesn't have anything to do with the question I just asked you."

Mike raised an eyebrow. "Are you saying that I did it?"

"Did you?" Libby asked.

"Why would I?" Mike countered, his voice rising. "What motive could I possibly have?"

A CATERED BAKE-OFF   199

"That's what we're asking you," Bernie pointed out.

"After all," Libby said, "you are familiar with this stuff."

"You mean explosives?"

"Obviously," Bernie said.

"You don't know much about the subject, do you?" Mike responded. "Otherwise, you'd know that anyone can build a small explosive device. All they need to be able to do is read well enough to follow instructions. You can find them on the dark web." Mike paused and gave his dog another quick pat on his head. "I wouldn't be surprised if there weren't instructions on YouTube as well. It's pretty easy to do, actually."

"But you know how to do it already, don't you?" Libby pointed out.

Mike rubbed his chin with his fist again. "Well, I worked as an ordnance officer, if that's what you mean, but I didn't build IEDs. Or bombs. I was one of the people in charge of logistics, meaning I oversaw moving explosives from one place to another without having any of them blow up."

"But you had access to materials," Libby insisted.

"So does anyone who shops at Ace Hardware or Home Depot," Mike countered. He put his hands on his hips and cleared his throat. "Anyway, why would I want to do something like that? What's my motive? Tell me that."

Bernie and Libby didn't answer.

"That's what I thought," Mike said, reading the sisters' faces. "You can't tell me, because you haven't a clue. This is a fishing expedition." He ran his hand through his hair. "I mean, I just know the kid to say hello to. He brought me some heavy cream when Adam and I ran out of the stuff, and that's about all the interaction I've had with him." He shook his head. "Poor guy. It sounds as if he has a long road ahead of him to recovery."

"Did you go to the Ed Smith High School in Oxford?"

200 *Isis Crawford*

Bernie asked suddenly, having decided to change the subject.

Mike gave her a quizzical look. "Why do you want to know? Is that a crime now, too?"

"No," Libby replied. "My sister is asking because it seems as if everyone else in the show's cast—except for us—did as well," she told him.

Mike shrugged. "What's your point?"

"No point, just an observation," Bernie replied. "Did you know Doug?"

Mike nodded. "Not very well. Just to say hello to, really." He smiled wryly. "Of course, everyone knew everyone in Oxford. It was hard not to, the town was so small, but Doug kinda kept to himself. And he wasn't around that long. His family moved out, about a year after they came into Oxford." Mike shrugged his shoulders. "I guess they didn't like small-town life." He thought for a moment and added, "A lot of people don't—you know, having everyone in your business all the time isn't to everyone's taste." He sighed. "It's a whole different universe down there. And now, if you don't mind, it's time for me to get some shut-eye." He turned to go again; then something occurred to him, and he turned back. "The contest is still on, isn't it?"

"As far as I know," Libby replied.

Mike grinned. "That's good. In case I forget to say this later, don't feel too bad when you lose the bake-off. It's always hard coming up against the best."

"Meaning you?" Libby asked.

"Who else?" Mike replied.

"Funny man," Bernie said.

Libby laughed. "Don't worry. We won't, since we're not going to lose."

"I wouldn't be too sure about that if I were you," Mike replied.

"Oh, I would," Libby told him.

A CATERED BAKE-OFF   201

"Care to make a side bet?" Bernie asked.

"I might be interested," Mike allowed.

"I don't suppose you had one of those with Dennis?" Bernie inquired.

Mike flinched. It was a quick, subtle movement, but Bernie caught it.

"You did, didn't you?" Bernie said. "It looks as if we may have something to discuss, after all."

"It was ten bucks, for heaven's sake," Mike protested. "Chill out."

"Some people take things like that very seriously," Libby observed.

"Maybe they do, but I'm not one of them," Mike told her.

"Who else in the group was in on the bet?" Bernie asked.

"No one," Mike said.

Libby snorted.

"What is that supposed to mean?" Mike demanded.

"That I'm having trouble believing you," Libby replied.

Mike shrugged. "Believe what you want."

Bernie changed the subject. "Aren't you afraid that you're going to be next? That something is going to happen to you, too?"

Mike shrugged again. "Not even a little bit. I can take care of myself, thank you very much. I don't need anyone to protect me."

"What is it you need to protect yourself from?" Libby asked him.

Mike pointed to Mathilda. "Get in that van of yours and go home. I'm done here." And with that, he turned around and motioned for his dog, Scooter, to follow him into the house.

"So, what do you think?" Libby asked Bernie as she and her sister walked back to Mathilda.

Bernie clicked her tongue against her teeth as she con-

202   *Isis Crawford*

sidered Libby's question. "I think something is going on that doesn't relate to pastry."

"Like what?" Libby asked.

Bernie shrugged. "I don't know." She watched the fireflies on the lawn. "But the kitchen has always been a dangerous place," she observed.

"Yeah. I suppose it is," Libby agreed. "Fire. Sharp knives. Boiling water. Bad tempers. I mean, what could go wrong?"

Bernie brushed a lock of hair out of her eye and changed the subject. "I'm beginning to get the idea that no one likes us."

Libby looked at her sister sideways. "Why are you saying that?"

"Because we weren't invited into the betting pool."

Libby laughed. "Maybe there isn't one."

"Also true," Bernie acquiesced. "But if there is," she persisted.

"Guess we're the odd guys out then," Libby noted as she and her sister continued walking to their van. Libby had just passed Mike's old Ford when she stopped. Something just occurred to her. "Bernie."

Her sister turned. "Yes?"

"Remember how Mike's van clunked right after we got out of Mathilda, and you said it probably needed an oil change?" Libby asked her sister.

Bernie nodded. "I remember. What about it?"

Libby pointed to Mike's Ford. "That just got me thinking about Dad's old Chevy. Do you recall how it used to make that clunking sound right after he parked it and turned off the ignition?"

Bernie smiled. "It did, didn't it? Oh," she said, her eyes widening as she realized the implications of her sister's statement.

"Exactly," Libby replied as she walked over to Mike's van and felt its hood. "It's warm."

"Fancy that," Bernie said as she went over and laid her hand on the hood to double-check. Her sister was right. The hood was still warm. "Mike lied to us," she observed. "We didn't wake him up, after all."

Libby nodded. "Evidently not. He must have come home right before we arrived. I wonder where he was?"

"Somewhere he didn't want us to know about. Otherwise, why would he have gone through that elaborate charade about us waking him up?" Bernie mused.

Libby scratched her cheek. "Good question. Of course, he could have been picking up groceries at the all-night corner deli."

"But then, he wouldn't be pretending that he'd been here, would he, Libby?" Bernie noted.

Libby sighed. "I suppose he wouldn't." She slapped at a mosquito buzzing around her head. Then she asked her sister where she was going as she watched her turn and head back to Mike's house.

"To ask him where he was, of course," Bernie replied.

"He's not going to tell you," Libby predicted. All she wanted to do was go home, take a shower, and hop into bed.

"One never knows, if one doesn't ask," Bernie said, drawing upon another one of her dad's maxims. By now, she was in front of Mike's door. "Here goes nothing," she said to Libby. Then she rang the bell. When Mike didn't answer, she started banging on the door with her fist.

A moment later, Mike stuck his head out of one of the second-story windows. "Hey, I already told you to get out of here!" he yelled. "If you don't get off my property in two seconds, I'm calling the cops."

"Go ahead," Bernie said. "Maybe they'd like to know where you've been as well."

"I've been here," he replied.

"That's not what the hood of your van says," Bernie told him.

Mike snorted. "I don't have to put up with this nonsense."

"Then answer my question," Bernie said.

Mike disappeared from the window. A moment later, he was back. "See this?" He held his phone out the window. "I'm giving you till three and then I'm calling 911." And he began counting. "One. Two—"

"Fine," Bernie said, cutting him off as she began backing away from the door. "We're going."

"And don't come back!" Mike yelled after her.

"Told you," Libby said to her sister, once they were sitting in the van.

"At least I tried," Bernie noted as she fastened her seat belt.

Libby grunted as she started up Mathilda. "Like I said, it's time we went home. I have a feeling tomorrow is going to be a busy day," she predicted.

And she was correct. It was.

Chapter 27

"Told you," Bernie said as she looked at the line forming in front of the cash register at A Little Taste of Heaven at eleven in the morning. It had been like this since they'd opened the shop at seven o'clock that morning.

Libby corrected her. "No, I told you." She'd just finished refilling the coffee machine and bringing out another tray of mini peach and blueberry crostatas. Now she was on her way back to the prep room to bring out their salad bowl special of the day. Today it was poached salmon, topped with a green sauce, on a bed of assorted greens, consisting of radicchio, watercress, purslane, and Bibb lettuce, and sprinkled with toasted, chopped walnuts.

Over the years, Bernie and Libby had noticed that whenever they were involved in some sort of criminal investigation, their business ticked up, and this day was proving to be no exception to that rule. Everyone who came into the shop wanted to hear the latest inside scoop on what was happening at the bake-off, served up with their coffees and breakfast pastries. So it was a little after two in the afternoon by the time Bernie and Libby were ready to drive down to Oxford.

206 *Isis Crawford*

"Good luck," their dad said, resting his book on the side table when Bernie and Libby went upstairs to tell him where they were going.

"How come you're wishing us good luck?" Bernie asked after she'd taken an Aleve for her shoulder. It was getting better, but it still felt achy around the middle of the day.

"Because I've found that usually places like that don't take kindly to strangers poking around and asking questions," Sean told her.

Libby leaned forward. "Places like what?" she asked.

"Isolated places," Sean answered. "Small-town places."

"Aren't you generalizing a bit?" Libby asked.

"No. Not really," Sean told her.

"Sounds as if you've had experience," Bernie noted.

"I've had some," Sean allowed.

"Have you ever been to Oxford?" Libby asked him as she took a sip of the coffee she'd just brewed. She frowned. It was a little weak for her taste.

"A long time ago, in a different lifetime," Sean replied as he took a bite of the scone with raspberry jam and whipped cream that Libby had brought up for him. "Delicious," he pronounced, savoring the combination. "Sometimes the classics are the best."

"Indeed, they are," Libby agreed. "That's why they're the classics. They always satisfy. So, why were you in Oxford?" she inquired, changing the subject. "Wasn't that out of your jurisdiction?"

Sean chuckled, remembering that day. "Indeed, it was. I was chasing down a couple of fugitives. I'd gotten word that they were hiding in a barn somewhere in that area, so I went there to see if I could locate them and bring them back here. Went straight to the sheriff's office to ask for some help."

"And did you find them?" Bernie asked.

Sean shook his head and took another bite of his scone. "Nope. Never did. Just got sore feet, a tick bite, and a twisted ankle for my trouble. Months later, I found out that the guys I was looking for were some of the sheriff's family, and he'd known where they were all along. He'd just chosen to send me on a wild-goose chase out in the boonies." Sean fell silent remembering. Then he said, "A couple of years after that, the Feds swooped in and cleaned everything up." He scratched the side of his nose. "Turned out the lot of them were dealing a variety of illegal substances. I guess you could call it a family affair."

Bernie started singing Sly and the Family Stone's "(It's a) Family Affair," but Libby hushed her. "So, Dad, you were saying?" Libby asked.

Sean finished the rest of the scone before answering. "All I'm saying is, don't go charging in there asking people questions and expect to get an answer. I mean, you might get one, but in my experience, the odds aren't in your favor," he replied as he wiped his hands on the napkin Libby had provided.

"What would you suggest?" Bernie asked him.

"I don't know," Sean said. "You're good at coming up with stories. Think of something. Of course," he reflected, "what I'm telling you happened a while ago. Perhaps things have changed since then."

"Hopefully," Libby said, although she could tell from her dad's tone that he didn't think they had.

"Okay," Sean said as he picked up the book on Antarctica he'd been reading before Libby and Bernie had come upstairs. "Call me on the way home. Let me know how things went."

"Will do," Bernie promised, getting up from the sofa, walking over, and kissing her dad on the forehead. Libby did the same.

208   *Isis Crawford*

"Stay safe out there," Sean called out to them as they went down the stairs.

"Always!" Libby yelled back, answering her dad's usual send-off with her usual answer. "So," she said to her sister when they were standing on the sidewalk, "I don't suppose you have a plan."

"Not really," Bernie told her. "Do you?"

Libby smiled. "Glad you asked. As it happens, I do. Bring pastries."

Bernie blinked. "Excuse me. Did you just say, *bring pastries?*"

Libby explained. "Well," she said, "we don't have a gun or a badge, so pastries are the next best option."

"As opposed to a handgun?" Bernie asked incredulously. "You mean the police would be better off carrying chocolate chip cookies around, instead of their service revolvers? Is that what you're saying?"

Libby stuck her jaw out. "As a matter of fact, I am. The world would be a better place if that were the case."

"You're right," Bernie conceded after thinking over Libby's statement. "The world would be a better place if it were all puppies and rainbows, and maybe it is in a different universe."

"I'm still bringing cookies," Libby told her. "You can't deny that everyone is more willing to talk after they've had something good to eat."

"That's true, up to a point," Bernie allowed. "However, I think we may be beyond that point right now. Like, way, way beyond it."

"Maybe, maybe not," Libby allowed.

"I guess we'll find out soon enough," Bernie said.

"I guess we will," Libby agreed as she started walking into the shop.

"Hey," Bernie called after her.

Libby stopped and turned around.

"Pack some for us, too, Libby," Bernie said.

Libby gave her the thumbs-up. "I was planning on it," she said.

"And coffee," Bernie added as she put her hand over her mouth to cover her yawn. "Lots of coffee." She could take a nap right now, and her day wasn't even a quarter through.

Bernie was thinking about whether or not it was possible to sneak a nap in, but Libby came back with the cookies. Then they drove over to Marvin's and talked him into letting them borrow his vehicle. It was less conspicuous than their van.

Chapter 28

The trip to Oxford took longer than expected. Libby ended up taking the back roads due to a truck and a passenger car colliding on Winton Avenue, backing traffic up for the next twenty miles or so. Ordinarily, she would have been annoyed, but it was bright and sunny, a beautiful day for a ride. The road they were on followed the Hudson for ten miles before it turned inland.

Libby and Bernie watched the waves sparking in the sunlight, listened to the seagulls squawking, and commented on the tugs guiding commercial barges down the river, the sailboats tacking in the breeze, and the ducks paddling near the shore. When they weren't doing that, they sipped their coffee and talked about the week's menus and about whether or not they should do another run-through of their signature piece for the bake-off, and why Dennis's house had been booby-trapped and what the relationship of that to the espresso machine exploding was. If any. Then, when they'd run out of topics to discuss, they sat quietly observing the wildflowers in bloom on either side of the road and the hawks soaring on the thermals.

"Look, Libby," Bernie said, pointing to an eagle, perched on an oak tree, devouring a fish he'd just caught. She'd read in the paper that the eagle population was making a comeback along the Hudson. She smiled, hoping that it was true.

At the Cloverfield Shopping Mall, the road they were following turned left, taking them through a landscape of abandoned farms, trailer parks, groves of scrub trees, and small, dilapidated houses in need of painting. Internet service was spotty, and after trying to look up something and failing, Bernie gave up and asked Libby a question.

"What did you bring anyway?" she inquired, pointing to the white bakery box tied with string that was sitting between them.

"Cookies," Libby promptly answered. "I already told you. Everyone loves cookies. And muffins. I threw a few in there as well."

"No cinnamon buns?"

"They were sold out."

"I guess we'll see if you're right or not," Bernie replied.

"I guess we will," Libby remarked as she slowed down for a tractor that had pulled out in front of her from a side road. She followed it into town.

As Marvin's Toyota bumped along, Bernie pointed to the white paper bag sitting next to the box. She was suddenly hungry. "What did you bring for us?"

"Open it and see," Libby instructed.

"Jam thumb-prints and raspberry muffins," Bernie said after she had. "Good choice." And she reached in the bag and took the cookies out. The thump-prints were butter cookies with a small amount of jam in the center. "Sugar and fat. What could be better?" Bernie observed as she ate hers and gave the other one to her sister. Then she handed out the muffins.

"We should have eaten lunch," Libby replied as she brushed muffin crumbs off her Bermuda shorts.

"We should make that our New Year's resolution," Bernie

212   *Isis Crawford*

said after she'd taken another sip of the coffee they'd brought along. Usually, they were too busy to eat. Most days, they grabbed a snack, instead.

By now, they were just a mile out of town. On the way, they passed the local high school/ middle school. It was a medium-sized, two-story, utilitarian-looking redbrick building, set back from the road and surrounded by playing fields. A couple of kids were playing baseball, while another group was throwing a football around. The sign in front of the school read: HAVE A SAFE AND HAPPY SUMMER. SEE YOU IN SEPTEMBER.

"Looks like a nice enough place," Bernie commented as they drove by it.

Three minutes later, they passed a small metal sign that read: THIS TOWN WAS FOUNDED IN 1805 BY JOHN OXFORD. POPULATION 3,000. PLEASE DRIVE SLOWLY. CHILDREN AT PLAY.

Five minutes after that, they were in the town itself. There wasn't much to it. From what Bernie and Libby could see, it consisted of several blocks of wood-and-brick Colonials fronted by large yards. They went by an old Victorian, which now served as a library, and a shop with dirty windows that sold antiquities. Then, a couple of blocks after that, they came to the town center. As Libby drove down Front Street, she took note of the post office, the grocery store, a diner, a bar called The Watering Hole, a bank, a gas station, and a newspaper named the *Oxford Outlook*.

"This is all very Norman Rockwell," Bernie commented, looking around. "I didn't think places like this existed anymore around here."

"Neither did I," Libby agreed. "It's a miracle the land hasn't been bought up yet."

"I guess the developers don't know about this place; otherwise, it would be," Bernie noted as Libby slowed down for a squirrel running across the road. "Heaven knows,

A CATERED BAKE-OFF   213

they're buying up everything else around here and in Longely."

"So, where do you want to start?" Libby asked her sister. "The bar or the newspaper?" She figured those were the best places to find someone who knew something about the town's past.

"Let's start with the bar," Bernie said. In her experience, bartenders were like hairdressers. They knew everyone's business.

Libby nodded and pulled up in front of The Watering Hole. Two men were standing outside, next to the door, leaning against the wall, watching them. *Of course,* Libby reflected, *there isn't much else to watch.* Aside from an Amazon delivery truck, a cat snoozing on a porch, and an elderly couple sitting on a bench, the street was empty.

"Those guys don't look friendly, do they?" Libby remarked as she parked Marvin's vehicle in front of the bar.

"Well, they don't seem like the types that love chocolate chip cookies, if that's what you mean," Bernie replied as she and her sister got out of the Toyota.

"You want to go in here?" the skinny one with the red bandana asked when Bernie and Libby approached them.

Bernie put on her best smile. "We were thinking about it. Why? Is there a problem?"

"As a matter of fact, there is, pretty lady. It's closed," the taller man said. He had a face scarred by acne and a mouth full of crooked teeth.

Bernie pointed to the OPEN sign in the window. "That's not what that says," she replied.

"You can't always believe what you read," the taller man said.

"Are you the bartender?" Libby asked.

"No. He stepped out for a while. Had an emergency he had to attend to. We're minding the store until he gets back," the skinny guy said.

214   *Isis Crawford*

"And when will that be?" Libby asked.

The guy with the acne scars shrugged. "Whenever he's done with what he's doing." He smirked. "But if you want a drink that bad, I can always let you in." He turned to his buddy and elbowed him in the ribs. "Right?"

"Oh, yeah," his friend said, leering. "It'd be our pleasure. Don't want pretty ladies like yourselves waiting out in the hot sun getting all sweaty and everything. Where you two from anyway?"

"Longely," Bernie said.

The tall guy gestured to the bar. "You want to go in and freshen up. You know, use the facilities."

"We're fine, thanks," Libby said.

"You sure?" the man said. "You look like you could use . . . a little . . . wash."

"Thanks, but we're positive," Bernie said.

"We don't usually get visitors in these parts," the tall man observed.

"We're just passing through," Bernie lied.

The tall man shook his head. "You sure you're not looking for real estate to buy and turn into one of those fancy places? You know, the kind with the pricey drinks, where everything is organic." And he turned and spat on the sidewalk.

"We're definitely not," Libby said.

The tall man smirked. "Because you look like those kinda people." He turned to his friend again. "Don't they?"

"They definitely do," his friend replied. He turned to Bernie. "But there ain't nothing for sale around here. Of course, for you—maybe I can find something if you ask me nice, if you know what I mean," he told Bernie. Then he reached over and touched her hair. "You get it done in one of those beauty parlors?"

Bernie knocked his hand away and took a step back.

A CATERED BAKE-OFF 215

"No need to be rude," the taller man said, his face turning into a thundercloud. "You one of those feminists or something?"

"Or something," Bernie replied.

"Hey," the skinny guy protested, "no need to act like that. My friend was just trying to be sociable."

"Is *that* what you're calling it these days?" Bernie demanded.

"Yeah, it is," the taller guy said. "You got a problem?" He took another step toward them. "You think you're too good for me and my friend?"

Libby looked at her sister. "Maybe we should get going," she suggested.

"Maybe we should," Bernie agreed.

"Hey, what's your hurry," the guy with the acne scars said. He took a step toward them. "You don't have to go."

"Yeah, stick around," his friend said. He grinned. "We can have a little fun. You two look like you can use some of that."

"Thanks, but no thanks," Bernie said, and she started backing away. So did Libby. A moment later, they were back in Marvin's vehicle. "No cookies for them," she noted. It was definitely time to leave before things got out of hand.

"Onward and upward," Libby replied as she started the Toyota. "So, now what, Bernie?"

"Let's try the newspaper," Bernie told her. "Hopefully, we'll have better luck there."

Chapter 29

Libby nodded, made a U-turn, and drove back the way they'd come. When they passed the bar, the two men waved. Bernie and Libby didn't wave back. They gave them the finger, instead. Two blocks later, she parked Marvin's vehicle in front of the store that served as a home for the *Oxford Outlook*. Then she and Bernie both got out and went inside.

"Yes?" the woman behind the desk said, looking up from her computer screen. "Can I help you with something?"

"Hopefully, you can," Bernie said. She put the woman she was talking to at about thirty. She was wearing an old pair of Bermuda shorts, a pair of Birkenstock sandals, and a T-shirt with a logo that read: I LOVE MY CAT. Her mousey-brown hair was in a ponytail, she wasn't wearing makeup, and her glasses were perched on top of her head.

"So, what's it going to be?" the woman asked. "Do you want to take out an ad? Sell something? Post a community event?"

"Actually, we're writing an article about the group of people participating in *The Longely Bake-Off*," Bernie said, improvising. "A human-interest piece. We were told several of the contestants used to live here." And she rolled the names off her tongue.

The woman repeated them back. Then she said, "Sorry, none of them ring a bell. You've made the drive for nothing. They were before my time. I just took over this paper four years ago."

"Is there anyone else I could talk to? Someone who worked here before you took over?" Bernie asked.

The woman shook her head. "Sorry again. Old Man McConnell did, but he died a couple of years ago. He did everything, and now I do it all," she went on. "I'm the reporter, the editor, the manager, the printer, and the chief cook and bottle washer." She stuck out her hand, and she, Libby, and Bernie shook. "My name is Claire, by the way."

"And we're Libby and Bernie," Libby said.

"I always wanted to own a newspaper, and when I saw this one was for sale, I couldn't resist." Claire shrugged. "I thought I could change it over from a pennysaver to something with more emphasis on local news. People told me not to, but I disregarded them, maxed out all my credit cards, and went ahead anyway." Claire held out her hands palm upward. "So here we are."

"How come they told you not to?" Bernie asked.

Claire grinned. "My lips are sealed."

"Would cookies unseal them?" Bernie asked.

Claire raised an eyebrow. "I'm listening. What do you have in mind?"

Bernie explained the situation.

"It's a deal," Claire said. "I've got a wicked sweet tooth," she told Bernie, while Libby went out and brought the box of cookies in. "You should sell these on Amazon," Claire declared after she'd taken a bite of a butter cookie. "You'd make a fortune."

218   *Isis Crawford*

Bernie laughed. "That's very sweet, but we have enough trouble keeping up with things as it is," Bernie told her.

Libby nodded. What Bernie said was true. She watched while Claire sampled a gingersnap.

"This is delicious," Claire declared.

"That's because it has two types of ginger in it," Libby told her. "Candied and grated."

"Do you think the high school would have any information?" Bernie asked, getting back to the topic at hand.

Claire shook her head. "I doubt it. There was an explosion in the school, right around the time you're talking about, and between the resulting fire and the blast, everything was pretty much destroyed."

Bernie perked up her ears. "Did you say explosion?" she inquired.

"They think it was a leaky gas pipe. In any case, the school was obviously rebuilt. There were a few other explosions as well, I was told." Claire narrowed her eyes while she thought. "If I remember correctly, one was in a house down by the pond, and there was another in a restaurant at the edge of town." She took a sip of water from the mug on her desk. "The gas company ended up investigating. They came to the conclusion that the gas lines hadn't been installed correctly by the initial subcontractor. They hadn't been dug deep enough, which evidently was pretty common back in the day when people first converted from coal to gas."

Libby made a face. "I didn't know that."

"Neither did I," Claire replied. "But I did a little research, and as it turns out, it wasn't that uncommon then."

"So, you're saying that the gas company's findings were correct?" Bernie asked, clarifying.

Claire nodded. "That's what the state investigators con-

A CATERED BAKE-OFF   219

cluded. Since the company changed the pipes out, there weren't any more explosions, so I think it's pretty safe to draw that conclusion. Of course," she continued, "there were a couple of folks here who said the explosions were on purpose, but they're the kind of folks who think there are aliens living under the Antarctic and that JFK is in Argentina running a fish store."

"Could we speak to them?" Libby asked, thinking it would be a good idea to double-check. Just in case.

"I'm afraid not," Claire said. "Edna Thomas is suffering from dementia, and her daughter moved her closer to her."

"Somewhere near here?" Libby asked.

"No," Claire replied. "Edna is in Austin now. Then Cal Williams had a stroke a while back, and he can't talk, and Roberta Quail died last week. At least those are the people that come to mind. So, then, the answer to your question off the top of my head is a no."

"I don't suppose you have old copies of the *Oxford Outlook* here?" Bernie asked.

Claire readjusted her glasses. "You mean, do we have a morgue?"

Bernie nodded.

Claire shook her head. "Nope. No one bothered. And to be fair, there's really no reason to save the paper. Most of the *Oxford Outlook* consisted of, and still consists of, ads and community service announcements, although I'm still trying to change that and get more news in there." She sighed. "Like I said, that's why I bought the damn thing. It's been an uphill battle, though. My boyfriend says I have delusions of grandeur, and I'm beginning to think he's right. I definitely bit off more than I can chew."

"Is there anyone you can think of who would be willing to talk to us?" Bernie asked.

Claire made a face. "Not really. I've found people around here are pretty closemouthed. They don't like speaking to people they don't know. Hell, they don't like talking to me, and I've been here for four years." She rubbed the side of her nose with her knuckle. "The truth is, if you're not born here, they don't want to have anything to do with you."

"Sounds like a friendly place," Libby observed.

"Maybe that's why the news thing isn't working so well," Bernie suggested.

"Ya think?" Claire said. She shook her head again. "Too bad I didn't know that before I bought the paper, although I can't say I wasn't warned."

Libby changed the subject. "And speaking of friendly, what's with the guys outside the bar?" she asked after she'd described her interaction with them.

Claire snorted. "Oh, them. They're just a bunch of morons," she said. "I try and stay clear of them when I can. You know, they're the kind of people who think it's funny to throw firecrackers at dogs."

"And the bartender?" Bernie asked. "Would he know something?"

"Jorge?" Claire replied. "I doubt it. He got here the year before I did. He inherited the bar from his uncle. I hear he wants to sell it, but my guess is that he's going to have a tough time finding a buyer. We're not exactly talking party central here. Frankly, I would leave if I didn't have all my money tied up in this thing." She sighed. "People told me to have an exit strategy. I should have listened."

"It must be tough," Bernie said.

"It is," Claire said as she reached into the box, took a mocha brownie, and ate it. She groaned with pleasure. "God, this is good. I can't decide which is my favorite."

She patted her stomach. "So much for my diet. But these are worth every pound. They're lethal."

Libby laughed. "I hope you mean that in a good way," she said.

"Totally," Claire replied. Then she added, "I know I'm eating my worries, but I don't care."

"And speaking of things that are lethal," Bernie said as she helped herself to a carrot cake muffin, "was anyone killed in the explosions?"

Claire shook her head. "The one at the school happened at night, and the houses happened during the day—luckily."

"Don't you think that's a little odd?" Bernie asked.

"Not really," Claire replied.

"Think about it," Bernie told her.

"I have," Claire replied. "I did a little research, and it turns out that most of the explosions were injury free."

"Maybe God was just watching over everyone," Libby observed.

"Maybe," Bernie replied. After all, it could be true, although she doubted it.

"I don't remember reading about the explosions," Libby remarked as she brushed an ant off her leg.

"That doesn't surprise me," Claire told her. "And frankly, even back then, no one cared about what happened here. We could be in Barrow, Alaska, for all the attention anyone ever pays us. Especially, since there weren't any fatalities. I think the whole town would have to go up in flames before it got on the media's radar . . ." She was about to continue, but her cell phone rang. She looked down at it, read the screen, and frowned. "It's been lovely, ladies," she said when she looked up, "but I have to take this. It's my printer."

Bernie and Libby nodded.

222　*Isis Crawford*

"Before you go, it sounded as if you were just about to say something else," Bernie told Claire.

"Just that things might be different now with social media," Claire replied, flashing an apologetic smile. "Just a random thought. By the way, my soul thanks you for the cookies, even if my waistline doesn't," she told the sisters as she got up and headed for the other room, phone in hand.

Bernie and Libby could hear Claire talking as they exited the building. It sounded as if she wasn't happy.

Chapter 30

On the way out of town, Bernie and Libby stopped at the library. Looking at the old Victorian, Bernie decided that once upon a time, it must have been a Painted Lady, the pride of the family who owned it, but that was ages ago. Now the colors had faded into nothingness, the paint was peeling, and Bernie and Libby could see wood rot on the windowsills, around the doorframe, and on the steps leading up to the front door.

"Sorry, we're closing," the librarian told them when Bernie and Libby walked in. They had to strain to hear her over the hum of the lawn mower next door.

"We'll be quick," Bernie promised as she glanced around at the bookshelves. Most of them were only halfway filled, if that. Then she took a good look at the librarian. On the heavyish side, she was wearing a pink headband, white peasant blouse, and a long, pleated skirt. She was young. Bernie put her in her early twenties, which was too young to have known Doug or any of the people in the bake-off who had gone to high school here. The likelihood of their getting any information was probably slight, but they were there, so she asked her questions anyway.

"Doug LaForte. Nell Pinto. Lori Peterson," the woman

224   *Isis Crawford*

said, repeating the first three names Bernie had just mentioned. "Doug LaForte was the one who got hurt by the exploding espresso machine, right?"

"Right," Libby said.

"I saw it in the paper. Weird way to die, that's for sure." She reached up and adjusted her headband.

"Yes, it is," Libby agreed.

"And the other names?" Bernie asked.

The woman grimaced. "Sorry, but they don't ring a bell. Should they?"

"Probably not, Candy," Bernie said, reading her name off the placard on her desk. "I suspect they were here well before your time."

"I remember Doug LaForte," a raspy voice behind them said. "Good riddance to bad rubbish, I say."

"Mrs. Halder," Candy cried as Bernie and Libby spun around. "That's not a nice thing to say."

"Too bad," Mrs. Halder replied. "It's true. He was a terrible person."

It took a moment for Bernie and Libby to spot the woman who was speaking. At first, they didn't see anyone, then they caught sight of a small, elderly lady seated behind a large fig tree. She looked frail, and even though it was a warm day, she was wearing jeans and a matching long-sleeved cotton shirt and sweater. Her snow-white hair was styled in a pageboy, and she was wearing a touch of bright red lipstick, which served to emphasize the whiteness of her skin and the creases on her lips.

"What did he do to get himself killed?" she asked.

"Nothing, as far as we know," Bernie said, which was true. She and her sister didn't know what, if anything, Doug had done to merit what had happened to him.

"He had to do something," Mrs. Halder insisted. "You don't kill someone for no reason," she observed. "The rest of them weren't so great, either."

"Who were the rest of them?" Libby asked.

Mrs. Halder frowned. "Those kids. The whole lot of them. Always sneaking around, up to no good, but that LaForte kid was the worst of the lot. I hope you're not thinking of going into business with any of them."

"We were considering it," Libby lied.

Mrs. Halder made a face. "You want to take my advice, don't!" she snapped. "But like I just said, LaForte was a terrible person. The worst."

"Why do you say that?" Libby asked.

Mrs. Halder grimaced. "Because he killed my cats. My precious Phoebe. With an axe. And he did other things, too. Bad things. That's why the LaFortes left, you know. They had to. Otherwise, Doug would have been in jail. He should have been in jail. Maybe that would have taught him something. I warned his parents that he was a bad 'un, but nobody wants to hear that about their own." And she waved her hand in the air to emphasize her point. Libby noticed her hand was shaking.

Candy got up, went over to the lady, and patted her on the shoulder. "Now, Mrs. Halder, no need to upset yourself."

"Don't treat me like I'm two, Candy," she said, pushing Candy's hand from her shoulder. "No one ever did anything when I phoned. I called and called, but no one ever came." She leaned forward and lowered her voice. "I think the police got paid off," she whispered. "That's what I think. Doug's dad was rich, you know. Rich people think they can do anything they want." She sniffed. A tear rolled down her cheek. "Poor Phoebe, Diana, and Apollo. They were my babies, you know. I raised them from six weeks. Why would someone do something like that?" she asked in a quavering voice. "My babies never hurt anyone."

"How about a cup of tea?" Candy asked her. "Would that make you feel better?"

226　*Isis Crawford*

Mrs. Halder's eyes brightened. She nodded. "That would be lovely, dear. Don't forget a drop of honey."

"I won't," the librarian said.

"Do you have any biscuits?"

The librarian nodded. "Of course. And after you're finished, I'll take you home."

"Yes, must feed the kitties," Mrs. Halder said as she went back to looking at a picture book of the national parks.

Candy beckoned for Libby and Bernie to follow her. They walked into a side room. Bernie guessed it used to be a utility closet, but at some point, it had been converted into a mini galley kitchen, with a microwave, a sink, a mini fridge, and an electric kettle on one side, and a counter holding several chipped white china mugs, two boxes of herbal tea, a handful of sugar packets, and a bag of Oreo cookies on the other side.

"Sometimes Flo gets confused," Candy said as she filled the electric kettle in the sink.

"So, you're telling me that what she said, isn't true?" Bernie asked as Candy put the glass kettle back on its stand and turned on the switch.

"The cat part certainly isn't," Candy said. "Flo never had any cats."

"Are you sure?" Libby asked.

"Pretty positive," Candy said. "She tends to imagine things and I go along with her. It's easier that way."

"Are you her daughter?" Bernie wanted to know.

The librarian shook her head. "No. Her niece. I bring her here, two or three days a week, and she sits here and looks at pictures until I take her home. For some reason, she really likes paging through our old copies of the Encyclopaedia Britannica and the World Atlas. Says they remind her of her dad. He used to sell them."

"That's nice of you to do that," Libby told her.

Candy smiled. "Thank you. It's good for her to get out, and it's actually good for me, too. That way, I don't have to worry that she'll fall when I'm not around. Saves on the stress." Then she noticed that the water was boiling. She shut off the kettle and asked Bernie and Libby if they would like a cup of tea as well. When they refused, she continued with what she'd been doing.

"So, how come you call her Mrs. Halder if you're her niece, if you don't mind my asking?" Bernie inquired as Candy put the tea bag in the water. "That seems rather formal, given the circumstances."

Candy smiled ruefully. "I call her that because that's what she wants to be called. She doesn't respond to her first name, Florence. She never liked it. Always talked about changing it. Or maybe it reminds her of Bill. Her late husband," the librarian explained when she saw the puzzled looks on Bernie's and Libby's faces. "And every time I call her aunt, she thinks I'm talking about someone else. I gotta tell you, dementia is a terrible thing," Candy observed. "I hope someone shoots me first."

"Same," Bernie said.

"Where did you get your librarian's degree?" Libby asked as Candy proceeded to take two Oreos out of the bag on the countertop.

Candy laughed. "Oh, I don't have a degree. I'm just filling in, doing the best I can. They can't get a librarian here," she explained. "There's no money to pay one. Actually, the only reason we're here is because someone left an endowment fund for the place. Anyway, I like to read, so this is perfect. I get first crack at all the new books coming in." Then she took the tea and cookies, walked over to where Florence was sitting, and put them in front of her. "Here you go, dear," she said.

Florence looked at them and her face twisted. "I didn't

228 *Isis Crawford*

order these," she told Candy. Then she said, "I told you. I want to go home. *Now.*"

The librarian sighed. She looked at Libby and Bernie and said, "Sometimes it happens. She forgets."

"I haven't forgotten anything," Florence snapped. She pointed to Libby and Bernie. "My taxi is here, and my pets are waiting for me to feed them."

"We can take her home if you tell us where we're going," Libby said to Candy.

"No. No," the librarian protested. "I couldn't let you do that."

"Don't be ridiculous. Of course, you can," Florence replied. And she stood up and marched out the door.

"It looks like the matter is out of your hands," Bernie observed.

"I just need fifteen minutes to close up here," the librarian said. "But the problem is, my sister is still at work. Usually, Florence waits with her, until her nephew gets home. I don't like leaving her alone. She tends to wander off."

"Don't worry," Libby said. "We can wait with her until someone gets there."

"Are you sure?" the librarian, who wasn't a librarian, asked.

"We're positive," Bernie and Libby said together.

"Okay, then," Candy said. She gave them her phone number. "Call if you need anything," she instructed. "Anything at all," she repeated. "I'll be there as soon as I can."

"Will do," Libby promised.

Bernie reached over and squeezed Candy's hand. "Don't worry, everything will be fine," she told her.

Chapter 31

Florence Halder's small, raised ranch needed a paint job, the brick chimney had to be repointed, the lawn mowed, and the white picket fence around it looked as if it would fall down any minute. In contrast, the front garden surrounding the house was a joy to see. It was edged and mulched with precision. Bernie decided it looked like a riff on an English garden. The purple cone flowers vied with the black-eyed Susans, and the ferns fought for space with the daisies; the zinnias showed their colors on the opposite side of the flower bed, and an old-fashioned rosebush stood sentinel by an old pickup truck without wheels.

"Your garden is beautiful," Libby said to Mrs. Halder as she pulled into the driveway, taking care to avoid the holes in the asphalt.

Mrs. Halder came to life. She smiled. "Thank you," she replied as Bernie helped her out of Marvin's car. "I try."

Bernie and Libby followed her into her house. The interior looked as if it could have come out of the pages of a 1950s *House & Garden*. Everything was immaculate. Everything matched. It was not what Bernie and Libby had expected. Mrs. Halder set her handbag down on the

230   *Isis Crawford*

coffee table in the living room and announced that she was going to take a nap. Bernie and Libby expected her to go into her bedroom, but she went out the French doors that led to a stone patio, instead.

"There," she said, pointing to an overgrown patch at the far end of the garden. "That's where my babies are buried."

Libby and Bernie nodded as Mrs. Halder walked over there. The sisters followed.

"See," she insisted, pointing.

The sisters nodded again, even though the only things they saw there were masses of hostas, goldenrod, and an old lilac bush that was past its prime, and needed to be cut back.

"I didn't want to do it here, but Dorothy Pinto insisted," Mrs. Halder said. She sighed.

"Dorothy *Pinto?*" Bernie asked.

Mrs. Halder replied, "I still think it was wrong, but what could I do? I didn't have much of a choice, did I? Otherwise, she said she'd tell my principal."

"No, you didn't," Libby agreed, because it seemed like the right thing to say.

"Were you a teacher?" Bernie asked.

Mrs. Halder nodded.

"Here? In this town?" Bernie prodded.

Mrs. Halder blinked. Her eyes started to mist over. "I don't remember," she said as her jaw began to tremble. "I can't remember."

"It's all right," Bernie said, hurriedly changing the subject. "What was wrong?" she asked, instead. "You just said that something was wrong. What was it?"

Mrs. Halder's eyes lit up. "It . . . was wrong. I kept on telling them that, but they didn't listen. They said I'd get in trouble if I told." Her voice rose.

Bernie could tell she was getting upset again, so she changed the subject. "Do you know Nell Pinto?" she asked.

"Nell? Nell?" Mrs. Halder repeated. She wrinkled her forehead. "Why does that name sound familiar?"

"We were asking your niece about her," Libby replied.

"And you just mentioned someone called Dorothy Pinto. Could that be Nell's mother?" Bernie asked, taking a guess.

"Dorothy had lots of babies," Mrs. Halder replied.

Bernie smiled, thinking they were finally getting someplace. "Do you remember any of their names?" she asked gently.

Florence Halder nodded vigorously. "She had Flopsy and Mopsy, and then she had Thumper and Cottontail and Moss."

Bernie and Libby exchanged glances.

"You mean bunnies?" Libby asked, thinking of Beatrix Potter and Disney.

Mrs. Halder shook her head. "No. Babies. I mean *babies*." And she pointed to the ground. "I helped bury them. See, we put stones down to mark their graves." She pointed again. "Look," she commanded. "See."

Bernie and Libby did. They caught glimpses of pavers peeping out of the speedwell and clover. "I see," Bernie said.

Mrs. Halder blinked. A tear ran down her cheek. "I miss them," she said. "We had nice talks."

"I'm sure you did," Libby told her, commiserating.

"And tea parties. We had tea parties, too. No one will help me weed now," Mrs. Halder said in a plaintive tone, swaying slightly from side to side. She held up her hands. They were gnarled, her veins running like road maps under her skin. "See." She wiggled her fingers. "They don't work so well anymore. Especially with thistles. I lost my gloves, you see." She leaned forward. "I think someone stole them," she confided in a whisper.

"I'm sure Candy will help you," Libby said, quickly stepping next to Mrs. Halder so she could catch her in case she fell. Then she patted her hand, took hold of it, and gently led her back inside her house to the tweed-covered sofa in the living room.

Mrs. Halder sat. Then she lay down on the sofa and closed her eyes. A moment later, she was asleep, her mouth ajar, a slight snore audible.

Libby covered her with the blue cotton throw lying on the sofa arm. "What now?" Libby said to her sister as she looked at her watch. They needed to get back to the shop soon. The evening rush was going to begin in a little while. Plus, Marvin was going to need his vehicle. He was supposed to go to the gym, and his father considered it bad form to drive around in the business's hearse.

"Now we wait," Bernie said, and with that, she went over to the bookshelves on the far side of the living room and took a look. There was an eclectic mix of romances, reference books, magazines, and old *Oxford Outlook*s housed on the shelves, in no particular order that she could see. While she waited for Candy to arrive, Bernie started going through them, hoping to find an article about the explosions that had rocked Oxford.

Halfway in, she found her first headline of interest. It was next to an article on what to do about ash borers and read: NOT BURIED DEEP ENOUGH? The byline was Dorothy Pinto's. *Now, that's even more interesting,* Bernie decided. She was in the middle of checking the publication date on the pennysaver when she heard a car driving up. A moment later, she heard the front door opening and closing.

"Candy," Bernie said. She turned around, expecting to find the librarian, who wasn't a librarian, standing in the living room. But she wasn't. It was someone else.

"What the hell are you doing here?" demanded the skinny guy who had been lounging in front of the bar, when she and Libby had driven into town.

Bernie stiffened. "We're waiting for Candy to get home. What are you doing here?" she demanded in turn of the man she'd privately christened the AH.

"I live here," he said.

"Oh," Bernie responded, shocked. She was momentarily at a loss for words.

Libby stepped into the breach. "Candy asked us to take your aunt home," she quickly explained.

The AH scowled and turned to Bernie. "So, you decided to look through her bookshelves?" he asked, his voice rising.

Bernie played it cool. She shrugged. "I like to see what other people read. Is that a crime?" she inquired, now all sweetness and light.

"I don't like people upsetting her," he said. He pointed to his aunt. "She's been through enough." His voice softened. "Poor dear."

"Does she have any pets?" Libby asked, changing the subject to a more neutral topic.

The man shook his head. "She never wanted any." His face clouded over. "She was mean. Real mean when she was younger. Killed Jack, my pet dog, because he ate her wallet. Shot him dead." He shook his head. "Funny, how she's gotten nicer since she's gone nutters."

"So, the pavers in the backyard?" Bernie asked.

"What about them?" the man responded.

"Your aunt said her pets were buried under them," Libby answered.

The man sighed. "There's nothing there." He tapped the side of his head with his finger. "She imagines things. You don't believe me?" he asked, reading the expression on the sisters' faces. "Here. Let me show you."

234   *Isis Crawford*

And before Bernie or Libby could protest, he took them outside and moved the pavers aside. "See," he said, pointing to the worms and the roly-polies wriggling around in the dirt. Then he moved the pavers back and motioned for them to come inside with him. "You can leave now. I'm here," he told them after he'd closed the screen door.

Bernie was just about to tell him she preferred to wait for Candy, when the librarian, who wasn't a librarian, appeared in the doorway. The sisters left immediately afterward.

On the way out of town, they stopped at the *Oxford Outlook* office to ask about Dorothy Pinto, but the office was closed, and Bernie realized she didn't have Claire's phone number, so she couldn't call her. She left a note for Claire, instead. The bar was closed as well, so Libby and Bernie decided to cut their losses and go home after they'd talked to Nell.

Chapter 32

The door to Nell's house was painted a bright blue, the trim was a light green, and the rest of the clapboards were painted a dark charcoal gray.

"Wow!" Libby said as Bernie knocked on the door. "I bet the neighbors aren't happy with Nell's paint job." It definitely stood out, since all the other houses on the block were pastel-colored Colonials, with white trim and black shutters.

"I bet you're right," Bernie said loudly, raising her voice so she could be heard over the rock music blaring out of the house. "I bet they don't appreciate the music, either," she observed as she knocked on the door again. No one answered.

"She probably can't hear you," Libby guessed.

"Probably not," Bernie agreed. On impulse, she twisted the door handle. It turned and the door swung open. The sisters looked at each other. "Should we?" Bernie asked Libby. Then she took a step inside before her sister could answer.

"Why ask if you're not going to wait for my answer?" Libby groused as she followed Bernie. They were standing

236 *Isis Crawford*

in the hallway. She could see that the living room and the sitting room were empty.

"Hello!" Bernie called out. Nell didn't answer.

Bernie tried another time. "Hello! It's Bernie and Libby," she yelled, but again no one replied.

Libby and Bernie looked at each other.

"I hope nothing's wrong," Libby said. She bit at a cuticle with her front teeth. The events of the past weeks had made her nervous.

"Me too," Bernie replied as she and her sister followed the music into the dining room and then into the kitchen.

"Nell," Libby cried as they entered the kitchen. She had to shout to be heard over the music.

Nell looked up. Her arms were in a mixing bowl up to her elbows.

"Don't look!" she yelled when she saw who it was.

"Why? What are you making?" Libby asked as she took in the baking sheets, the parchment paper, and the piping bags on the table. "Anything interesting?"

Before Nell could answer, Bernie grabbed her sister's upper arm and pulled her out of the kitchen and into the dining room.

"Obviously, she doesn't want you to see what she's doing," Bernie explained to her sister.

"Oh," Libby replied, understanding. "Right. Sorry," she called out, apologizing to Nell.

"I don't think she heard you," Bernie said as she led Libby into the living room.

A moment later, the music went off. A couple of minutes after that, Nell appeared in front of them. She had a streak of flour on her left cheek and her hair was pinned up on top of her head. The apron she was wearing had a picture of Lucy van Pelt of Peanuts fame on it, and that was covered with dabs of chocolate icing and vanilla custard.

"What's the matter? What happened?" Nell demanded,

looking from one sister to the other and back again, a panicked expression on her face.

"Nothing happened," Libby told her.

"Whew," Nell said, putting her right hand over her heart. "That's a relief." Then she wiped her hands on her apron and asked another question. "Then I don't understand. Why are you here?"

"We're here because we have a few questions we need to ask you," Bernie told her. "Sorry if we startled you before. We knocked, but you didn't hear."

Nell waved a hand in the air, indicating it wasn't an issue. Then she laughed. "I'm not surprised. I guess I got carried away with the volume. Good thing my neighbors are at work—otherwise, they'd probably have called the cops on me." She plopped down on an armchair and indicated Libby and Bernie should sit on the sofa. "So, what's the question?" she inquired once the sisters were settled.

"You lived in Oxford, right?" Bernie wanted to know.

Nell nodded. "Right. For a little while."

"But you went to high school there, correct?" Bernie inquired.

Nell nodded. "About a year or so. Why do you want to know?"

"We found a picture of you and Doug in his briefcase," Bernie told her.

Nell waited. "And?" she finally said when Bernie didn't add anything to her statement.

"We just wondered why he had it with him," Libby explained.

"If I remember correctly, I think he'd gotten a new camera and we were trying it out," Nell replied.

"So, you guys were friends?" Libby asked.

"No. Not at all," Nell replied immediately. It was obvious to the sisters that she didn't have to think about her

238   *Isis Crawford*

answer. "If I was friends with anyone, it was Adam. We even went out on a couple of dates."

"How about Lori, Mike, and Adam?" Bernie inquired. "Were they friends with Doug?"

"We all knew each other, but none of us were buddy-buddy, if you know what I mean."

"I find that strange," Bernie observed, "Oxford being such a small town and all. I would have thought you guys would have hung out together. I mean, you all went to the same school."

Nell shrugged. "Then you would have been wrong."

"About the school?" Bernie inquired.

"No, about us hanging out together," Nell replied. "Lori and Mike had jobs, I had to help my nana with chores on her farm, and Adam had to babysit his little sister."

"And the judges?" Libby asked. "What about them?"

"Same thing," Nell replied. "The two of them had jobs after school and on the weekends. Most of the seniors and juniors did. They had to. Their families needed the money. All of our families did." Then Nell changed the subject. "Are you ready for this weekend?"

"I guess I'm as ready as I'll ever be," Libby said. "They say that *the show must go on*. Hopefully, it will, in this case."

"What do you mean by *hopefully, in this case*?" Nell asked, repeating Libby's last words.

"I think what my sister means is, who knows what's going to happen, given everything that's been going on," Bernie answered.

Nell's eyes widened slightly. "You think something else will happen?"

"I don't know," Libby responded. "I sure hope not."

"Me too," Nell replied. She shuddered. "I don't think my nerves will take anything else. I'm having nightmares."

"So am I," Libby confided. She leaned forward. "Not to change the subject or anything, but what's your mother's name? I know it's an odd question, but humor me on this."

Nell wrinkled her forehead. "Tell me why you want to know."

Bernie answered for Libby. "We want to know because we found an article in the *Oxford Outlook* by a Dorothy Pinto on the gas leak problem in Oxford. We thought we'd like to talk to her about it, and since your last name is Pinto . . ." Bernie stopped talking, leaving Nell to fill in the rest of the sentence.

"Oh, that," Nell replied, momentarily distracted. "Yeah. Evidently, it got pretty bad for a while. I guess they had a fair number of accidents when they first started introducing gas into homes in the area. They didn't know to bury the pipes deep enough. Who would have thought that was a thing?"

"Not me," Libby said.

"So, was Dorothy your mother?" Bernie asked Nell.

Nell shook her head. "She was my aunt on my father's side. She was the reason my dad wanted us to move there in the first place, but then there was this big argument, and everyone stopped speaking to everyone else."

"I don't suppose you kept in contact?" Bernie asked her. "We'd like to hear more about the explosions."

Nell shook her head. "You'd have to hire a medium to do that. I heard she died a while ago. Heart attack."

"And your dad? Would he know anything?"

"Doubtful," Nell replied. "He got divorced from my mom and met some lady and moved to the Philippines. Last I heard, he was selling fish and eggs at the local town market. And as for my mom," Nell continued, anticipating Bernie's next question, "she passed a couple of years ago. Cancer."

240 *Isis Crawford*

"I'm sorry," Libby and Bernie both told Nell at the same time.

Nell smiled sadly. "Don't be. It was a mercy in the end. She was praying for it. But enough of that." And she changed the subject. "On a happier note, what do you think the technical challenge is going to be?"

"Good question," Libby said. "I'm betting something using some sort of pastry, like a strudel or a baklava. Pastry is always hard." Then she had another thought. "Or maybe something like apple cider doughnuts. Frying is always tricky."

"True, but I'm going with French macarons," Nell said.

Bernie tucked a strand of hair behind her ear. "I hadn't thought of those, but you might be right," she admitted. "They're tricky," she continued, thinking of the meringue confections. "They have to look good, as well as taste good," she observed.

Libby scratched an itch on her elbow. "I don't know," she said. "If I had to bet, I think the judges will go with something English. I mean they are replicating *The Great British Bake Off,* after all," she continued. "So I'm thinking they'll pick something like an Eccles or Chorley cake, for example."

With her thumb and forefinger, Nell squished a stray ant that was crawling up the arm of the chair where she was sitting. "What the hell is an Eccles or Chorley cake?" she demanded.

"Some sort of little pies filled with dried fruit," Libby replied. "I watched a lot of reruns of *The Great British Bake Off* when I heard we were on the show," she replied before Nell could ask her how she'd come up with those examples. "That was one of the contestants' assignments."

Nell laughed. "Nice to know. I guess that we'll see what we can see," she commented. Then she added, "Whatever that means."

"I guess we will," Bernie replied. She looked at her phone. "And speaking of baking, I guess it's time we got back to the shop. Peach crostatas await."

Nell raised her hand in a gesture of farewell. "See you this weekend. And may the best baker win."

"Absolutely," Bernie said as she and Libby walked out the door.

"Maybe we should bake a batch of macarons," Libby said, once they were back in Marvin's vehicle. "I haven't made them in a while," she reflected, thinking of the recipe. Although the recipe looked easy—after all, what were macarons but fancy meringue sandwiches with filling— they were anything but. What they were, were complicated and time-consuming. Libby was about to say that it wouldn't hurt to make a practice batch before the weekend; Bernie spoke at that moment.

"So, what do you think?" Bernie asked her sister.

"About what?"

"About Nell."

"What about her? Aside from the fact that she might have been responsible for letting the goats out."

"Yes, aside from that." Bernie fingered her pendant. "I had the feeling she was holding something back."

"Like what?"

Bernie shook her head. She couldn't say. It was just a feeling she had in her gut. "I think we should go back there," she said, instead.

"To Oxford?" Libby asked.

Bernie nodded. "Yes."

"Why, Bernie?"

"I don't know," Bernie admitted. "I just feel as if we missed something. Something important."

"Well, I don't," Libby told her.

Chapter 33

It was a little after nine that evening. Bernie, Libby, and their dad had just settled down to watch the latest episode of *Blue Bloods*. They were eating peach and blueberry crumbles and arguing about the differences between a cobbler, a crisp, a crumble, and a brown Betty.

Just then, Libby got a text from Adam. **There's something I need to tell you. Something to do with what's happening.**

Libby showed the text to her sister and Dad, then wrote: **Are you talking about the bake-off?**

Yes, the answer came back.

"Ask him what he means," Bernie instructed Libby. By now, Bernie and her dad were looking over Libby's shoulder.

"I was going to," Libby told her. Then she texted: **Like what? What's going on?**

The answer came back a moment later: **I have some information you'll find interesting.**

What is it? Libby typed.

I can't text it, Adam responded.

"Tell him we'll call him, or he can call us," Bernie told her sister.

Libby nodded. Adam's reply came back a minute later: **No. Don't trust the phones. We need to meet in person.**

A CATERED BAKE-OFF   243

Sean raised an eyebrow. Everyone looked at each other.

"Very mysterious," Sean said.

"I'll say," Bernie agreed. "Libby, ask him when he wants to get together."

Libby did. The answer came back quickly: **Tonight.**

Bernie shook her head. She was in her pj's and had no desire to change out of them. "Tell him tomorrow."

"Okay." And Libby typed: **How about tomorrow?**

TONIGHT came the all-caps response.

"Ask him why it has to be tonight," Bernie commanded.

It's time sensitive, Adam wrote back.

Sean frowned. He didn't like the way this was going. "May I?" he asked, gesturing to Libby's cell.

"Be my guest," Libby said, handing the phone to him.

What's the hurry? Why can't we meet tomorrow morning? Sean wrote.

The three of them huddled around Libby's cell phone waiting for an answer, while *Blue Bloods* continued playing in the background.

"Maybe you scared him off," Bernie said when Adam didn't answer.

"We'll see," Sean told her. Then he wrote: **What's the holdup? Changed your mind?**

The response was immediate: **I'm thinking.**

Well, think faster, Sean shot back, after which he handed Libby's phone back to her.

"Maybe you shouldn't have said that," Libby remarked when Adam didn't reply.

Sean snorted. "If that's the case, then what this character has to say can't be that important."

"I guess we'll find out," Libby said as she rested the phone on the table and took a bite of the crumble. It was perfect. Just the right balance of sweet and taste, juicy and crunchy. Only one thing could make it even better: home-made vanilla ice cream. She was about to offer to go downstairs and get some, but her phone dinged.

"That's Adam," Sean predicted.

"You're right, it is," Libby said after she glanced down at her cell. She read the message. "He says tonight, or not at all."

"Great," Bernie said. She sighed and turned to her dad. "What do you think? Should we meet him?"

"I don't like it," Sean replied.

"Tom Selleck would go," Bernie said, pointing to the television.

"But you're not Tom Selleck," Sean replied, stating the obvious.

"You would go," Bernie countered.

"That's true, I would, but I would have had backup keeping an eye on me, not to mention I'd be carrying a weapon," Sean told her. "Plus, I don't have to get up at five in the morning to start the cinnamon buns."

"This is true," Libby said. She'd been thinking the same thing.

"Libby, ask him where he wants to meet," Bernie instructed.

Libby asked, and the answer came back a few minutes later. "He says, at River Park, by the swings, in an hour."

"Now, I *really* don't like it," Sean commented.

"As opposed to *mostly* don't like it?" Bernie asked.

"I'm with Dad on this one," Libby said.

Sean rubbed his hands together and studied a moth fluttering on the other side of the window screen. "I mean, why there?" he asked.

"Because it's deserted," Libby answered.

Sean leaned forward in his chair. "Exactly. Ask him if he wants to meet at RJ's or come here, instead." Then he added, "Tell him we'll feed him some peach or blueberry crumble."

The answer came back a minute later: **Sorry. Thanks, but**

A CATERED BAKE-OFF 245

no thanks. No sweets for me. I'll wait ten minutes. If you're not there by then, I'm gone.

"I think he's bluffing," Sean said. He rubbed his hands together again.

"But what if he's not?" Bernie asked.

Sean shrugged. "There's always a work around."

"So, you don't think we should go?" Libby asked her dad.

"Obviously, he doesn't," Bernie replied. "But I don't think we have an option. We have to go."

Sean snorted. "That's ridiculous. Of course, you have a choice. No one is holding a gun to your head."

"I meant that we aren't making any progress with this case. Maybe Adam has the information we need to help us solve it."

"That's not true. You have something," Sean objected.

"Really? Like what?" Bernie asked.

"The explosions here and in Oxford, for openers," Sean replied.

Bernie objected. "I'm sorry, but I just don't see how they can be related. I mean, we're talking different places and different times. They're separated by what? Twenty years apart, more or less? Not to mention they're qualitatively different."

Sean ate a bite of peach crumble, then told his daughters how much he liked it, before replying, "I know it's a stretch—"

"That's an understatement."

Sean put up a hand. "Let me finish, Bernie."

She apologized. "Go on."

Sean cleared his throat and continued. "Well, for openers, the two things could be related if the explosions in Oxford weren't caused by the gas lines not being buried deep enough."

Libby put her fork down. "So, what you're saying is

246   *Isis Crawford*

that the same person who caused the explosions in Oxford rigged the oven here and wired up Dennis's house?"

Sean nodded his head. "I'm saying that's a possibility. Something to be looked at."

"An unlikely one," Libby told him. "I mean, if that's the case, why did the gas company say it was their fault if it wasn't? After all, companies don't usually take responsibility for something like that if they had nothing to do with it."

"That's also true," Sean allowed. "However, you don't actually know what the gas company said. Your information comes from a secondhand source," he pointed out. "Maybe your informant got the information wrong."

"Maybe," Bernie said. She thought of Claire. "Although, given the source, I tend to doubt it."

Sean nodded. "Okay. How about this, then. Maybe most of the explosions were caused by the pipes not being buried deep enough, but perhaps not *all* of them. Maybe someone got *inspired*." Sean bracketed the word *inspired* with his fingers. "You know how some people like to set fires, maybe someone liked to blow things up."

"Maybe, but then how would you explain the gap?" Bernie persisted. "Why do it, then stop, then start again?"

"Several reasons." Sean ate another piece of the crumble, pausing to savor the flavor before continuing to speak. "In my experience, people who like to set fires continue to do so. Perhaps that's true with people who like to set explosives as well."

"That doesn't explain the gap, Dad," Bernie pointed out.

"Well," Sean continued, "how about if whoever is doing this was hospitalized or incarcerated or living someplace else and moved back into the area. Or maybe they've been here all along, but they're going through a bad patch, and this is how he or she deals with it."

A CATERED BAKE-OFF 247

Bernie nodded. Her dad made sense.

Sean went on: "And you do know one other thing, right?"

"What's that?" Libby asked.

"You and your sister are the odd people out. Everyone else involved in the bake-off lived in Oxford at one point or another. Maybe something happened back there."

"Maybe," Bernie agreed as Sean looked at his daughter's face and sighed.

"You're still going, aren't you?" he asked.

Bernie nodded. "Adam is a sweetie, Dad. I can't image him hurting anyone. Ever."

Sean frowned. "That's what serial killers' nearest and dearest always say."

Bernie rolled her eyes.

"I'm serious," Sean said.

"I know you are," Bernie told him.

Sean sighed. "Why are you so stubborn?" he asked.

"Because I take after you," Bernie said.

Sean opened his mouth to answer, then closed it again. For once, he didn't have an answer. What his youngest daughter said was true. He glanced at his watch. A half hour before they had to leave.

Chapter 34

Bernie, Libby, and Sean spent the next twenty minutes watching *Blue Bloods,* finishing their crumbles, and discussing whether Pennsylvania peaches were better than the ones grown in Georgia. Then it was time to go.

"We'll be careful," Libby told Sean, looking to reassure her dad.

"I know *you* will," he replied in a pointed tone, looking at Libby.

Bernie put her hands on her hips. "What is that supposed to mean?" she demanded.

"What you think it means," Sean shot back.

"I'm not reckless," Bernie protested.

"I never said you were," Sean answered.

"No, you didn't say it, but you implied it," Bernie told her dad.

"If the shoe fits," Sean retorted. "I can come with you if you want," he offered a moment later, the idea just having occurred to him.

Bernie and Libby both shook their heads.

"We'll be fine, Dad," Libby reassured Sean.

"Honest," Bernie said. "Really. I'll be careful. I swear I will."

A CATERED BAKE-OFF   249

Sean grunted. "I guess that will have to do," he said as he glanced at the clock on the wall. "Aren't you going to change?" he asked.

Libby looked down at her pj's. They looked okay to her. "I wasn't planning to."

"Neither was I, Dad," Bernie said.

"You're seriously going like that," Sean said.

"Yes, seriously," Bernie said as Sean shook his head. "I mean, it's not as if we're wearing negligees."

"Now, there's a word I haven't heard in a long time," Sean remarked. "Do they even sell those things anymore?"

"Of course, they do," Bernie told him. "You should get around more. I can help you set up a dating profile if you like."

"I think I'd rather eat raw eel," he said. Sean shook his head. Sometimes he didn't understand this generation. He didn't understand them at all. It would never have occurred to him to walk out the door wearing his pajamas. Not unless the house was on fire. But this he did know. Their mother would have had a fit if they'd gone out like that. Of course, he reflected, she would have a fit about what they were going to do. Five minutes later, he wished them luck as they walked out the door.

It was still raining when Bernie and Libby left for the park, but at least the downpour had abated, turning to sprinkles.

"I don't get it," Bernie said as she and Libby headed toward the park. "Why all the big hoo-ha? Why couldn't Adam have met us?"

Libby smiled. *Hoo-ha* had been one of her mother's terms. "Hopefully, we'll find out. All I can say," she told her sister, "is that this better be worth it."

Bernie grunted her agreement. She would have much rather been home watching TV with her dad at the moment, than heading off to the park. She was sure her sister

250   *Isis Crawford*

would too, but here they were driving over there anyway. She decided to close her eyes for a moment. *I'll just rest them for a minute,* she told herself.

When she opened them again, they were at the park. "Wow," she said, stretching, "I didn't realize how tired I was." Bernie looked around. They were the only vehicle there. She glanced at her phone. They were right on time. "So, where is Adam?" she asked.

"Not here," Libby said.

"Obviously," Bernie replied.

"Maybe he ran into traffic?" Libby conjectured.

"At this time of night?" Bernie asked.

"Okay. He could have parked at the other lot and walked up," Libby suggested, although she couldn't think of any reason why he should have done that. It was a ten-minute walk on an unlit path that was in even worse shape than the one they were about to take.

"Hopefully, he'll be at the swings," Bernie replied.

"Hopefully," Libby said as she shut Mathilda's engine off and got out of the van. She was beginning to wish they'd listened to their dad. "This doesn't feel right," she told Bernie. "Do you think we should go back?"

"You can wait here if you want to," Bernie told her.

Libby thought about it. She was tempted, but then she decided she wouldn't be able to live with herself if anything happened to her sister, so she followed along. The sisters walked down the path that led to the playground. It was dark. The moon wasn't out and the streetlights that lined the path were old and emitted a pale, sickly yellow glow. The sisters walked carefully, since the path's macadam had long dissolved into dirt, gravel, and small pieces of tar that were easy to trip over.

"We should have brought a flashlight with us," Bernie observed.

"We shouldn't need to bring a flashlight. What I want to know is, when are they going to fix this?" Libby complained as she avoided a puddle of mud in the middle of the path. "Isn't this what we pay taxes for?"

Bernie didn't answer. She knew her sister's question was rhetorical. Everyone who came here had been asking the same question for years. Instead, she kept her eyes on the ground and concentrated on listening for the sound of someone walking in back or to the side of them, in case Adam was sneaking up on them. Although, why he would do that was beyond her. So far, though, all she had heard were the crickets and the roar of a motorcycle on the roadway that went along the river.

During the day, the path they were on was lined with benches filled with parents and their children. Tonight there was silence, the benches acting as sentinels as the sisters passed them, hurrying toward the playground. The path curved, so they couldn't see the playground in the distance, but when they got beyond the large clump of overgrown laurel bushes on the right-hand side, it became apparent that the playground was empty. No one was there. Bernie stopped.

"So, where is he?" she asked.

"I don't know," Libby said. "All I do know is that he better show up," she said, a grim tone to her voice.

"Text him," Bernie told her.

Libby did: **We're here. Where the hell are you?**

Around, the reply came a moment later. Libby watched the dots on the screen as Adam added: **There's a package for you over by the swings. Open it.**

"Great," Libby said as she showed the text to Bernie.

"I think I don't like this," Bernie said.

"I know I don't like this," Libby told her sister as Bernie held out her hand and asked Libby for her phone. Libby

252   Isis Crawford

handed it to her. "Dad was right. We shouldn't have come," Libby commented.

Bernie didn't answer. Instead, she texted Adam.

"What are you writing?" Libby asked.

Bernie handed Libby's phone back to her. "This," she said. **This better be good.**

Oh, it is. Trust me on this, Adam texted back a minute later.

"Yeah, right," Libby muttered as she showed Adam's latest text to Bernie.

The sisters were now at the playground. Bernie opened the gate. It creaked. They went in. At first, the sisters didn't see anything and then Bernie did. She pointed it out to Libby.

There was a gallon jug standing to the left of the swing set.

"Over there," she said.

The sisters walked toward it. It looked as if the jug was half full of some sort of liquid. Inside was a square of tin foil. There was a note attached to the top of the jug with a pink ribbon.

"What the hell?" Libby said as Bernie approached it. "Is that it? Is that why we're here?"

"I don't see anything else. Do you?"

Libby said she didn't, but suggested that maybe there was something behind the jug.

"Maybe," Bernie agreed, although as she walked toward it, she couldn't imagine what it could be. She was a little over three feet away when her phone rang. She looked at it and saw it was her dad. She didn't answer it. *I'll get it later,* she decided, letting the call go to voicemail.

Then her cell rang again. She looked. Her dad. Again. She let out an exasperated sigh. A couple of minutes later, she heard a ding.

A CATERED BAKE-OFF 253

A text was coming in: **Answer your goddamned phone**.

"Okay. Okay. Chill out," Bernie groused. She stopped and called Sean back, knowing her dad wouldn't stop calling until she did.

Sean answered immediately. "Thank God," he said.

"Come on, Dad. I'm not two," Bernie replied when she heard his voice.

"Where are you?" Sean demanded.

"Where I told you we were going to be," Bernie replied impatiently. "At the park, in the playground."

"And?" Sean prompted.

"Adam isn't here, but he left something for us," Bernie replied, switching her phone from one hand to another.

"What is it?" her dad asked. Bernie could detect the tension in his voice. "Describe the object to me."

"Dad."

"Just do it."

Bernie sighed again and did as her father had requested. "It looks like a gallon jug with some sort of liquid in it and what looks like a piece of tin foil," Bernie answered. "Very weird. The label on it says white vinegar. I'm going to get closer and get a better look."

"No, don't do that," her father ordered. "Stay away and whatever you do, don't touch that jug," he instructed.

"Dad," Bernie cried. "You're being ridiculous. This isn't a bomb—"

Sean interrupted her. "Bernie, I want you to listen to me very carefully."

Bernie stopped talking. She recognized her dad's tone of voice. It was the tone he used when something bad was about to happen. She took a deep breath and let it out. "Okay, Dad. I'm listening. What's going on?"

"Adam Borat is dead."

"What?" Bernie asked. Her voice came out in a squeak.

254   *Isis Crawford*

"Clyde just called to tell me."

"Then who was texting Libby?" Bernie wanted to know.

"I have no idea," Sean replied. "What I do know is that in no circumstances are you to touch that jug."

"But—"

Sean interrupted again. "No *but*. I know this sounds silly, but there's a good chance that you have Drano, water, and tin foil in that jug."

"So?" Bernie said.

"So, if I'm right, touch it and the whole thing will explode. Even the slightest movement could set it off," Sean explained.

"Holy crap!" Bernie exclaimed.

"Exactly, Bernie," Sean responded. "I remember watching it happen to Al Hecht when I was on patrol. Second day on the job for him, too."

"Was he badly hurt, Dad?"

"You could say that. He was blinded. It got him right in the eyes."

"Oh my God," Bernie cried. She could feel a chill creeping up her spine.

Sean continued to speak. "I'm hanging up and calling Clyde now and asking him to alert the bomb squad. I'll tell him you and Libby will meet the team in the parking lot."

Bernie was still holding her phone when Libby tapped her on the shoulder. Bernie let out a shriek and jumped around. "Don't do that," she cried, putting her hand to her chest. "You almost gave me a heart attack."

"What's going on?"

"You're not going to believe this," Bernie said, and she told her sister what their dad had told her.

"See," Libby said. "I was right. I knew we shouldn't have come. I knew something was off."

"You didn't *know*—you *thought*. There's a difference," Bernie countered.

"I most certainly did know," Libby responded as she and her sister started walking back toward the parking lot. They were still arguing when they heard the police sirens in the distance.

Chapter 35

Ninety minutes later, Libby and Bernie were looking down at Adam Borat. He was lying on his side, curled up in a semi-fetal position next to the estate koi pond. He was wearing a pair of blue shorts and a white T-shirt, with a picture of a golden retriever on it, and Bernie reflected he looked eighteen under the glaring spotlights the police had set up around the crime scene. A trickle of white foam ran down from his mouth to his chin. Bernie noticed an empty wineglass lying near his outstretched hand. A few dregs of what looked like red wine coated the bottom of the glass.

"That's interesting," she said as she squatted down to get a better look. She wondered if Adam had been sharing a drink with someone. If so, who? Or had he been drinking alone. And where had the wine come from?

"What happened?" Libby asked Clyde as Bernie stood up. A moment later, the coroner's people started the process of collecting Adam's body.

"Best guess," Clyde replied. "Henry"—the coroner—"thinks Adam was poisoned. Someone put something in there." Clyde pointed to the wineglass, after which he gestured to the white foam on Adam's mouth and chin. "It's probably cyanide, but Henry thinks there's a chance it could be something else, too. We won't know until we get the tox screen back."

"And how long will that take?" Libby asked.

This time, Henry answered as he stripped off his gloves. "Considering the way things are going, between six to twelve weeks. Maybe even longer."

"You're kidding," Libby said.

Henry shook his head. "I wish I was. We are extremely short-staffed. We always have been, but now things have gotten worse. It's like everyone has disappeared."

Bernie sighed as she watched Adam being zipped into a body bag. She remembered last weekend when they'd all been cooking together. As she swatted at a mosquito that had landed on her shoulder, she wondered if Adam had an inkling about what was coming. "How long ago do you figure that he died?" Bernie asked Henry Field.

He was a short man, with a receding hairline, bushy eyebrows, ice-blue eyes, and an expression on his face that showed *I've seen it all*. He scratched his chin before replying. "I'd say three or four hours, but I'll know more when I get him back to my place." He nodded for his assistants to take the body away.

Bernie and Libby watched as the EMTs lifted Adam's body bag onto a stretcher and carried him toward the waiting ambulance. Then they noticed Sam and the goatherd standing behind the ambulance. They were talking to a policeman, who was writing down what they were saying.

"Are they giving their statements?" Libby asked Clyde.

Clyde nodded.

"Who found Adam?" Bernie wanted to know.

"Sam," Clyde responded. "He was going out for his last stroll around the estate before he went home for the night.

258   *Isis Crawford*

He told me that since the incidents began, he's been doing it every evening, to make sure things are in order."

"And the goatherd? What's his story?" Libby asked.

"He came on the scene at almost the same time as Sam did," Clyde responded. "Claimed he was looking for a lost goat."

"Did he find it?" Bernie inquired.

Clyde nodded. "Not it, her. She was eating the weeds around the pond."

"Any confirmation of Sam's and the goatherd's alibis?" Libby asked.

"We've just got their words for their movements," Clyde replied. "No one else was around. Except for the estate's owner. Not that he was much help."

"I take it he didn't see or hear anything?" Libby inquired.

Clyde shook his head. "He was asleep."

Libby thought back. "So Adam couldn't have been texting us."

"Not unless he was doing it from the great beyond," Clyde replied.

"And we don't know who was doing it," Libby said.

"Aside from the fact that it wasn't Adam's ghost, no, we do not." Clyde stifled a yawn. He'd been about to go to bed when the call had come in. "Adam's phone is missing, so my guess is that whoever has the phone is the person who was texting you. But I could be wrong. It has happened on rare occasions."

Bernie slapped at a mosquito. There were a lot of them near the pond. "Do we know where everybody who is participating in the bake-off was tonight?" Bernie asked.

Clyde shook his head. "We're working on it."

"Why was Adam here in the first place?" Libby wanted to know. "Was he supposed to be meeting with Sam?"

"Not according to Sam, he wasn't," Clyde responded.

A CATERED BAKE-OFF 259

"Sam told me he didn't know what the hell Adam was doing here. You were lucky," he said, changing the subject. "Very lucky. I know that jug didn't look like much, but the slightest motion—"

Bernie interrupted. "And everything would have gone *boom*. I know. Dad told us about what happened with the rookie back in the day."

"I was there," Clyde told her. "It was awful. Thank heavens your dad called you in time."

Bernie shuddered, remembering what had happened when the bomb squad robot had picked the jug up. The movement had caused a large explosion. Bernie shuddered again, thinking of what would have happened if the Drano had gotten in her eyes. "But why target us? I don't get it."

"Maybe you're getting too close to figuring out who killed Doug LaForte," Clyde suggested. It was the only explanation he could think of at the moment.

"I wish. We don't know anything," Bernie protested.

"Zero. Zip. Nada," Libby agreed.

"He gets it, Libby," Bernie told her sister.

"Yeah, but I'm betting our killer doesn't know that," Clyde replied as Bernie watched the fireflies dancing around her and smelled the faint river smell of the Hudson riding in on a gust of wind. A moment later, Clyde and Henry both excused themselves and went to talk to one of the policemen standing by his patrol car.

The moment the two men left, Sam came over and joined Bernie and Libby, while the goatherd headed back to his domicile.

"Are you guys okay?" he asked them.

"We are," Bernie answered for both her and her sister. "It looks like the bake-off participants are dwindling."

"That's one way to put it," Libby said. She turned to Sam. "Do you know why Adam was here?"

"I wish I did," Sam replied. "Like I told your buddy

260   *Isis Crawford*

Clyde, I haven't got a clue. We didn't have an appointment. I didn't see him around, and neither did the guard at the entrance. The way I figure it, Adam must have come over the wall." Sam rubbed his chin. "Had to have. Although, according to Clyde, they haven't located Adam's vehicle on the road."

"Maybe he walked here?" Libby suggested.

"From where he lives? Doubtful," Sam scoffed. Looking at Sam, Libby reflected that he seemed to have aged twenty years in the past two weeks.

"And the wine and the glass?" Libby asked. "It doesn't make sense that he brought them with him. Especially if he came on foot. I mean, who breaks in by climbing over a wall with a glass of wine in their hand?"

"Someone who likes to drink," Bernie suggested.

"Or maybe he got here and decided he was thirsty," Sam said.

"Most people carry bottled water for that eventuality," Bernie noted.

"Evidently, he wasn't one of them," Sam responded.

"Where do you think he got the wine from if he didn't bring it with him?" Libby asked.

"Maybe from the tent," Sam suggested. "We have wine stored in there."

"Let's check," Bernie suggested.

Sam nodded. "I was just going to. Why don't you guys come with me and take a gander?"

Bernie and Libby both nodded. They'd been hoping Sam would say that.

"The police didn't go through it?" Libby asked.

"They did, but you know what was in there and what everything is supposed to look like, they don't. Anyway, I want to go through all the supplies and make sure nothing has been tampered with. Just to be on the safe side."

"So I'm getting from what you just said that the bake-off is still on," Bernie stated. She'd been positive the show would be canceled.

"That would be a yes, if everyone else still wants to, of course," Sam answered. "Do you?"

"Definitely," Bernie said. She'd answered without thinking. She was damned if she was going to let someone scare her off.

"Absolutely," Libby agreed. She felt the same way as her sister. "We should dedicate the next episode to Adam."

"Good idea," Sam said.

Libby nodded. By now, the three of them were at the tent. It sat there silently, waiting for the baking to begin. "It makes no sense," Libby began, getting back to what had happened earlier in the evening. "Why leave that jug?" she observed. "It wouldn't have killed us."

"No, it wouldn't have, but it would have scarred me or you up pretty badly," Bernie replied as she lifted the tent flap and walked inside. Everything seemed the way they'd left it.

"Three days until the weekend," Libby noted as she followed Bernie in.

Sam brought up the rear. "What else could go wrong?"

"Don't say that," Bernie cautioned as she went over and turned on the nearest stove's burner. It worked. Then she turned on the other three. Those were fine, too. "Well, here goes nothing," she said as she said a short prayer to the cooking gods and put her hand on the oven dial. Libby and Sam instinctively backed away when Bernie turned the knob. There was no explosion. "Thank heavens," she said. "One oven down, and three more to go."

Sam, Libby, and Bernie spent the next ninety minutes testing all the ovens, inspecting the refrigerators, the mixers, and blenders. Then they started on the supply closet. There were four bottles of wine there, two red and two white, all of which were still sealed.

"So Adam didn't get the wine from here," Bernie commented as she finished inspecting them. "Plus, there are no wineglasses."

Next they went through all the stored staples. They made sure that all the bags of sugar, flour, the boxes of salt, and jars of herbs were sealed, as were the rest of the miscellaneous boxes, bags, and cans that had been laid in. Bernie was just about to suggest that they take everything with them, and then put them in a securer location, when Sam got a phone call. Turns out, it was from a security firm.

"One of my cousin's friends runs it," he explained after he'd hung up. Five minutes later, a Jeep pulled up with the logo FRED'S SECURITY written across the sides. "Clyde's suggestion," Sam explained as two geared-up guys exited their vehicle. "Extra, extra security. They'll be guarding the place until we go live on Saturday," Sam explained as one of the guys gave Sam a half salute before he and his partner walked toward the tent. "It's probably overkill, but given the circumstances." And his voice trailed off.

"They look serious," Bernie observed.

"That's the idea," Sam responded. He frowned and sighed. "I just wish I'd thought of it sooner even if it is costing me a bloody fortune. Maybe if I had, this wouldn't have happened."

"No one could have foreseen something like this happening," Libby told him as she watched the two guys take up their positions. One stayed outside the tent, while the other one went inside.

"They'll change shifts with another team every twelve hours," Sam informed Libby and Bernie. Then he turned and headed toward his office. The sisters followed, even though Sam hadn't invited them along.

Chapter 36

Libby watched the clouds drifting over the slim crescent of the moon hanging in the sky.

It was a dark night and the fairy lights on the paths gave off a pale diffused light. Bernie, Libby, and Sam walked slowly, sidestepping low-hanging tree branches, as they smelled the honeysuckle, listened to the frogs croaking in the brook, and discussed what had just happened.

"I liked Adam," Sam reflected.

"He seemed like a good guy," Libby said. "Not that I really knew him that well," she added, "but he was always nice when I ran into him at the farmers market."

"He made the best doughnuts at the home fair," Bernie recalled.

"They were good," Sam echoed, "especially the ones filled with apricot jam."

"They weren't good, they were great. So were the ones with raspberry jam, for that matter," Libby said as a mosquito buzzed around her head. Then she changed the subject. "I wonder what's going to happen to his pub?"

"I assume it's going to close," Bernie said as the trio continued along the path they were on.

"That's a shame," Sam observed. "I liked the place."

When they reached the main house, Bernie, who was in front, made a left, walked another ten yards or so, and turned the corner. The others followed.

"Oh! Oh," Bernie said, stopping suddenly.

"What's the matter?" Libby asked, bumping into her.

"That," Bernie said, pointing.

Libby looked. At first, she didn't see anything and then she did. The door to the office was slightly ajar.

"Oh, no," Sam cried. He was bringing up the rear, and was the last to see what was in front of him.

Bernie, Libby, and Sam glanced at each other.

"This is not turning out to be a good evening," Libby observed.

"Maybe it isn't what we think it is," Bernie replied as she turned to Sam and asked him the obvious question.

"No, I locked it," Sam answered. "I'm sure I did."

"How *sure* is *sure*?" Libby inquired.

"Pretty sure," Sam responded. He swatted a moth away. "Although," he belatedly added, "sometimes the lock doesn't catch." He bit the inside of his lip as he tried to remember whether he'd shut the door all the way and heard the telltale click. "I think I double-checked."

"But you're not positive?" Bernie asked.

Sam thought some more. Then he shook his head. "Well, not one hundred percent positive. Maybe like eighty-five percent."

"Okay, then," Bernie said, and she took out her phone and turned on the flashlight. "Let's see what's going on." She walked over to the door and played the light over the lock and the doorframe. When she was done, she straightened up and, with a nod of her head, indicated the marks on the wood next to the plate. "It looks as if someone jimmied the lock," she announced.

"Are you sure?" Sam asked.

Bernie nodded. "See those?" she asked Sam and Libby as she pointed to the marks on the wood.

"Yes," Sam said.

"It looks as if someone used a screwdriver," Bernie told him.

Sam came over and leaned in to get a better look. "At least I locked the damn thing," he commented. "These days, with everything that's happening, I don't know whether I'm coming or going—metaphorically speaking."

"I know how you feel," Bernie responded. She stifled a yawn and asked another question. "So, is this door the only access to the office, or can you access it from the house's inside as well?"

"This is the only access," Sam told her. "They added the office"—he paused to think—"maybe two years ago. They wanted it separate from the rest of the house. Easier to keep track of visitors that way, I guess."

"We need to report this to the police," Libby said.

Sam sighed. "Indeed, we do." He shook his head. "This is just the icing on the cake, although now that I think about it, that metaphor makes no sense whatsoever."

Libby, Bernie, and Sam looked at each other again.

"It just gets better and better, doesn't it," Libby observed.

"I don't know what's in the office that anyone would possibly want," Sam said, continuing to speak. "I guess I should take a look and see what's missing." He shook his head and sighed again. Then he stepped across the threshold. Libby and Bernie followed.

"What a mess," Sam declared as he took a look around.

"I take it that this isn't your mess?" Bernie asked Sam.

"Hardly," Sam replied indignantly.

"Just checking," Bernie said.

266   *Isis Crawford*

With the light on, it was even more apparent that some-one had been looking for something. The file cabinet and desk drawers had been opened. Papers were strewn all over the Oriental rug, the cushions were off the sofa, and whoever had done this had taken half of the books off their shelves and stacked them on the floor.

"That's weird," Libby said, pointing to the piles.

"Whoever did this was probably interrupted," Bernie suggested.

Sam put his hands on top of his head and groaned as he thought about what it was going to take to clean the mess up. "What the hell were they looking for?" he demanded.

"Funny thing," Libby replied. "That's what I was going to ask you."

"I have absolutely no friggin' idea," Sam responded. "Not unless they want to see my rejected movie scripts."

Bernie noticed that his jaw muscles were working, and his hands were clenched into fists.

"But I can tell you this. If I ever catch the SOB who did this, he's a dead man. That I can promise you," Sam concluded.

Bernie grunted. She was focusing her attention on the bar next to the bookshelf. "That's quite a selection of liquor you've got there," she observed. All the bottles were high-end stuff.

Sam smiled. "I'm not a heavy drinker, so when I do drink, I like to drink the best."

"Me too," Bernie said, picking up a bottle of fifteen-year-old Macallan Scotch whisky. She was thinking she could use a shot of this right about now, and then she noticed the top of a bottle of Montrachet. She put the scotch down and picked up the wine. "Did you open this?" she asked Sam, showing him the bottle.

"I had a glass a couple of days ago," Sam replied. "Why?"

"Who else uses this office?" Libby asked.

"People come and go all the time," Sam replied. "You know that. Cast. Crew. It's supposed to be mine for the duration of the show. Why are you asking?" His eyes widened as an idea occurred to him. "Do you think that's the wine Adam was drinking? Do you think someone poisoned the bottle?"

"Could be," Bernie said, remembering what Clyde had said.

"Damn!" Sam cried. "I was looking forward to killing the bottle with Nell, too. She really wanted to taste it."

"I think you guys are going to have to wait on that," Libby said.

"I think you're right," Sam said. "Too bad whoever did this couldn't have picked a cheaper bottle of wine."

"Would that have made it better?" Libby asked.

"Well, it wouldn't have made it worse," Sam noted. He stared at the bottle for a moment while the implications of what he'd just said sank in. "So Adam probably wasn't the intended target—"

"No, you were," Bernie said, interrupting.

Sam grimaced. "I know I piss people off, but never like this. And I thought producing this show would be easy." Sam laughed bitterly. "Imagine that." He sat down with a thud on the only upright chair in the room.

"Who have you pissed off?" Libby asked.

Sam rubbed his chin. "Believe me, I would tell you if I knew."

"That is the question, isn't it?" Bernie said as Libby chimed in with another observation.

"Maybe there wasn't anything in the Montrachet," she said. "Maybe Adam got the wine that poisoned him somewhere else. Maybe his killer forced it down his throat."

"That seems unlikely!" Sam exclaimed. He rubbed his

268   *Isis Crawford*

eyes with the heels of his hands. "I bet the tox lab will find something in the wine."

"It wouldn't surprise me," Bernie said softly.

Sam took his hands away from his eyes and stood up. "So Adam was collateral damage." Sam pointed to the wine. "And that was meant for me."

"We don't know that for sure," Libby told him.

"Yeah, I think we do," Bernie said. "If the wine was meant for Adam, that means that someone would have had to have known he was planning on coming in here."

"And that he would sample the Montrachet," Libby added.

"All the other bottles of wine are sealed," Bernie noted.

Libby bit at her thumbnail. "Do we still think Adam broke into the office? Someone else could have come and gone. Maybe they lured him here, killed him, stole his phone, and texted us."

"Anyone could have come and gone," Bernie said. "Getting over the wall is pretty easy."

"If not Adam, then who?" Libby asked.

Sam shook his head. "Ya got me. And what did they want?"

"Maybe something in your records?" Libby asked.

"My records," Sam echoed. He snorted. "I don't know why anyone, aside from my accountant, would possibly be interested in them. They're just records for the show. Tax stuff. Workman's comp."

"I don't know, either," Bernie allowed as she bent down and studied the framed pictures someone had swept onto the floor. Presumably, they'd been on the desk.

Bernie, Libby, and Sam spent the next half hour picking everything up and checking to see what, if anything, was missing. When they'd finished, Bernie called Clyde and told him about what they'd found. Then they left.

"You're awfully quiet," Libby said to Bernie on the way home.

"I was just thinking," Bernie said.

"Always a bad sign," Libby observed.

Bernie frowned. "Ha. Ha. Very funny. No. I think we goofed. We need to revisit Sam's office."

"Why?"

"Because I just realized something," Bernie replied as she started making an illegal U-turn on Grey Street.

"Are you trying to get us killed?" Libby screeched as the car coming toward them slammed on its brakes.

"No. Other people are trying to do that. I'm trying to get us back to the estate," Bernie told her.

"Great," Libby said, folding her arms over her chest and leaning back in her seat. Returning there was the last thing she wanted to do. Another five minutes and they would have been home.

Chapter 37

When Libby and Bernie arrived at their destination, the police had packed up and were leaving. "Good," Bernie said as she watched the coroner's van and two police cars drive by them on Allen Street. Then she counted a third and a fourth one bringing up the rear. "The less we have to deal with them, the better," she noted.

Unfortunately, there was an unmarked police car sitting by the estate's entrance and its officers waved the sisters away when they tried to drive in.

"Can we go home now?" Libby asked Bernie. "I have a feeling those guys," she said, referring to the cops, "are planning on staying for a while."

"Someone just tried to kill us," Bernie said as she backed up.

"Believe me, I'm aware," Libby said.

"Don't you want to find out who?"

"Obviously," Libby replied.

"Because I think we might have missed something in there," Bernie said, pointing in the direction of the office.

"Like what?" Libby demanded.

"If I knew that, we wouldn't have to go back, would we?" Bernie asked her.

A CATERED BAKE-OFF 271

Libby sighed. Much as she hated to admit it, her sister was correct. "I guess we go over the wall, then."

Bernie nodded and made a left. "That's what I was thinking. We can park on Valesco Road and hop the wall from there," Bernie told her.

"We should be in bed," Libby noted.

"Agreed," Bernie said.

"All I can say is, this better be worth it," Libby declared while her sister parked the van behind a large black walnut tree and shut off Mathilda's motor. Then she and Libby got out of Mathilda, walked over to the wall, and climbed over it. It proved easy to scale, indeed.

"I bet this is the way Adam came in," Libby postulated as she bent down and retied her sneaker.

"I bet you're right," Bernie agreed, since, according to Clyde, Adam hadn't signed in with the guard at the front gate.

"In any case, someone's been here," Libby said as she pointed to a couple of fresh cigarette butts nestled in the laurel bush.

"Someone other than Adam," Bernie observed. "Because I don't recall Adam smoking, do you, Libby?"

"Not really," Libby allowed. "Who else in the group smokes?"

Bernie thought for a minute. "No one. Or at least no one that I know of."

"Maybe someone in the group is a closet smoker," Libby suggested.

"Or maybe one of the camera crew or one of the estate employees came out here for a smoke break. Besides, Adam could have climbed over the wall in any number of locations," Bernie said. The more she thought about it, the more she was having doubts about her original thesis.

"True, but if he did come over, this would be the place

to do it," Libby pointed out. "We're fairly near the office here. It isn't a long walk to it, so he probably climbed over the wall somewhere in this general area."

"But if he had, then his car would be parked somewhere around here," Bernie noted. They'd driven around the perimeter of the estate on their way there and hadn't seen it. "He didn't get here by foot, that's for sure," Bernie said.

"Someone could have dropped him off," Libby suggested. Then another idea occurred to her. "Or he could have left his car in the lot behind the Regal movie theater. It's not that far away."

"True," Bernie conceded. Then she closed her eyes and she tried to visualize the scene. "More to the point, why did he come here in the first place?" she asked when she opened her eyes again.

"To look for something?" Bernie suggested.

"Or to meet someone?" Libby guessed.

"Why here?" Bernie asked. "There are lots of other places to go."

"I don't know," Libby allowed. "Maybe he had a thing going on with the goatherd."

Bernie laughed.

"It's possible," Libby said.

"Anything is possible," Bernie responded.

"True," Libby said. She gnawed on her lower lip. "But the probability is that he went straight to the office and jimmied the lock."

"Then he decided to pour himself a glass of wine after sneaking onto the grounds, breaking into the office, and searching it. Then when he's done, he takes a leisurely stroll through the grounds, sipping his wine and texting us," Bernie hypothesized.

"Well, when you put it that way . . ." Libby said.

". . . it doesn't sound very plausible," Bernie stated, finishing her sister's sentence for her.

"I guess it doesn't," Libby said. "What are you saying exactly?"

"That on reflection, I think Adam's murder was probably staged," Bernie replied. "I think it happened somewhere else."

"Then what about Clyde's theory that Adam was poisoned?" Libby asked.

"One thing doesn't necessarily preclude the other," Bernie said as she started walking toward the office. Libby followed. "What we do know," Bernie continued, "is that someone stole Adam's phone and tried to lure us out." She stopped and took a breath. "I'm guessing that whoever has Adam's phone is the person who broke into Sam's office."

"Hopefully, they'll have left fingerprints," Libby said.

"That would be nice, but I wouldn't count on it, if I were you," Bernie told her sister.

"I'm not, but one can always hope," Libby replied.

"Yes, one can," Bernie replied, even though she wasn't big on the concept these days.

The grounds were quiet, except for a goat's occasional bleat. The police were gone, the guards were doing their guarding around the tent, and Sam had left for home. The only things moving at this time of night were the leaves, rustling in the slight breeze that had sprung up, and the moths that were flitting around in the darkness. Bernie stopped when she got to the office door. The door was festooned with crime scene tape. She reached out and turned the doorknob, even though she expected the police had locked it. And she was correct. They had.

"Now what?" Libby asked.

Bernie went over and tried the nearest window. It opened. She gestured to it and said, "Do you want to go first or should I?"

274   *Isis Crawford*

"How am I supposed to get in?" Libby demanded. "The window is too high."

"Or your legs are too short," Bernie told her as she spotted a plastic bucket a short distance away.

"They are not," Libby protested as Bernie went over, got the bucket, flipped it over, and put it just below the window.

"There," Bernie said. "Now you're all set."

"Terrific," Libby said. "You first."

"Not a problem," Bernie answered, clambering in.

Libby followed a moment later, scraping her leg in the process. She looked around while she rubbed her ankle. The placed looked the same, except for the residue of black fingerprint dust scattered over things.

"I would hate to be the one cleaning this stuff up," Libby noted.

"Me too," Bernie replied as she started laying out the five pictures she'd picked up, and put back on the desk, when they were there a little while ago. When she was finished, she turned to Libby and asked her what she saw.

"Kids playing ball," Libby replied.

"Look closer," Bernie said.

Libby did. The first picture showed three kids throwing a basketball around in someone's backyard; the second photo showed a grinning kid, with a gap in his front teeth, holding up a baseball in one hand and a bat in the other; the third picture showed ten boys in front of a dugout; the last photo showed a team posing with a trophy.

Libby straightened up and turned to her sister. "I don't get it. What am I looking for?" Bernie tapped the fourth picture with one of her fingernails. "Does anyone here look familiar?"

Libby concentrated. She didn't see anything. And then she did. "Is that who I think it is?" she asked her sister.

Bernie smiled. "Yes."

Libby inspected the picture again. "I'll tell you one thing. Sam has certainly changed since he was a teen."

"Yeah. He had a lot more hair," Bernie said.

"He was really chubby," Libby noted as she studied the photo. It looked as if it had been professionally done. All the kids were sitting on the bleachers in the first and second row. Sam was sitting in the center of the group. It was spring and everyone looked happy. Sam was holding up a trophy. Libby tried to read the writing on it, but she couldn't. It was too indistinct. She turned to Bernie. "Okay. So Sam played baseball, so what?"

Bernie pointed to the hats all the boys were wearing. It had a small picture of a flying bird. Underneath the picture was the word *soar.*

"What about them?" Libby asked.

"We saw this logo in Oxford," Bernie remarked.

"You're right. We did. In the library," Libby said, remembering. "It was the high school logo."

"Ergo, Sam went to high school in Oxford," Bernie said.

"So it would seem," Libby said as she stifled a sneeze. For some reason, her allergies were getting to her this season.

"Let's make sure, shall we," Bernie said, and she reached for her phone and called Sam. When he answered, she put him on speakerphone. "Quick question: Is that you in the picture with the trophy that's in your office?" she asked, getting directly to the point.

Sam laughed. "As a matter of fact, it is. Are you back in the office?"

Bernie lied and told him they weren't—that she'd just made the connection.

"You've certainly changed a lot," Libby noted.

276   *Isis Crawford*

"Well," Sam replied, "I guess it's safe to say I'm not that chubby kid anymore."

"I didn't know you lived in Oxford," Libby observed.

"For a little while," Sam replied. "My family wasn't there for long," he explained "For maybe four months. If that. Then we came back for about three months when I was a senior."

"How come so short?" Bernie asked.

Sam cleared his throat. "The place where my dad had been working hired him back. We moved around a lot in those days. Baseball was my passion. I always wanted to pitch in the majors, but my speedball never clocked faster than seventy-five."

"What did he do?" Libby asked.

Sam didn't answer immediately. After a minute or so had gone by, he said, "A little of this and a little of that. My dad had a problem with alcohol."

"Sorry," Libby said,

"Don't be," Sam told her. "It wasn't your fault."

"So you know the other people in the bake-off," Bernie observed.

"Obviously," Sam responded.

"Sorry. I misspoke," Bernie said. "I meant, you knew them when you were in Oxford, didn't you?"

There was another moment of silence on the line. Then Sam said, "I knew who they were, if that's what you mean."

"But you lived in the town," Libby emphasized.

"Actually," Sam said, "we lived outside the town on a farm. I wasn't in school a lot back then. I spent a lot of time hanging out in the woods, getting stoned and drunk." He sighed. "Let's just say, I didn't put my time to good use back then. It's a period I would rather forget about, and now, if you don't mind, I'm going to say good night. It's late and I need to get to bed. It has been, as you know, a very long and stressful day, and I have to get up early to-morrow morning." Then Sam hung up.

Bernie and Libby looked at each other.

"He's the last one," Bernie observed.

"Do you think he's involved?" Libby inquired.

"That he killed Adam? That he could be behind every-thing that's going on?" Bernie mused.

"Yes!" Libby said. "On the one hand, he could have jimmied the door, to make it look like a break-in; he could have doctored the wine; he might have paid Dennis to write those notes; and he could have fooled around with the espresso machine. But on the other hand . . ."

"What's his motive?" Bernie inquired. "After all, he ini-tiated the show. He's going to lose money if it doesn't air."

Libby nodded. What Bernie said was correct. They had the *when* and the *where*, but not the *who* or the *why*.

Chapter 38

It was a quarter to eight the next morning when Ellen Green walked into A Little Taste of Heaven and headed for the counter. The morning commuter rush was ending and there were just a handful of moms sitting around and chatting as they sipped their second cups of coffee and ate their pastries after dropping off their kids at day camp.

"Smells nice in here," Ellen commented to Bernie and Libby as she breathed in the odors of butter and cinnamon and coffee. Bernie was just about to thank her, when Ellen added, "I heard about Adam. Lori and Nell both called me at seven. They saw it on the national news."

"So did I," Bernie said. Adam's death had been the lead story on the local morning news as well. She shook her head. "Talk about not seeing something coming," she remarked, straightening up. Bernie had been bent over, in the middle of sliding a tray of strawberry corn muffins into the display case, when Ellen had walked in.

"I don't think anyone did," Ellen said as she retied the light blue, wraparound dress she was wearing.

"Except for the person that killed him," Libby couldn't help adding.

A CATERED BAKE-OFF 279

"It has to be the same person who has been doing all the other stuff, right?" Ellen asked her.

Bernie answered for her sister. "How can it not be," she replied, hitching up the strap of her red-checkered sundress.

"I don't know what to think anymore," Ellen said. She leaned forward slightly. "I'll tell you what I don't believe," she confided to Libby and Bernie. "I don't believe we're still going on with the show in three days."

"To be honest," Libby said, "I can't believe it, either. If you had asked me, I would have sworn Sam would have canceled."

"I think his sponsor threatened to sue him if he did," Bernie said as she wiped off her hands on her apron. "At least that's what Sam told me," Bernie continued. She and Libby had spoken to him first thing that morning.

Ellen brushed her bangs away from her forehead with the tips of her fingers. "Adam used to work for Red Fern before he opened the pub. In fact, he was the one who put Sam in touch with Jeff."

"Talk about how no good deed goes unpunished," Libby said.

Ellen shook her head. "I don't understand."

"I think what my sister means is that if it weren't for the show, none of this would have happened and everyone would still be alive," Bernie explained.

"I hadn't thought of it like that," Ellen said.

"The show seems to have been the catalyst," Bernie told her.

"I suppose you're right," Ellen said, her eyes turning to the display case.

Bernie pointed to the muffins she'd just placed in the case. "Would you like to try one? They just came out of the oven."

280 *Isis Crawford*

"Is this a bribe?" Ellen asked.

Bernie grinned. "It absolutely is," Bernie told her.

Ellen laughed. "Then I accept," she said.

"Would you like some coffee with that?" Libby asked. "I've just brewed a fresh pot."

Ellen nodded. "That would be brilliant." She sighed. "You know, if this keeps up, I don't know if anyone is going to be left in the contest to judge."

"Sam was thinking about us all competing separately," Bernie said as she handed Ellen her muffin and coffee.

"Interesting." Ellen thought for another moment before she replied, "I can see why Sam said that, although I'm not sure what that would mean for the specials. Mike would be on his own then. He'd have no one to partner up with, although maybe that's the way he wants it. He might be happier," Ellen noted. She took a bite of the muffin and sighed in pleasure. "Delicious," she said, changing the subject.

Libby smiled and thanked her.

"The fresh strawberries aren't too mushy, are they?" Bernie asked. She'd used two types—dried and fresh in the recipe.

"Not at all," Ellen replied. "They lend a nice soft note to the muffin." She took a sip of coffee and another taste of the muffin. "These are definitely keepers. They're pretty and they taste good." She took another bite. "And I love the pink sugar sprinkled on top. You should serve these on Valentine's Day."

"Good idea," Libby said, signaling to Amber to take care of the customer in front of the display case, while she moved out onto the floor. "Why did you say what you just did about Mike?" she asked Ellen.

"That he would be happier without Adam?" Ellen asked.

"Yes," Bernie replied.

A CATERED BAKE-OFF 281

Ellen shifted her weight from her right to her left foot. "Actually, that's what I came to talk to you about." She took another bite of her muffin before continuing. "It's probably nothing, but I was driving by Mike's place the other day and he and Adam were outside arguing. I couldn't hear what they were saying, but they both looked pretty upset."

"How upset?" Bernie asked.

"Upset enough that Mike pushed Adam, and Adam pushed back. Then Mike turned and went back in his place, and Adam got in his car and drove away."

"That's pretty upset," Libby conceded.

"But not upset enough to kill someone," Ellen replied.

"People have killed for a lot less," Bernie pointed out. That's what her father had taught her.

"Well, like I just said, I'm probably making a big deal about nothing. On the other hand . . ." Ellen stopped talking. Her voice trailed off.

"You don't want it on your conscience if their argument turns out to have been something?" Bernie suggested.

Ellen smiled in acknowledgment. "I really don't. But if it turns out to be nothing, I don't want to get Mike in trouble with the police, either."

"I understand," Bernie said.

"I figured you would," Ellen replied. "That's why I came to you." She paused for a moment, gave a wistful sigh, and said, "I liked . . . those guys. Both of them. They were really funny together . . . when they weren't at each other's throats."

"They were," Libby agreed. "Listen," she continued, "as long as you're here, let me ask you a question. Did you know Sam before he picked you for the show?"

"I didn't know him as a friend or acquaintance, if that's what you mean, but I've seen him around," Ellen replied.

282   *Isis Crawford*

Bernie clarified. "I think what my sister meant is, did you know him when he lived in Oxford for a while?"

Ellen smiled. "That was a long time ago, but yes, I did," she replied. "I stayed with my aunt while my parents went on a field trip to Ghana. They were anthropologists," Ellen explained, seeing the puzzled looks on Bernie's and Libby's faces.

"So, were you friendly with Sam?" Libby asked. "For that matter, were you friendly with everyone else on the show, since they all lived there?"

Ellen shook her head. "I knew who they were, but that was about it. My aunt homeschooled me. Me and my sister didn't get out much. We had school and then my aunt had us doing chores around the farm. By the time four o'clock rolled around, I was too tired to move. Besides, that was the only time my aunt let us watch TV. She was really strict. Actually, she told me she didn't want me playing with the other kids, that they'd be a bad influence."

"You must have been glad to see your parents," Bernie remarked.

Ellen laughed. "Now, there's an understatement if ever there was one. Oxford was a bad-news place—at least according to my aunt."

Libby raised an eyebrow. "How so?" she inquired.

"You know how sometimes there are places where bad things happen?" Ellen explained. "Well, Oxford was one of them. That's what my aunt said anyway. Lots of freak accidents. I mean, my aunt fell down this boarded-up well that she didn't even see."

"Was she okay?" Bernie asked.

Ellen grimaced. "Fortunately, someone heard her. Otherwise, she would have died, but she broke both her arms. I don't think she was right after that. Claimed that she heard the voice of Saint Joan telling her to be strong."

"Is she still in Oxford?" Libby asked.

Ellen shook her head. "She died a couple of years ago in a nursing home in Miami."

Bernie decided it was time to change the subject. "So let me get this straight. You're saying you weren't friends with any of the contestants when you were in Oxford?"

"Not really," Ellen told her. "I mean, I knew who everyone was. Sometimes we'd see each other when my aunt took us to the general store once a week to get our groceries, or I'd see them in the library, but I really didn't hang out with them. I mean, most of the kids there were farm kids. They went to school and then went home and did chores. They didn't have a lot of free time, and speaking of which, neither do I. Good luck," Ellen added. "I have a feeling we're going to need it."

"So do I," Libby remarked as she watched Ellen walking out the shop door at the same time that their dad was walking in.

"I just found out something you might be interested in," Sean told his daughters.

Libby handed him a strawberry corn muffin as she asked him what they'd be interested in.

He took a bite of the muffin first. "This is delicious," Sean told her. "This is why I love summer. The produce." Then he took another bite.

"So, what did you find out?" Bernie prodded after her dad took a third bite.

"Sorry about that," Sean said, and he told them what he'd come to say.

Chapter 39

It took Libby and Bernie a little over two hours to finish up their chores at A Little Taste of Heaven, after which they drove to Mike's place, but he wasn't there. According to his brother Leon, he'd gone to the estate to talk to Sam.

"I think he wants to quit the contest," Leon told the sisters. "I mean, who can blame him?"

"Not me, that's for sure," Bernie replied. "I don't suppose you happen to know what Adam and Mike were fighting about?" she asked.

"They had a fight?" Leon asked, looking surprised. "When?"

"A couple of days before Adam died. At least that's what we were told," Bernie replied.

"If they did, it's news to me," Leon said. He wiped the sweat off his brow. He'd been loading his brother's truck and it was a hot day, with the temperature supposed to climb into the nineties. "I mean, I know they had their differences . . ."

"About what?" Libby asked.

"Baking stuff." Leon shrugged. "I think they were arguing about what kind of shortening to use in pastry. Something about butter or lard. Or maybe it was Crisco." He frowned. "The truth is, I don't really know. Cooking. Baking. They're not my thing. I don't know a pie plate from a spring blade—"

"Do you mean springform?" Libby asked.

Leon laughed. "Yeah," he said. "That's the word I was looking for. I mean, it's weird. My brother always liked baking from the time he was a little kid. He even wanted to make his own birthday cakes. Two of them were these exploding volcano cakes. He even made one for me." He gave a wry smile. "They were great, even if one of them spewed cake all over the walls." He laughed. "You should have seen my mother's face. Then when he was older, he used to bake cookies and bring them to school. I thought the guys would give him a beatdown, because the cookie thing was something that the girls did, but they didn't. They liked him." "Was this in Oxford, by any chance?" Bernie asked, hazarding a guess.

"Sure was," Leon said.

"So, Mike knows everyone in the contest? He went to school with them?" Bernie asked.

"For a little while," Leon replied, "and then my mom and dad moved when we were sophomores."

"In high school?" Bernie inquired.

Leon nodded.

"How come?" Bernie wanted to know.

Leon shrugged. "I don't know. They just said something about it not being the best place for us, but they never told us why it wasn't."

"Ellen Green said Oxford was a strange place," Libby observed.

"Maybe it was," Leon said after a moment of thought. "I thought it was okay, but what did I know? I'm just the kid brother. No one ever told me anything."

286   *Isis Crawford*

Bernie laughed. "I know the feeling."

Mike's brother smiled. "I remember thinking that maybe Mike did something he wasn't supposed to do."

"Why do you say that?" Bernie asked him.

Leon shrugged. "I don't know." He thought for a moment. "Maybe it was because we left in such a hurry. My mom and dad were whispering a lot. You know, like something was going on. Or maybe because Mike looked really scared." Leon shrugged again. "Or maybe I was seeing things that weren't there. Maybe I just made the whole thing up. Who knows?" He looked at his watch. "Sorry, guys, but I gotta go. Otherwise, I'm going to be late with my cookie deliveries."

Bernie nodded. "Thanks for taking the time," she told him.

"Not a problem," Leon replied, and he jumped in his vehicle and took off.

Bernie and Libby watched him round the bend and head to his first delivery. Then they got into their van and made their way to the estate. They got there fifteen minutes later.

"We're here to see Mike," Bernie told the guard.

"Good for you," the guard told them, interrupting the conversation he was having on his phone.

"Not having a good day?" Bernie asked.

The guard grunted. "That's one way to put it." He looked at them, sighed, and told the person he'd been talking to that he'd call them back in a few.

"What's going on?" Libby asked. "More problems?"

"Yeah. You could say that," the guard said. "Damn goats got out again." He pointed to the bottom of his pants. "One of them ate the hem off these. I look like a bum."

Bernie started to laugh.

"It's not funny," the guard said. "I'm supposed to go on a date when I get off. I was planning on going straight from work."

"Sorry," Libby said, but she was laughing, too. She couldn't help herself.

"Your friend Mike wasn't too pleased with the goats, either," the guard remarked. "One of them ran across the road. He nearly hit him with his car."

"Is Mike with Sam now?" Libby wanted to know.

"I think he went to talk to Ed," the guard said.

Libby scrunched her eyebrows together. "Ed?"

"Yeah, Ed. The goatherd," the guard said. "I don't know why his dad lets him keep the damn things," he continued. "I mean, what's wrong with using a riding mower, for heaven's sake?"

"The goatherd's dad?" Libby repeated at a loss.

The guard nodded.

"Who's that?" Bernie said.

The guard gave her an incredulous look. "The guy who owns this place, of course."

"He's the goatherd's father?" Libby asked.

The guard snorted. "That's what I just said. You didn't know that?"

Both Libby and Bernie shook their heads.

"How do you know?" Libby asked the guard.

"Because my dad used to work here back in the day when the Valle family owned the estate. Things were different then," the guard went on. "Then things got nuts—that's what happens when you gamble—and they lost the estate. Eventually, it got bought out by someone else." The guard frowned. "Then that person died and his brother inherited."

"The one who's partially paralyzed and never comes out of his room?" Bernie asked.

The guard nodded. "Yeah. That one. Lots of comings and goings over the years, my dad said. Evidently, lots of fights over this." The guard waved in the direction of the house. "Lots of family drama. I guess, owning stuff will do that to you—not that that's my problem. I rent."

"Ours either," Bernie said.

"Of course," the guard continued, "I wouldn't want to be him." He nodded in the direction of the estate. "Tied to his oxygen machines. Can't walk. Can't talk, hardly at all. I mean, what's the point keeping this place running if he can't enjoy it?" The guard shuddered as he brushed away a bee that was buzzing around his head. He swiped it with his hand before tapping his fingers on the chair he was sitting on and changing the subject. "Now, do you guys want to see your friend the goatherd or not, because I have things to do."

"See him," Bernie replied.

The guard grunted, gave them directions, and waved them through. As Bernie and Libby drove away, they could hear him talking to someone on his phone. Five minutes later, they arrived at the goatherd's cottage.

Chapter 40

"It's pretty," Libby said as she studied the cottage. She was surprised. She didn't know what she'd expected, but this wasn't it. "It looks like something out of the English countryside."

Bernie nodded. It was true. It did. "It's the ivy," she said as she knocked on the bright blue oval-shaped door. No one answered. Bernie knocked again, and when no one replied this time, she peered in the mullioned windows. She didn't see any movement inside.

"Maybe the guard was wrong," Libby said. "Maybe Mike and Sam are somewhere else."

"Maybe," Bernie said as she tried the door handle. The knob twisted in her hand and the door swung open. Bernie called out Mike and Sam's names. There was no reply. The sisters looked at each other.

"I guess no one is here," Libby said.

Bernie raised her hand. "Not so fast," she said. "Methinks, I hear a noise." Bernie cupped her hand behind her ear and pretended to listen. "Don't you, Libby?"

"Not really, no."

"I'm going to check," Bernie said, stepping inside.

290   *Isis Crawford*

"What the hell," Libby told her as she joined her sister. "Sure. Why not?"

The two sisters paused for a moment and listened. The cottage was quiet. The only sounds they heard were the goats bleating.

"Maybe we missed them," Libby suggested. "Maybe they're up at the house. Or they could be with the goats." The goats were penned up near the tent.

"They could be anywhere around the estate," Bernie said as she took out her phone and called them. The calls went straight to voicemail. "So much for that," she said as she looked around.

The place was small, cozy, and exemplified the saying *There's a place for everything, and everything in its place.*

"Wow," Bernie said, taking in the chintz-covered sofa, leather chairs, Oriental rug, Chinese scroll, and the fireplace with the fan in front of it. "This is not what I would have expected." She went over and looked at the pictures hanging on the walls. All of them were Impressionistic landscapes. A few were pencil sketches, but most were pastels, watercolors, or oils. As Bernie studied them, she realized the pictures reminded her of . . . somewhere. She just couldn't put her finger on where that somewhere was. When she looked closer, she realized all the pictures had been signed by the goatherd. And then she realized where she'd seen the landscapes.

"Do you think they could be in trouble?" Libby asked her sister.

"Hopefully not," Bernie said as she left off studying the pictures and walked into the dining area. The dining-room table was covered with papers. Bernie went over and had a look. The first thing that caught her eye was a stack of mail on the table. Bernie picked up the letters and flyers and leafed through them. Probably 90 percent were addressed to the goatherd's father. The other 10 percent belonged to the goatherd. She put the mail down and turned her attention to the other items lying on the table.

A folder marked *Longely Bake-Off* was sitting on the table's edge.

"Let's see what's in here," she said, opening the folder and reading the letter on top. It was from the goatherd to Sam proposing the idea for *The Longely Bake-Off* and telling him that if he was interested, he had a possible couple of sponsors for the project, and that they would be happy to host it at the estate, gratis.

"Now, that's interesting," Libby said when Bernie read the letter aloud to her. "I thought that the guy that owns the flour mill came up with the idea."

"I did, too, but that's not the case. Well, according to this letter, it isn't," Bernie said. "Makes me wonder what else we don't know," she commented as she continued to rummage through the folder.

There were scribbled notes about the show's production values, lighting, tent, and equipment rentals, as well as notes about the time of year for the production and possible sponsors. When Bernie was done, she closed the folder, passed it to her sister, and began leafing through some of the other printed matter. She found pictures and newspaper articles from the local paper about *The Longely Bake-Off*. Then at the bottom of the pile, she found an old crumpled-up article from twenty years ago. Bernie smoothed it out and started reading it. Halfway through, she started wondering if what she was thinking was correct. That's when she called her dad and asked him.

"What was that about?" Libby asked her sister when Bernie got off the phone.

"This," she told Libby. She tapped the newspaper article she'd been reading and handed it to her sister. "Tell me what you think," she instructed.

Libby read the article. Then she read it again, just to

make sure. She looked up at Bernie when she was done. "Holy crap," she said.

"*Holy crap* is right," Bernie said.

"Is this for real?" Libby asked.

"So it would appear," Bernie said as she opened a binder that was sitting next to the mound of papers. When she began flipping through the pages, her breath caught in her throat as she passed the binder to her sister.

Libby stared at the photos on the pages. They were all there. Her, Bernie, Mike, the entire cast of *The Longely Bake-Off*. She shook her head. "I don't get it. We didn't give Sam our picture, did we?"

"No, we didn't," Bernie said.

Libby tapped the photo of her and Bernie. "That was taken last winter by the river. Where did the goatherd get it from?"

"He must have taken it then, Libby," Bernie guessed.

"The goatherd?"

"That's what I'm thinking," Bernie said. "Him or someone else."

Libby swallowed as she realized the implications of her sister's statement. "He was stalking us?"

"It would appear to be the case," Bernie replied. "Unless you can think of another explanation."

Libby couldn't. Her glance turned to the other photos. They looked recent as well. She turned the page and came across a picture of Adam in front of his place of business. It had a big X drawn over it. The one of Doug had an X as well. "This is not good," Libby observed. She shut the binder with a snap.

"No, it is not," Bernie agreed.

"We need to talk to the goatherd," Libby said.

"But first we need to talk to Sam and Mike and see what they know," Bernie told her as she checked her phone again.

A CATERED BAKE-OFF 293

Neither of the men had texted her back. "So, what do you think?" she asked Libby.

"I think we should check out Sam's office," her sister replied.

"Me too," Bernie replied.

"Are you thinking what I'm thinking?" Libby asked as they drove over there.

"I think I am," Bernie answered. "You know, if you had asked me that question a couple of weeks ago before this thing started, I would've said you were nuts to suggest something like that, but now I'm not so sure. I'm not sure at all."

"Me either," Libby said as she pulled up to Sam's office and Bernie jumped out of the van and peered in the window. Everything looked the way it had the last time she'd been there. Then Bernie tried the door, just for the hell of it. It was locked. No big surprise there.

"Maybe they're in the house," Libby suggested.

"Let's find out," Bernie said as she jumped back in the van.

Libby drove around to the house's main entrance. Mike's vehicle was parked in the driveway. "Well, at least that answers one question," Libby declared as she parked next to the Camry and she and Bernie exited Mathilda.

Chapter 41

Bernie glanced inside Mike's Camry. Nothing looked amiss. Then she and Libby walked down the brick path that led from the garage's driveway to the house. The front of the house was partially hidden by overgrown laurel and azalea bushes. Purslane was creeping over the path, and the sisters had to step onto the grass to avoid the stinging nettles growing out of the soil between the bricks. As they got closer to the house, they noticed that the door was slightly ajar.

Leaving the door open is getting to be a thing, Bernie decided.

"Maybe Sam or Mike forgot to close it all the way," Bernie said as she rang the bell.

"Maybe," Libby replied as she and her sister stood there, listening to the chime echoing inside the house. They waited for someone to answer the door, but no one did. The sisters looked at each other.

Libby shrugged. *What the hell,* she thought. She nodded and Bernie pushed the door open and stepped inside. Libby followed her. It was hot, dark, and stuffy in the hallway.

"I think someone needs to turn on the air-conditioning,"

A CATERED BAKE-OFF 295

Bernie observed as Libby called out Mike's and Sam's names. The men didn't answer.

"Not to mention getting a decorator in here," Libby agreed as she and her sister glanced around. The hallway looked dingy. The paisley print wallpaper on it was yellowing, the gilded mirror on the wall had a small crack near the bottom of its frame, and the table under the mirror was piled high with junk mail and old newspapers.

"Letting some fresh air into this place wouldn't hurt, either," Libby observed, making a right turn into the living room. That room, like the hallway, looked as if it had been furnished thirty years ago and left to its own devices after that. The curtains in the living room were drawn, as were the ones in the dining room, giving the place an abandoned feel.

"I don't think anyone has prepared a meal here in a long time," Bernie commented when she and her sister entered the eat-in kitchen.

Like the hallway and the living and dining rooms, the room had good bones, but time had ground them down. The appliances looked tired, the checkered vinyl floor was scratched, and the white enamel sink had seen better days. A light layer of dust lay over the Corian countertops and the table in the alcove.

"I don't think anyone has touched this kitchen since the fifties," Libby observed as she opened the avocado-green refrigerator door. The only things in it were a couple of bottles of water and a wrinkled apple, with a bite out of it, that needed to be thrown out. "I mean that literally," she continued. "From the looks of things, they certainly haven't cooked a meal in here in a while, that's for sure."

The sisters exited the kitchen and walked into the utility room next. It was a mess of old cardboard boxes, bundled-up newspapers, old raincoats, and bags of potting soil.

296   *Isis Crawford*

Bernie sighed. She was just about to ask Libby whether she thought they should check the basement or the second floor next, but she heard a noise behind her. Surprised, she spun around. The first thing she saw was the goatherd; the second thing she saw was the gun in his hand.

"Nice to see you, too," Bernie told him.

The goatherd laughed. "Really?"

"I thought you might be the one behind everything," Bernie replied as Libby turned around.

The goatherd raised an eyebrow. "And how did you come to that conclusion?" he asked.

"By process of elimination," Libby answered.

"I don't believe you," the goatherd said.

"Actually, it was the papers in your cottage that sealed the deal," Bernie added.

"I don't get it," Libby continued. "Why? What did any of us do to you?"

"Let me show you my father," the goatherd said. "Then you'll understand." He nodded toward the stairs that led to the second floor. "After you," he told them.

"And if we don't want to go?" Bernie asked.

"I'll shoot you now, instead of later," the goatherd replied.

"In that case, let's go," Libby said, and she and Bernie started climbing.

Libby and Bernie led the way, with the goatherd bringing up the rear. Bernie was hoping the goatherd would get near enough to her so she could fall backward onto him and hopefully dislodge his weapon, but he was careful to keep his distance.

When they got to the head of the stairs, the goatherd told them to go right. They did. The room they entered was the second one to the left. It smelled of sickness. The room was spacious, the three large windows facing north making it seem more so. Both Libby and Bernie were surprised to see the windows provided a view of the tent where the bake-off was being held.

"So my dad could see what's going on with you guys," the goatherd explained, answering Libby's question, even though she hadn't asked it.

The room itself was crammed with hospital equipment. The man lying in the bed looked wizened, or maybe he looked that way because of all the equipment he was hooked up to, Libby reflected. Lights flashed on and off around him. Equipment beeped. An electric wheelchair sat off to the side, while Alexa sat on a night table next to the bed, along with multiple medicine bottles.

"I take it that's your father?" Bernie asked, pointing to the man in the bed.

The goatherd nodded.

"What happened to him?" Bernie inquired.

"Ask your dad," the goatherd said.

"I'm asking you," Bernie said.

"Fine," the goatherd replied. "Your dad tipped off the Feds."

"That's not strictly true from what I heard," Libby told him. "He complained to a few of his friends—"

The goatherd interrupted. "Who happened to be in the law enforcement business. He started the ball rolling."

"But he wasn't the one that was ultimately responsible for what happened," Bernie pointed out. "My dad wasn't the one selling drugs."

The goatherd snorted. "That's because he got a living wage. Workers at Mickey D's were making more than my dad was."

"Okay," Libby said. "I could argue that point, but I won't. Why go after us, though?"

"That's simple," the goatherd answered. "Your dad helped take my dad and my brothers away from me, so I'm taking you away from him. I want him to know what it feels like."

"Because they landed in jail?" Bernie asked.

The goatherd nodded.

"And the rest of the people?" Bernie asked. "Why them? What did Adam or Doug ever do to you?"

"They did plenty," the goatherd replied. "Plenty."

"Like what?" Bernie demanded.

"What do you think?" the goatherd replied.

Libby answered the question. "I'm guessing you think everyone in the cast had something to do with the drugs your dad was selling."

"That's one way of putting it," the goatherd said, clenching his jaw, the words coming out in a hiss. "He was doing everyone a favor."

Libby was incredulous. "A favor?"

"Yes, a favor," the goatherd said. "He was being a nice guy. He didn't want to sell to them, but they begged and begged, so he finally did, and look what happened. They turned on him. If it wasn't for them, your dad would never have known what my dad was doing. Then they stole his drugs and testified against him and my brothers. He wasn't doing anything that everyone else wasn't doing," the goatherd added, nodding in his father's direction.

"They stole?" Bernie prodded.

"Yes, stole. From the farmhouse," the goatherd replied. "They must have followed my dad to his stash one day."

"You know that for a fact?" Bernie asked.

"As a matter of fact, I do," the goatherd responded. "What did he do that was so wrong? Sell to guys that like to party?"

"Is that what you really think?" Bernie asked.

"Yes, it is," the goatherd replied. "Your friends stole my dad's life from him. It's their fault he landed in jail. If he hadn't been there, he never would have been beaten up the way he was. If they hadn't set him and my brothers up, no one would have gone to jail. You know what they do to lawmen in jail?" the goatherd asked, his voice quavering in indignation.

"Nothing good, that's for sure," Bernie replied. "But why now?" she asked, changing the subject. "We're talking about something that happened twenty—"

"Eighteen," the goatherd corrected her.

Bernie gave an impatient wave of her hand. "Fine. Eighteen years ago."

The goatherd wiped his chin with his free hand. "I'll tell you why. Because I promised him I would when everything happened. But then . . . I got distracted. I'm back in the saddle now, though," the goatherd replied as Bernie spied the control to the electric wheelchair on the table next to the bed.

Bernie nodded to Libby as she began to inch closer to it. She figured she wasn't that far away. Just a couple of feet. It could be a good distraction, if what she was thinking worked. She'd seen an ad on TV a couple of weeks ago that had featured a remote- controlled wheelchair that you could summon from ten feet away. She just hoped that this wheelchair was like the one in the ad.

"Okay. Would you mind telling me what brought on your change of heart?" Libby persisted, hoping to keep the goatherd's interest on her. She'd seen the same ad her sister had. "I mean, it's not as if we're going to tell anyone."

"Because he's dying, that's why, and he deserves to die in his bed, not on the street," the goatherd replied.

"Why would he die on the street?" Libby queried, attempting to prolong the conversation. "He doesn't look homeless to me."

"Don't play dumb. You know why," the goatherd snapped.

"No, I really don't know," Libby protested. And she really didn't.

"You're lying, and I don't like liars," the goatherd snarled. Then he lifted his weapon, aimed, and started pulling back the trigger.

"Please don't," Libby cried as Bernie took a deep breath.

Then she leaned over, grabbed the wheelchair's remote, and pressed down on one of the buttons. *Let this work,* Bernie prayed as the wheelchair jerked. She watched as it started moving toward the goatherd. Startled, he jumped back, and as he did, Libby gave him a hard push from behind. He stumbled and his weapon discharged into the floor. Then Bernie stomped on his hand with her high heel. The goatherd screamed in pain and dropped the gun. Libby kicked the 9mm away from him, bent over, picked it up, and aimed it at the goatherd.

"You won't shoot," the goatherd sneered.

"You're right," Libby told him. "I won't shoot, but my sister will." And she handed the gun to Bernie.

Bernie smiled. "Now, I, on the other hand, have no problem whatsoever discharging this weapon," she said. "In fact, I'll probably enjoy doing it."

The goatherd's eyes widened.

"So, why don't you tell me and my sister the whole story," Bernie continued. "Because otherwise, I will shoot you."

"You won't," the goatherd said.

"Wanna bet," Bernie asked him, and she fired the gun into the floor. "Believe me, I won't miss next time," she added, raising the gun and aiming it at the goatherd's head.

"Well, when you put it that way," the goatherd said, and he started talking.

Chapter 42

Three days later, *The Longely Bake-Off* finished filming its last segment inside the tent.

"That's a wrap," Sam declared, and everyone, including the crew, clapped.

"I didn't think we'd make it," Nell said.

"I was beginning to wonder myself," Libby allowed.

"Poor Adam," Mike said as Sam opened the fridge and brought out two bottles of champagne, while Ellen went into the pantry, got glasses, and set them next to everyone's technical challenges. "Too bad he didn't make it." Mike swallowed. "We should dedicate next season to him."

"Is there going to be a next season?" Ellen asked.

"We're thinking about it," Sam responded. "I mean this wasn't really a bake-off."

"No. It was a kill-off. Too soon?" Bernie asked when no one laughed at her joke.

"Definitely," Libby said.

"We began with champagne and we're ending with champagne," Sam said as he popped the cork and began to pour the champagne into the glasses Ellen had laid out. When he was done, everyone took a sip and toasted each other.

"To next year and your participation trophies," Sam said, raising his glass.

"Just like Little League," Bernie quipped. No one laughed at that, either. "Guess I'm losing my touch," Bernie said, looking around.

"You never had it," Libby told her.

"That's harsh," Bernie replied.

"But true," Libby answered.

Bernie was just about to reply, but Mike spoke first. "I still can't believe it," he said as he finished off a piece of Bernie and Libby's Battenberg cake. He lifted his fork. "And by the way, this cake is excellent."

Bernie and Libby beamed.

"Our pleasure," Libby said.

"We want to thank you for everything," Sam said to them.

"Glad we could help," Bernie told him.

"So are we," Nell agreed while she turned to Sam. "I still don't understand," she said.

"It's complicated," Bernie said.

"That's an understatement," Libby added.

"What don't you understand?" Sam asked Nell.

"How you didn't recognize him, for openers," she told him.

Sam raised an eyebrow. "Him?"

"The goatherd," Nell clarified.

"You didn't recognize him, either," Sam pointed out.

"That's because I didn't see him," Nell reminded him. "I was in the bathroom when he came to round up the goats, if you recall."

Sam sighed. "That's right. You were."

"But you, on the other hand, were there," Nell reminded him.

"I wasn't exactly concentrating on him at the moment," Sam told her.

"And before?" Nell asked.

"You're kidding, right?" Sam replied. "He was a little kid back in Oxford when I was there. How old was he? Maybe seven? How would I recognize him from then? If I saw him at all. I mean, it's not like we'd be running into each other." And he took a bite of Nell's Bakewell tart and nodded his appreciation of it. "Anyway, he has a beard and a mustache now."

"But who did you arrange this thing with? Who suggested the bake-off? Who made the arrangements for the estate?" Nell demanded, continuing with her line of questioning.

Sam sighed. *"Lawyers."* Sam made the word sound like an obscenity. "They were the ones who contacted me. They were the ones who gave me the list of the cast members they wanted."

"Didn't that seem strange to you?" Mike asked.

"Not really," Sam replied. "I was talking to some people at the Longely Community Center when I was playing pickleball a while ago, before the show was in the works, and everyone agreed it was a great idea. You know, showing off Longely's assets. We do have some great food shops and restaurants here. I just thought it had come from that. What do they call it?" He snapped his fingers as he tried to remember the word he was looking for. *"Synergy.* That it was synergy. That's the word I'm looking for. I was trying to figure out where to hold the show when the lawyers offered the estate. I mean, it was perfect.

"Then we got to discussing how we were going to pick the judges and the contestants. We agreed they had to be local. And your names came up. In fact, they refused to do the show without any of you." Sam finished his glass

304   *Isis Crawford*

of champagne. "And as for recognizing the sheriff, I only saw him for a couple of minutes, maybe five at the most, and I sure as hell didn't recognize him, either. I mean, he was this big guy back in the day, imposing, but when I saw him . . ." Sam's voice trailed off for a moment. He shook his head. "I never would have thought . . . Anyway, he looked really small in bed, and his mustache was gone, and there was something weird going on with his chin. And it wasn't like I recognized his voice. It had changed."

"That's what happens when you become an invalid," Mike commented.

"And get old," Bernie added.

Sam took another bite of the tart and swallowed. "Anyway, what happened, happened a long time ago."

"Exactly," Nell said.

"A very long time ago," Lori agreed, taking another bite of her Battenberg cake as she observed that it went well with champagne.

"Some people have long memories," Bernie observed.

"What did the goatherd tell you?" Lori inquired.

Bernie repeated what the sheriff's younger son had said to her about the drugs.

"He's full of it," Mike said when Bernie was through. "We didn't do anything wrong, right?" he turned and asked everyone.

"How can you say that, Mike?" Ellen replied. "Of course, we did. We stole."

"Not really," Lori said. "We did a public service and turned in a corrupt public official."

Nell shook her head. "Yeah, and then we did the same thing he did."

"You're being ridiculous," Mike told her. "We just used for free what we paid for before. And so what if we gave out a few party favors? We were just making people happy."

A CATERED BAKE-OFF 305

Bernie put her hands on her hips and looked around the group. "I suppose that depends on how you define *making people happy.*"

"What do you think?" Lori asked Bernie.

"Why ask her?" Ellen demanded. "She wasn't there."

"But *you* were," Bernie said, emphasizing the word *you.*

There was a moment of silence; then Nell said, "We were just kids."

"We thought we were so smart," Sam reflected. He rubbed his nose with his knuckle, before turning to Bernie and Libby. "How did you find out?"

Bernie reached over and took another sip of her champagne, savoring it before she answered. "My dad used to be head of the Longely PD," she replied.

"Duh," Nell said. "We know that."

"Well, he still has friends in high places," Bernie told her.

"And?" Nell said.

"And," Bernie continued, "he has a couple of friends in the FBI whom he contacted, and they did a little digging for him. You know, talked to some of their retired friends. It seems that back in the day, the FBI got an anonymous tip about the sheriff and his sons."

"I thought getting rid of drug dealers was a good thing," Nell protested. "You sound like you don't think so."

"More to the point, I don't think the dealers you're referring to see it that way," Libby replied. "Especially when you take over their business, steal their weed supply and all the cash they had—cash they were counting on to get out of town with. I think that's called *adding insult to injury.* I mean, I can see why that would piss them off, can't you?"

"You don't know that," Lori said, swallowing.

"We have the words of a couple of ex–FBI agents, so I think we do," Bernie said, noting as she talked that every-

306   *Isis Crawford*

one in the room was looking everywhere, but at each other. She smiled. "I have to hand it to you. It was a stellar way to get rid of the competition."

"Are you saying we dealt dope?" Mike demanded.

"That's exactly what my sister is saying," Libby answered.

Bernie smiled. "You know, it always puzzled me that you guys all said you weren't in Oxford for that long and that you didn't hang out together."

"We weren't, and we didn't," Lori said.

"That's not quite true, is it?" Bernie replied. "I know because I checked."

"What's your point?" Ellen asked her.

Bernie replied. "Why did you and your families all leave town around the same time? Coincidence? The zombie apocalypse? Probably not," Bernie said, answering her own question when no one said anything. "I'll tell you what that says to me. It says that something bad happened and your families wanted to get you all the hell out of town, and we know what that bad thing was, don't we? And then there was the whole *I didn't know anyone when I was in Oxford.*"

Bernie looked around again. Everyone was still studying the tent walls and ceiling. "That seemed fairly unusual in a town as small as Oxford. Do you know that according to my dad's friends, the Feds had a couple informants in the high school?" Bernie turned to Nell. "And guess what? They caught you and you—"

"Nell, you ratted us out?" Lori cried, disbelief written across her face.

Nell bit her lip and folded her hands across her chest. "Hey, I'm sorry. I really am, but I didn't have a choice. They were going to put me in jail forever." She turned to Bernie and Libby. "Okay, we made a mistake. Big deal. It all turned out fine in the end."

A CATERED BAKE-OFF   307

"Not for the sheriff or his two older sons," Libby noted.

"It's not our fault Zach and Geoff got killed in a prison riot or their dad got a beatdown," Mike said.

"Unfortunately, the goatherd's dad doesn't see things that way," Libby said. "He sees it as you guys killing his sons and destroying his life."

"Okay," Lori said. "I get that. But why wait till now to get revenge?" Lori asked. "Like you said, what happened, happened a long time ago."

"Ask Mike," Bernie replied.

Everyone turned toward him.

"Well," Nell said.

"I don't know what you're talking about," Mike protested.

"I think you do," Libby told him.

"No, I really don't," Mike countered. "Honest."

"That's funny coming from you," Bernie replied. "What about your real estate deal?"

Mike fake laughed. "Oh, that."

"Yes, that," Bernie said. "I'm guessing our former sheriff was upset when he found out you were going to screw him over again and take his home away from him. I think that reawakened old feelings, so to speak—old feelings, as in the desire for revenge."

Everyone turned back to Mike.

Mike put his hands up. "Adam and I didn't know who was living there," Mike told the group. "If I had, believe me, I never would have started things moving."

"How could you not know?" Ellen demanded.

"Because he was a recluse," Mike said, "and his name isn't on the deed. His brother's is. Was."

"Why not take it out on his brother?" Nell asked.

"Because, according to my dad's sources, Adam was the one who persuaded his brother to sell," Bernie answered.

"He owed money," Mike said. "There's an outstanding

308 *Isis Crawford*

lien on this parcel of land." And with a sweep of his hand, he indicated where they were standing. "We were doing him a favor."

"That's what he thought anyway," Bernie told him. She brushed a wisp of hair off her face. "According to my dad, you promised him you'd let everyone stay where they were, right?" Bernie asked.

Mike nodded.

"And then a venture capitalist came calling," Bernie said.

"Hey," Mike said, "when someone offers you three or four million, it's hard to say no."

Bernie ignored him and continued with her explanation. "Mike and Adam sold the lien to a venture capitalist company that is planning to sell the acreage to a company in California that is going to build a multiuse development on it, which means that our former sheriff and his son are about to lose their home. PS: This time, the word is that the zoning board is going to approve the request."

Mike shrugged. "That's what happens in the real world. Money talks. You snooze, you lose."

"So, you're the person responsible for what happened?" Nell demanded of him. Then she balled up her fists and took a step toward him.

"That's not fair," Mike said, taking a step back as Bernie stepped between him and Nell. "How did I know the guy was going to go full-on crazy? Anyway, it was Adam's idea, not mine."

"Yeah, blame the dead person," Lori said. "Talk about a cheap shot."

Sam shook his head. "I guess losing their home was the last straw," he observed.

"I'll tell you one thing," Libby said. "Those guys spent a long time planning this. Maybe if we'd quit when they started with the nursery rhymes."

"No. They would have done it anyway," Bernie said.

"You don't know that," Libby protested. "If Dennis—"

"What about him?" Nell asked, interrupting. "How is he? How did he get involved in this whole thing anyway?"

"He was the one that did the rhymes," Bernie told her. "The goatherd paid him to do it."

"Then why booby-trap his house?" Sam asked.

"Because Dennis decided the goatherd wasn't paying him enough," Bernie said.

"And Dennis decided to blackmail him," Libby added.

"Not smart," Ellen observed.

"It certainly wasn't," Bernie agreed. "Dennis is going to survive, but he's going to be left with some pretty bad scarring."

"Why didn't the goatherd just shoot him?" Mike asked.

"Because the goatherd was trying to point the finger at you," Bernie told him. "He figured if he couldn't get you one way, he'd get you another. After all, you were the one that set up the deal."

"Wait a minute," Ellen said. "You're telling me that this whole thing was about real estate."

"Let's just say, it's what started the ball rolling," Libby replied.

"So, what's going to happen to everyone?" Nell asked.

"The goats are going to a sanctuary, the son is being charged with two homicides, and his father is being charged as a co-conspirator, but he doesn't have that much longer to live," Libby answered.

"I never would have figured this out," Nell said.

"We nearly didn't," Libby remarked.

"Speak for yourself," Bernie told her.

"I say we stop bickering and open another couple of bottles of champagne," Sam offered.

"Works for me," Bernie said.

310   *Isis Crawford*

"Ditto," Libby agreed, and she went off to get two more bottles. "A toast," she said when she came back and had poured the champagne into everyone's glasses, "to food, fun, and laughter."

"And the time to enjoy them," Bernie added.

"To next year's bake-off," Sam said. "May your cakes be tender, your meringues fluffy, and your icings sweet."

At which point, everyone raised their glasses and drank.

Recipes

This recipe comes from my longtime neighbor and friend, Ruth Federman Stein. Don't let the name of this recipe dissuade you—this is an easy recipe that everyone will enjoy snacking on.

VEGETARIAN CHOPPED LIVER

1 small can of Le Sueur peas, drained
2 medium onions, diced and sautéed in oil until golden brown
½ cup of lightly toasted walnuts
2 hard-boiled eggs
½ teaspoon salt
½ teaspoon pepper

Chop walnuts until very fine in a food processor. Add peas, onions, and eggs and process thoroughly. Add salt and pepper, to taste. This can be frozen. You can double the recipe and freeze half.

312　*Recipes*

This next recipe comes from my cousin Joan Bernstein. Like the previous one, it's easy, quick, and delicious. It's a nice recipe to have in your repertoire during the holidays.

DATE-ALMOND BALLS

1½ cups pitted dates
1½ cups toasted almonds
¼ cup cocoa
1 teaspoon vanilla extract
¼ teaspoon salt

Roast the almonds in a 350-degree oven until lightly browned.

Combine all the ingredients in a food processor (metal blade) and blend until ground. Form into 1-inch balls. Leftovers can be refrigerated.

Note: If the balls are not holding together, add more pitted dates to the mixture in the food processor.

RECIPES 313

This recipe comes from my mom, Florence Spencer, by way of my grandmother Dora Bruckner. While this recipe isn't fast, these cookies are delicious and welcome at any time of the year.

RUGELACH

2 cups all-purpose flour
½ teaspoon salt
2 sticks softened unsalted butter
8 ozs. softened cream cheese
½ cup plus 4 teaspoons sugar and 1 teaspoon cinnamon
1 cup apricot preserves or strawberry jam
1 cup finely chopped walnuts (optional)

To make dough, combine flour and salt in a bowl. Beat butter and cream cheese together until combined, then add flour mixture until a soft dough is formed. Roll into a bowl, cover with wax paper, and refrigerate for 8 to 24 hours.

When ready to make, preheat oven to 350 degrees and place oven rack in the center of the oven. Then line the bottom of 2 baking pans with parchment paper.

Take dough out of fridge, cut into 4 pieces, wrap 3 in plastic wrap and put back in the fridge. Roll the remaining piece out into a rectangle on a well-floured board or use wax paper. When the rectangle is about 12 by 8 inches, put back in fridge to chill, and roll out the other 3 pieces. When they are done, take them out, each individually, and sprinkle with the sugar and cinnamon mixture, then brush with ¼ cup jam or preserves, and ⅓ cup of the walnuts if desired. Roll up tightly into a log. Do the same with the others and place them onto the trays. Using a sharp knife,

314 *Recipes*

make ¾ of an inch cut—not all the way through—at 1-inch intervals. Bake for 45–50 minutes or until golden brown. Take out of oven and cool. When the rugelach are still warm to the touch, cut all the way through. The cookies can be stored for up to a week in a container in the fridge.